My heart pounds as the engine whines with the steep incline of the road coming out of the wash valley. I hit the top and push the gas up to thirty—dangerously fast in this terrain. I hit a rocky curve and almost flip. I correct the wheel just in time. I fly over the rough terrain, sneaking nervous glances in the rearview and waiting to see lights behind me. I follow the road out of the desert and onto the highway. I'm alone. For some reason they let me go. Why? Why the fuck would they do that?

WORLD
OF
VACANCY

CHARLES SCHMIDT

 Lucky Bat Books

WORLD

OF

VACANCY

CHARLES SCHMIDT

Chapter 1: HACK

MY HANDS ARE FUCKING FILTHY from handling this cab's steering wheel for twelve hours. The company buys the old cop cruisers. We drive them into the grave, along the way the sweat and grime from a thousand filthy fucking cabbies soaks right into the steering wheel. After a shift my hands look like I've been mining coal.

I pick up a stripper that's getting off work. She chain–smokes menthols and has me stop off at a corner store so she can buy a few tall cans of some foul malt liquor. She's white but talks black, has poor teeth. I let her out at some shitty apartment building. She tips me a dollar and I watch her walk away, her acne–scarred face floating above one hell of a body. My attention to the glory of her ass and its battle with her mini skirt is rudely interrupted by a spook crackhead banging on my window. He tries to pull the door open. It's locked. I tell him to fuck off and I leave.

I'm sorry for what I've done. I'm even sorrier for what I want to do.

I have been pretty good lately; maybe I rolled a drunk or took an extra buck or two from a drunk broad. I might have kicked a homeless guy in the face and knocked out a few teeth. I just get so fucking bored, driving this fucking cab all day, working my ass off to barely afford a shitty life.

Next stop I pick up an aging racist at a dive bar in a strip mall. He slumps into the back, mumbles something about "spics and beaners." He has faded prison tats up and down his arms. He tells me a story about how the devil came to him while he was in the joint, a few days in on a week–long stint in solitary.

"He didn't say nothing," the con says. "He didn't have to. This face just came out of nowhere, right through the dark. That fucking face, man."

He pauses. His whiskey–stench breath fills the cab.

"That face said it all, man, said everything I ever thought was true."

"Yeah? And what's that?"

"That there ain't nothing good about none of us," he says.

We stop in front of a cinderblock house with a dust–covered lawn. He pays his fare and walks inside.

The dash computer beeps with my next fare. I go to the local ER, pick up a borderline, morbidly obese black woman. She gets in and tells me about her losing battle with type 2 diabetes.

I try to tune her out. She steers the conversation to her daughter, how her daughter was gang–raped at a party last month. The story goes from mildly uncomfortable to just dreadful within a few sentences..." they held her down and raped her anally, over and over."

I accelerate and get her home as fast as I can. I can't look her in the eye as she thanks me and gets out.

There are people out there worse than me. It should make me feel better but it doesn't.

CHAPTER 2: NICK

SO JORDO TELLS ME THIS STORY about how this one night he looked out the window and saw his neighbor cram a hunting rifle into his mouth. Jordo shouted no–no–no but the guy pulled the trigger and the top of his head split open "like a popped zit." I tell the story about how I saw a woman tackled by a slow–moving city bus, how she let out a hoarse yelp when the bus hit, how she went unconscious after she hit the ground and her head bounced on the pavement like a basketball. She lived, though. It was in the paper.

We do our third set of push–ups for the day. There's nothing to do but roam the yard, sweat, talk, and do push–ups. It's hot as fuck in tent city; temperatures in the tents have hit as high as one hundred forty. We take showers with our clothes on to cool off but it's short–lived relief; a few minutes later you're just as hot and now humid fucking damp too. Fuck you, Sheriff Joe. It's a hundred and nine today in the city of Phoenix, but tent city is always hotter. And the air is fucking toxic. Tent city is sandwiched between an animal crematorium and some industrial wasteland. That's the air we breathe. This is fucking punishment, no arguments here.

I take naps on my bunk, the top bunk. I sleep underneath the pitifully underpowered fan. I can't sleep for more than twenty minutes; I always have the same dreams, dreams about sharks. It was shark week on TV the week before I got pinched. I had just relapsed. Again. I drank all day while Sarah worked. I drank in that ice–cold apartment, dumb drunk in front of the TV, watching people dive and swim with sharks, people living actual fucking lives, sitting in a fucking cage while massive prehistoric beasts prowl around.

It's two weeks later and I'm locked in a cage too, surrounded by a few beasts as well, I suppose, but it's mostly just guys who had one too many and drove home, or got caught with a bag of grass, or shoplifting, or some other chickenshit stuff. Some of us are going away for a while, prison maybe, but most of us will be home in a month or two.

We don't have shit to do but talk, so the stories float around, and every storyteller always gets back to the concrete belief that life has dealt them a shitty hand.

That's what I like about Jordo. He doesn't blame the world for his own bullshit. He was on probation and went out and partied a couple of nights, pissed dirty for his PO, and is now doing a one–month vacation in the tents. He and I, we're alike: we don't fucking complain, just joke about the fact that we're lucky to only be here for a matter of weeks. If they knew all the shit we've done, they'd probably lock us up and throw away the key.

Jimmy the Tweaker, though, he never stops talking. He tells that us that there are fenstitutes that stop by the tents, bottom–of–the–barrel whores that'll blow guys through the fences for as little as five bucks. He tells story after story, each more bold and absurd. We yawn in response. He tells us about how he'd go down by the border by Douglas and shake down border jumpers for whatever they had on them, and he says he found this drug smuggler in the desert, dehydrated and collapsed under the sun, a huge potato sack full of brick weed next to him. Jimmy says he took the bag of weed and left the smuggler a bottle of water and hiked out with his huge score, but he saw a Border Patrol vehicle on the horizon and had to bury the grass and come back for it later. Of course, sometime after he supposedly buried this loot he ended up in Phoenix, spun out of his mind, and the cops found him stealing copper from a job site. Now he's stuck in the tents till his court–appointed lawyer gets him a plea deal.

"As soon as I get out of here, man," Jimmy says, "Fuck, two months at the most, my lawyer says. When I get out of here I'm going to dig up that big bag of grass and get paid, man, and fucking leave that awful bitch and the kids and this fucking state forever. A fresh fucking start, amen." Jordo laughs. "Yeah, right, Jimmy. You're going to get out of here, keep your nose clean for a few days at most, then you're going to get a few too many Coors deep and end up smoking a glass dick, again, and you're going to do the same dumb shit, again, and end up here once more, sweating through another hundred days or so, daydreaming and telling a bunch of bullshit stories to make the days go by."

The guys laugh and clap at that. Jimmy, all hundred thirty pounds, he gets butthurt, jumps up and gets in Jordo's face. Jordo smiles and shoves Jimmy back.

"Take it easy, peckerwood; we're just fucking around, man."

Jordo and I split off and do another set of a hundred push–ups, then go get a couple of smokes from the work–release guys. Boredom is a good punishment, no arguments here. I have nothing do but sit here and wonder if Sarah is fucking that guy from work, the one she claims is "just a friend, he's not like that." I told her that all guys are "like that," he's just playing an old and well–worn angle, putting in his time until he can pounce. I close my eyes and I see them fucking, her getting railed out on that queen–sized bed in that ice–cold apartment, him behind her all worked up and sweating all over my goddamned bed. She loves me, I think, and she's a good girl, but that doesn't change the fickle nature of her kind, the insecurity and the loneliness that is her Achilles heel. Fuck, any guy with decent game can take advantage of that. I'm stuck in this fucking hell and she's probably getting her brains fucked out.

I imagine myself getting out of here, going home and catching them right in the act. I imagine slashing them up with a kitchen knife, them all naked and screaming. I feel the warmth of their blood; it splashes all over me as I hack away in that cold apartment.

These fucking tents are really starting to fuck with my head.

Jordo tells me to forget about it, "Just try and imagine that the world outside is frozen while we're in here, like someone hit a giant pause button or something."

I tell Jordo I'm going to kill if I find out she fucked around on me while I was locked up.

Jordo smiles and tells me he understands. He says he'll even help me bury the bodies. That's a good fucking friend. I'm sure we'll never see one another on the outside, but for now he's the best I've known. He has plans about running a numbers racket at an OTB, or maybe setting up one of those private poker rooms to get knocked off. He has big stuff going on in Tucson, he says, and that's where he's headed when he gets out. Me, I'll probably go back to working the door at one of the titty bars, try to not drink myself into a blackout every goddamned day. I guess we don't know what we're actually going to do until that day arrives. We are always the last to know.

We do another set of push–ups and then watch a couple of chiefs swing on each other until the D.O.s break it up. Some clouds move in and it is monsoon season, so we get a good show of lightning and rain and dust whipping around us that serves as entertainment in this shithole. I fall asleep and dream about all sorts of vile shit. I wake up often, almost moaning in the torture of the swampy humid air left over from the storm.

Jordo gets a surprise the next day and gets out early. We exchange phone numbers and do one of those awkward bro hugs and he walks out, a free man, and he ceases to exist; like he said, he has entered that giant pause button world, and I feel some despair with him gone, so I spend the day singing the entire Nirvana Nevermind album to myself, song by song, just killing time and waiting.

CHAPTER 3: HACK

AFTER DROPPING OFF THAT WOMAN that wouldn't stop talking about her daughter getting raped, well, I guess I sort of snapped. I went home and slept for two weeks straight until whatever it was passed and I got up and showered and shaved and got back in my cab. I try to do something nice every day. I feed a stray cat. I give a piss–reeking bum a free ride to the VA. I smile here and there. I do my best, but I still feel like I'm rotting inside.

I take the cab to the nicer part of town, cart around drunken twenty–somethings that laugh and generally seem to really enjoy their places in life. They tip well, and generously avoid conversation with me. The girls, they sit on the boys' laps and giggle and sing and shout out the window. Their perfect white teeth glow inside the dark cab. The boys grin that drunken sheepish grin and their minds are stuck on one thought: fucking; I watch them skip and stumble up the stairs into their homes. I don't resent them for what they are, I'm glad they're here, glad there are some people that will never have to struggle. That's a good thing. They have no skeletons in their closets. I can see that.

At four in the morning the streets are dead, pretty much anywhere in town. It's a good time to set something on fire. I find a dull–looking empty car lot with a rundown office building. The economic shit–spiral has made a whole world of vacancy in this town. I make three Molotov cocktails, and in almost slow motion I light them one by one, toss them in a great leaping arc. The structure is engulfed in flame in a matter of a couple of minutes. I watch the fire lick and burn and roar, and the building partially collapses upon itself. I even get a rare hard–on. I stay not one moment too long. I drive away and I look back to see a great balloon of orange in my rearview mirror; I look back until I'm far away and it's just night again and I feel relief in the oddest of ways. Regardless of what I've done or continue to do with my life, I've done some things that very few people get to do. That's good enough for me.

CHAPTER 4: NICK

I'VE BEEN SOBER FOR ABOUT FOUR DAYS. Sarah doesn't know about my slip–up earlier this week when I guiltily chugged two pints of vodka while she was at work.

Sarah picked me up from Tent City when I got released two weeks ago. She was happy to see me; she smiled that suburban beauty of a smile. She brought me an energy drink and smokes. She kissed me long and hard. I did my best to act like I was happy to see her again; I mean I was happy, happy to see her, happy to be out, fuck, I was thrilled to be free and to be with her again, but in the back of my mind I couldn't shake that question as to whether or not she had fucked that guy from work.

I didn't come out and ask about it as she drove us home; no, I'm too much of a pussy to be that upfront. I knew that the first chance I had I was going to inspect every square inch of that apartment for some evidence of another man being there. She worked that night, tending bar at one of those trendy lounges in Old Town. Before she left for work she told me that she loved me but if I got drunk again she was kicking me out of the apartment and we were through for good.

"I won't drink," I said," I promise."

She left, and the second I heard her car start I tore the sheets off of the bed and buried my face in the mattress, straining and inhaling, looking for any suggestive scent or stain. I moved on to the sheets and pillows and comforter after that. It all smelled that lovely girl smell of body cream and fabric softener. I then got on my knees and crawled throughout the house, looking for hairs, a piece of a condom wrapper, anything. I looked in the trash cans and studied the floor of the bathroom. I found nothing.

She came home late and we fucked. She rubbed my ribs and said I looked skinny, skinny from the dog food diet they serve in the tents. She fell asleep easily afterward, but I did not; as exhausted as I was from the untold days of fitful sleep, I couldn't stop worrying that she had been fucking someone else in this very bed while I was away.

Before I fell asleep it dawned on me that there is really, really something fucked up with my head.

So yeah, a couple of days after that I walked to the Circle K down the street to grab a pack of cigs and an energy drink and again I went into zombie mode, found myself buying a pint of Vodka and slamming it on the way back to the house. About twenty minutes later I walked back to the store and bought another pint and slammed that, too. I think I repeated this process once more before I finally bought a fifth and I got real fucking drunk and passed out.

I woke up later, woke up to Sarah nudging me with her knee. She had two bags packed for me, packed with all my crummy shit. She dangled my keys in front of my face. "Get out," she said. "This is over. You have to leave now."

I protested. My fucking hung-over head pounded as I offered apologies and promises, but she all but pushed me through the door and I stopped resisting, deciding that for the near future another drink sounded like a much better immediate option than begging her to take me back after yet another broken promise. It's a well–worn scene.

I had about two hundred bucks to my name. I got a shitty hotel room and I drank. I drank through the two hundred in a couple of days and then surveyed my earthly possessions for what could be pawned. I pawned my pistol, a Glock, for one seventy–five, my laptop for ninety bucks, and a watch my father gave me for another hundred bucks. I drank that cash up quickly–three or four days, between the bottles and the hotel room. A pretty little nineteen–year–old Latina escort came over and drank with me all night and snorted speed off my stomach then fucked me for a hundred bucks. She left and I woke up flat broke with a soul–crushing, suicide–potential hangover.

I got in my Jeep and went to an AA meeting where I cried on a stranger's shoulder and left feeling a little better. Next I took a title loan out on my Jeep for a grand and checked into a pay–by–the–week apartment building. I collapsed on the bed and took four over–the–counter sleeping pills. I fell asleep reminding myself what an utter fucking loser I am. I slept on and off for three days, fitful depressed sleep. I resisted the urge to call Sarah and beg her to take me back. I went to an occasional AA meeting and spoke to some familiar faces. I couldn't gather the nerve to call my old AA friends, too ashamed to have them see me come back from yet another failed recovery.

Last night I went to the casino and blew all but fifty bucks at a blackjack table. I drove home, stopping at a convenience store on the way. I wanted to buy a bottle but resisted the urge. I got home and slept and woke up and here we are.

Now I'm driving through all one hundred and nine scorching degrees of Phoenix with the windows down, hot as fuck, but AC burns gas and I have to preserve every drop. I swing by a couple of strip clubs to look for bouncer work. Nothing. Same goes with a bunch of other bars and nightclubs. No spots open. I get an offer for some hours in a week or so, but nothing in the near future. I have a day left on my weeklong lease at the apartment and not much else. I'm just about tapped out.

I lie in bed and think. I think about Jordo, how we talked about teaming up to make some cash when we got out. It's worth a shot, I suppose. I want a straight job but I'm not having a lot of luck finding one. I could, and probably will, go out on my own later and shake down some street drug trash for a few bucks, but for now I'll at least see if there's a slight chance Jordo can help me out.

Chapter 5: HACK

I GET A PICK–UP CALL IN CENTRAL PHOENIX at one of those yuppie condo complexes that keep popping up all over the place. The fare is a kid, nice enough kid, Eddie is his name. He needs a ride to the MVD to get his license reinstated. He's from Minnesota. Strange thing about the kid, I can tell by what he says and how he says it that he knows the streets and how they work, but he lives in that nice fucking yuppie condo with a Mercedes in the garage. I figure he's a dealer or something, but it doesn't matter, I guess. He asks me about the P.O.W. patch on my backpack on the front seat, and I forget about trying to read him when the subject of 'Nam comes up.

I find myself telling a story I rarely tell, there is rarely the right audience for it, but something about this kid makes me feel like this is an okay time to let an old favorite out.

"There was this dink whorehouse we all used to go to, all the guys, these girls took goddamn good care of us. But these dink bitches were crafty, some of 'em even spoke English pretty well, and some of the GIs got to talking to them and I guess they talked too much because whatever these guys told the whores somehow got back to some VC. I guess some if not all of these dink whores were VC, and I guess some of the shit they leaked to their gook brothers or whatever ended up getting some of our guys killed."

This kid is a good listener, he lights a smoke and nods. He is really into it. Kindred spirit.

"So, needless to say, we find out about these dink whores using their dink whore magic to get info from the guys about where we'd been, where we're going, what we're doing, and all that. The word gets out and a group of us decides that we're going to march up there in the middle of the night and toss grenades into the place and blow them to fucking bits. These Aussies, man, the Aussies were fucking great, man, these Aussies get in on it and a couple of 'em convince us to let them take care of it, say they have something planned and to give them a day or two to see it through. We agreed, and a day or two passed and we figured the Aussies didn't get it done so we we're preparing to go handle business on our own, then word gets around that a couple of the girls from the whorehouse went missing and then came back home gift wrapped in a couple of oil drums. The Aussies had nabbed a couple of the girls, two that were known to be the more talkative types, they took them and strangled them and then chopped them into pieces and filled up two oil drums with the parts and left the drums on the door step of that dink whorehouse. So yeah, that spot closed down not long after and you can be damn sure that any nearby dink whore with half a brain didn't ask any soldiers any questions after that."

The kid laughs. "That is a great story."

"Yes it is. A lot of shit happened like that over there, shit that never gets talked about. Crazy fucking war, man. Some real savage shit."

We don't talk for a couple of minutes, until we get close to the MVD, and I have to ask him. "Can I ask you something, Eddie?"

"Of course," he says.

"Are you running from something, my man?"

His face goes sort of blank. He readjusts his shirt and shrugs. "What do you mean?"

"Nothing, man. It just seems like there's something about you that you aren't quite right with."

He grins. "Well, I can't dispute that," he says. "I wouldn't want to know a guy who is one hundred percent all right with himself."

I nod. He gets out a minute later, pays me, and then gives me a ten–dollar tip.

"You're a good kid, Eddie. Don't worry about what I asked you about before. You're going to be okay, man. You have nothing to worry about."

"Thanks. See you around."

"Probably not," I say. "But that's good for you."

I give him a thumbs–up and I drive off.

Chapter 6: NICK

I FIND JORDO'S NUMBER AT THE BOTTOM of one of my bags. I call him and leave a message. He calls back a couple of hours later. It's dark out and I'm getting ready to head out and do some fundraising.

"Holy shit, Nick. I never thought I'd talk to you again. I wanted to see how you're doing, but I lost your number, shit, you know how it is."

"It's all good, Jordo. How are things?"

"Fucking good, man, I'm down in Tucson, fucking shithole, but I got a few things brewing, shit, if you want to come down here and help out in a couple of weeks I got some real solid stuff lined up, would love to have you around. You looking for work?"

"Yeah, that's one of the things I'm calling about. I'm not finding much in the way of work at the clubs and I'm pretty much tapped out. Just making some calls, seeing if I can get something going. Sarah kicked me out, so yeah, shit kind of sucks right now. I'm glad you're doing well, man. That's good stuff."

"No worries, Nick, I think I can find something for you, no problem, something to tide you over until I get this shit down here straight and you can come work with me. I'm going to call a couple of people, I'll ring you back in like a half hour, okay?"

"Sure, I really appreciate it."

I hang up. I sit on the couch for forty–five minutes and wait for the phone to ring. An hour passes and I'm getting ready to leave again when the phone rings.

"Hey, it's me," Jordo says. "You mind getting up real early tomorrow? I talked to my Uncle Tim and he has some work tomorrow he needs help with. He's kind of a prick, but if he likes you he takes pretty good care of his crew. I put in a good word so just do your best, huh?"

"Awesome. Thanks man, I owe ya one."

"My pleasure, buddy. I'll call you in a week or so and we'll get you down here. Make some serious money. In the meantime, just stick with my uncle, man. It'll get you through."

Nick gives me an address before he hangs up and tells me to be there at six a.m. I get undressed and turn out the lights. My mind starts with the *drink drink drink* song but I manage to fall asleep.

I get up at five thirty and get dressed. I drive twenty minutes to the edge of Phoenix and Chandler. The address is an old car lot, pavement with cracks and weeds. The lone building on the lot has been burnt to the ground; all that's left is its charred foundation of torched wood, concrete, and steel. A couple of pickup trucks are parked in the lot. A few guys mill around.

I ask around for Tim and find him behind the building surveying the damage.

"Hey, are you Tim?"

"Yeah. I am. Who're you?"

He looks me up and down. He looks like the typical contractor, obviously done plenty of work with his hands, definitely the boss. He has jarhead–like features and graying black hair. He bears a striking resemblance to Jordo.

"I'm Nick, your nephew's friend. He said you needed some help with some work?"

He turns to me and stares for an uncomfortably long time.

"I don't *need* anything," he says, then pauses. "I have some work that *can* be done. Do you want to do it?"

"Uh, sure. What is it?"

He points to the burnt wreckage of a building. "See all this shit? I want you to grab a sledgehammer and go to work and break this shit up until we can load it all up in the truck and go dump it. You up for that?"

"Yeah, I can do that," I say. I wasn't really looking for manual labor work, but fuck it, I need money.

"Well you're a pretty big guy, so I assume you can do it. Last time Jordo sent me a guy that needed work he was one of his coke–snorting buddies, a real fucking pussy. Are you one of them, one of Jordo's coke–sniffing buddies?"

"No, I don't touch that shit."

"Good. Usually I'd hire some day laborers for this kind of shit, pay them eight bucks an hour. You being Jordo's friend and all, I'll give you ten bucks an hour provided you're a hard worker. Sound good?"

"Yes. Thanks."

"Okay, grab a sledgehammer out of the truck and get to work. The more you get done now the less you have to do when it's a hundred and seven fucking degrees out in a few hours."

I grab that hammer and get to it. It's tough fucking work. I swing the fucker as hard as I can; every time it hits, the impact spreads through my body and vibrates my bones. I swing through it. When I get tired I think about what a fuck–up I am, that pisses me off, and I swing the hammer that much harder. When that stops working, I think about how I'm sure that Sarah was fucking someone else while I was in jail, *that* was why she kicked me out, and I get furious again and I smash and smash the concrete and charred wood and metal. The sun gets higher and it gets hotter and hotter. I'm pouring sweat by eleven o'clock. Someone brings me a jug of water. I don't take more than thirty seconds or so to break for a drink, and I smoke while hammering. My hands get raw and blistered but I do not fucking stop. I destroy the

remnants of the charred building as best as I can. Memories of old high
school wrestling workouts pop up, reminding me of how they drilled
into us the ability to push our bodies far past the point where our minds
insist that we're tired. I cling to that and push myself.

After almost five hours, I've slowed down a bit but I'm still swinging.
One of my hands is bleeding. Tim comes over and tells me it's good
enough. We load a trailer bed with the fruits of my labor and everyone
but Tim gets in the truck and leaves to dump it off.

Tim pulls out a wad of money and counts out three twenty dollar
bills and hands them to me.

"You aren't one of Jordo's faggoty coke friends, I'll give you that,"
he says. "You got some work ethic, huh?"

"Thanks."

"See you around, Nick," he says.

He turns around to get in his truck. I follow after him.

"Hey, Tim, if you don't mind me asking, is there any more work I
can get soon? I'm kind of hard up and looking to get whatever I can."

Tim turns around and looks at me for a moment. Again, he looks me
in the eyes for a little too long. It gets uncomfortable. Finally he says,
"Sure. Come for a ride in my truck and we'll talk about it."

We get in his truck; it's well–worn but clean on the inside. He pulls
out of the lot and we leave the edge of Chandler and Phoenix and
hop onto the I–10 and head west. He doesn't talk. I get the impression
I'm not supposed to either. I figure we're heading to another worksite
or something; I don't really care at this point. The exhaustion of the
day's work is catching up with me. I'm gonna be pretty fucking sore
tomorrow, that's for sure. I could easily fall asleep right now.

He stops at a gas station and comes out with a sports drink and
sandwich for me. "You look like you need it," he says. I thank him and
he nods.

We drive in what seems like circles, down side streets, through strip
malls and alleys. He peers out the window often. Finally we stop in an

alley behind a strip mall, behind a check–cashing joint, next to a salon and a liquor store. He asks me to step outside of the car so he can make a phone call. He taps on the glass a minute later and motions me back in.

"In about five minutes a car is coming, a Nissan Titan pickup. The driver is going to park right where we are right now, and wait for someone. That someone is not going to show up. I'm going to park at the other end of this lot, down by that fast food joint. When the guy in the Titan shows, I want you to wait for him to get out of his truck. When he does, you're to inform him that he owes Roy one thousand dollars, and that he has been dodging his debt for long enough, and that if he doesn't pay it on the spot you'll be forced to take his account into collection. Got it?"

My heart skips a little, fuck, I was not expecting this. "Sure. And if he refuses to pay, you want me to, well…"

"Whup his fucking ass. Take whatever he has on him or in the car. If he doesn't have cash or a card, you can take the fucking Titan for all I care. Just take something of value. And hurt him. Don't kill him or anything, but definitely break something. And not a finger, something that lets him know the severity of his situation. You up for that? If you aren't, just get the fuck out of here right now."

He looks at me. The motherfucker is pretty intense. Fuck it, I got this.

"Yeah, no problem. I got this."

He nods and I get out. He parks the car down by a Jack in the Box.

I light a cig and wait by a dumpster behind the checks–cashed joint. The Titan shows up ten minutes later. I stay crouched by the dumpster where this guy can't see me. I wait for him to get out of the truck. A few more minutes go by and he still hasn't gotten out of the car. I make a judgment call and spring out from behind the dumpster and rush up to the driver door, which the moron left unlocked. I drag him out of the car. He is not a big guy but not a small one either, maybe 160–180 pounds. He doesn't have his seat belt on, so pulling him out of the truck isn't much of a problem. He frees one hand on the way out and tries to grab a .45 underneath his seat. He doesn't succeed. I drag him to the ground and put my weight on top of him, keep him pinned. He struggles but even as tired as I am, I'm much, much stronger than him. My heart pounds with fucking adrenaline rushes. Just get this over with. "Listen, man, it's like this. You owe Roy money and you've been dodging him. I'm going to offer you a simple and relatively pain free way out of this. Give me the money you owe, get back in the truck, and get the fuck out of here. Otherwise I'm going to have to break something. Or break some *things* rather. So just pay up."

"Fuck you, faggot," he says.

I head butt him hard, an old bouncing trick. His nose shatters in a mess of blood.

"Your account has now gone into collections. I told you this could be easy, but I guess you'd prefer it this way. I'm going to break your collarbone now."

I hold him down by the neck with one hand. His blood flows down his face onto my hand. I make a fist and prepare to smash it down on his collarbone.

"Wait," he says. "I have some money in my pocket, not the full seven hundred, but at least a couple hundred–"

"Your debt is a thousand dollars, and that's what you're going to pay, right now."

"That's bullshit," he coughs through the blood, "I owe seven hundred!"

I slap him hard, right on his broken nose. He yelps in pain.

"One thousand. Non–negotiable," I say.

"Okay, well, I got two hundred in my pocket and we can go to an ATM and get"

I hit him again, this time on the side of his head. "We aren't going anywhere. Pay up, pay now."

He digs a hand into his pocket and pulls out a crumpled wad of twenties.

"There," he says. "It's all I have, but I swear I'll have the rest tonight or tomorrow, I just need —"

I move my hand toward his pockets and he gets really fidgety and squirms, tries to prevent me from emptying them. I cock back and sock him right on the jaw. He goes limp for a moment and then resumes his feeble struggle. I dig through his pockets and find another wad of bills, another two hundred dollars. I drag him up off the ground, he struggles a bit more so I punch him in the gut and knock the wind out of him. He collapses and gasps for air.

I take his keys out of the ignition and put them in my pocket, then grab the pistol from underneath the seat and tuck it in my waistband under my shirt. Last, I check the center console, where there's another wad of bills, these hundreds. I jam them in my pocket.

I get out and open the back door of the truck and start to jam this guy into his backseat. Tim then pulls up, followed by another car, a Grand Cherokee. Two guys get out of the Cherokee and advance toward me.

"Nice work, kid," one of them says to me. "Keys?"

Tim rolls down his window. "Give them the keys, Nick, they got it from here."

I do as he says.

They hop into the Titan and pull away, followed by the Cherokee. I get in Tim's truck and we leave. Casually. My heart is still pounding. I light a cig, notice the blood all over my hand. Tim hands me a towel and I wipe off. I'm stunned, I can't fucking believe I just got through all that, in broad fucking daylight. I mean, we were sort off hidden behind the checks – cashed building, I mean, I've ripped off and beat on street trash and petty drug dealers before, but always at night, never anything close to this.

"That shit with the hammer today, that was impressive, Nick. But what you just did there, I mean, you took a little longer that you should have, but still, that was fucking beautiful work, Nick."

I see Tim smile for the first time.

I dig through my pockets and hand him the wads of cash. He keeps the wad of hundreds but hands the rest back to me, five hundred bucks all in all.

"For a job well done. You can keep that pistol, too, though you need to unload it pretty fast. You don't want that piece of shit's piece on you. It probably has some interesting history on it, you know?"

"Okay, I'll get rid of it."

"Good. You familiar with guns, Nick?"

"Yes," I say. "Well, I grew up hunting and target shooting quite a bit."

He nods.

We don't talk for the rest of the ride back to the car lot. I'm spent every which way, but for the first time in as long as I can remember, I don't feel an overwhelming need for a drink. That is a fucking miracle.

Tim drops me off at my car.

"You did good today, Nick, real good. You follow orders and don't ask a lot of questions. I like that. You keep your mouth shut and don't talk to anyone about this, okay? You passed the test today. Go home and get some sleep. We'll talk soon."

Chapter 7: HACK

I'VE BEEN DRIVING FOR ABOUT sixteen hours, at least two hours too long. A sea of coffee isn't going to set this weariness straight. This is my last ride, I need some fucking sleep. I'm stuck in traffic on the 202–Loop, bringing a boring but talkative woman (the worst combination) to the airport for some vacation to Georgia or some other southern shithole she won't stop blabbering about. I'm sure she's a nice broad, I don't see anything in her that suggests otherwise, but my fucking nerves are frayed. Please, lady, will you shut the fuck up? Nothing puts me in a foul mood like looking around and seeing a sea of people, fresh–faced and ready to tackle the day, and here is me, dirty and still awake from a bleary–eyed night of carting around the night's dregs. Forgive me for not giving a shit about your exciting vacation, sweetheart.

I turn the radio up to drone her out. The reporter on the news channel talks about a grisly discovery out in the desert off of Table Mesa Road. Some ATVers found a torched Nissan Titan at the bottom of a ravine. Upon further inspection they found a charred corpse in the backseat, the reporter says, and the sheriff's office is looking for anyone with information…

The broad in the backseat is so self–absorbed; she talks and talks but I don't listen. I think about this charred truck out in the desert, I picture the killers rolling that Titan truck off the road; it falls down the ravine…I wonder if they started the fire first and then rolled it, or maybe they didn't plan a fire at all and the truck just happened to catch on fire as it crashed and rolled, or best of all, maybe they rolled the car down the ravine and then hiked down and torched it; did they walk back to the road with that furious orange glow of fire lighting up the desert, that awesome heat at their backs, that loving sound of flames feeding?…Fuck…

I drop blabbermouth off at the airport. She tips me well and now I sort of feel bad about ignoring her, but goddamn, the thought of that Titan burning bright out there alone in the desert, now that's something. The image of that fire tumbling yellow and orange, billowing clouds of rubbery black smoke, it gives me a much–needed second wind. I say fuck it and pick up one more fare; just one more and then I'll go home and finally get some sleep.

Chapter 8: NICK

HAVING CASH IN MY HAND IS TEMPTING. I almost buy a few bottles of booze, but I keep my head straight and pay another week's rent and get some groceries instead. I unload that pistol for four hundred bucks to a friend of a friend. Holding this much cash in my pocket is trouble; it's a lot easier to stay on the straight and narrow when you don't have shit. I do the things I'm supposed to do. I go to a meeting and go out for coffee with some guys afterward, shoot the shit about what's going on in the sober world. I steer the conversation away when anyone asks what's going on with me. I sleep pretty damn well; this first week of sobriety is easier than it has traditionally been.

I wake up to the phone ringing. It's still dark out; phone says its five thirty a.m. I answer. It's Tim.

"Nick. You up for some work today? And by today I mean right now," he says.

"Sure, just tell me where to be."

I write down the address, get dressed, and head out.

I stop for a cup of coffee and something to eat on the way. The cashier tells me it is supposed to be at least a hundred and twelve degrees today. I head out toward Fountain Hills, a decent drive down the 101 and down

Shea toward the reservation. I pound the coffee–fuck; I didn't sleep more than three or four hours. It might be a long day. A cab swerves into my lane and I react just in time and lay on the horn. The fucking cabby flips me off and I return the favor. The sun's coming up as I reach the heart of Fountain Hills, a nice sprawl of moneyed suburbia, sprawling single–level houses carved onto the edge of hills for good desert views. I follow the GPS directions on my phone and find Tim's truck at the end of a cul–de–sac. I roll my windows down and am greeted with a slight desert breeze. The night's insect drone is just starting to die down. Mornings look a lot more hopeful when I haven't been up drinking all night, that's for sure. Yes, it's a beautiful fucking morning. I get out of the car and study the house Tim and his crew are working on. I wouldn't mind waking up in a house like this, maybe with a sweet and quiet wife next to me, maybe a kid or two down the hall. I've been through enough craziness. The simple shit in life, all the normalcy that I used to look at with pure dread, it's starting to look pretty damn good.

Tim and his guys are putting in a new patio on the side of the house, digging and leveling out the desert landscaping to make way for a new brick patio next to the pool and hot tub. Tim nods at me as I approach and motions me aside. We talk underneath a huge grapefruit tree.

"I'm going to need you to put some hours in with my work crew at least three or four days a week. You're going to want that W–2 to help wash your cash. Cool? Okay, get a shovel and get to work."

I grab a shovel and start picking at the tough sand and rock to make a foundation for the porch. Scorpions scurry as I get a few inches deep. We dig down for an hour or so, then grab hoes and levelers and flatten the area out. A truck shows up with the tile bricks and we go to work carefully laying them out in perfect, flat order. It's tedious work but the time flies by. We wrap up the job around one or so. Tim tells me to meet him at a diner in Fountain Hills.

I find him sitting in a corner of the restaurant and join him. I wait for him to start some conversation. He takes his time, preoccupied with reading the classified ads. A waitress arrives and we order breakfast. She leaves and Tim starts to talk.

"So you met Jordo in the tents, huh," he asks. "What charge they get on you?" he asks.

"Disorderly conduct, fighting. Misdemeanor assault. Failure to pay fees. My lawyer pled it down to misdemeanor disorderly conduct, but I still ended up doing around thirty days."

"You a felon?"

"No."

"Good. Was this your first charge?"

"No, I had a DUI a few years back and some other minor shit. This was my first time locked up for more than a day or two."

"So what happened? Those petty cases don't usually get that much time."

"This guy, he was my ex's old boyfriend, he was still stuck on her I guess, he found out where I worked and came in and started some shit. The other bouncers tossed him out before anything really happened. I returned the favor, went to the bank where he worked and broke his jaw. I got away from that, but a week later I was walking to my car when he and a few of his friends tried to jump me. I knocked the first guy that came at me out cold, then the rest scattered like pussies. I chased one down and put a beating on him. The cops rolled up and got the story, but decided that even though they came at me, the fact that I chased one of 'em down was good for an assault charge."

"So what, you like fighting, huh?"

"No. Not at all, actually. I guess I just have a bad habit of always wanting to even the score."

"Jordo tells me you're a pretty bright guy. Went to college and everything."

"Yeah. ASU. Sociology major. I wanted to be a social worker."

"Yeah? And what happened to that?"

"I got drunk. I'd been sober for five years. I started drinking and everything went to shit. I've spent the last, I dunno, four years or so repeating the same stupid shit–sober for a few months, drunk for a few more, that cycle."

"You drinking right now?"

"No. I've managed to put some days together."

"Good. I can't have you drinking if you want to work with me, not if you're a drunk. So if you get drunk and fuck up you're liable to get hurt–or worse. You got that?"

"Sure." I swallow. I don't typically react well to threats, but the way Tim does it, so calm—effortless even—so matter of fact, it's pretty fucking intimidating.

"That guy you worked over the other day, the shithead in the Titan? He used to work with me. Shit, I even considered him a friend at one point. But he fucked up, and you saw what happened to him."

"I got it," I say, curt enough to let him know I understand, but at the same time I'm not going to be bullied around. You can't just be too meek and submissive around guys like Tim; you let the wrong people push you around too much and they lose respect for you. My time on the streets has taught me that much.

"You seem like a smart kid," Tim says. "You're obviously big and tough, but I don't need another meathead to bust heads. Those are easy to find. I need someone with half a brain that can keep a low profile and do some very simple, simple but profitable, work. I think you might be a good fit."

Our food arrives and we dig in. I am fucking starving from digging and hauling tile all morning. The violence of the other day not lost on me, I have to let Tim know what's what before this conversation goes any further.

"Look Tim," I say. "I'm looking to work, and I can do whatever it is you need, and I'll do it well, but I gotta let you know that there're a couple of things I don't do. I don't kill people and I don't move drugs. I figure I should let you know that now before we go on with this."

Tim smiles. "I don't need you to kill anyone. There're plenty of fucking killers in this town, maybe too many." He laughs. "And I don't fuck around with selling dope either. Too much heat in that. Too much competition. I have a family, a wife and two girls. I have the contracting business. I keep it all regimented. Tightly."

He passes me the classifieds he's been looking at. "This is what I want you to do." He points his finger at the Sporting Goods listings, which are almost all ads for guns for sale. I look over them and pass it back to him and shrug.

"I want you to buy guns, private sale only," He says. "As you probably know, private sales are perfectly legal here in the great state of Arizona. All you need is cash. Some pricks might want to see an Arizona driver's license or write down the numbers or even make you sign a bill of sale. That's no problem, I can get you a phony license for that, and you learn how to sign a good fake signature. Most people selling guns don't give a fuck. They just want the cash and maybe a sweaty handshake. It's very simple."

"So you want me to buy guns? That's it?"

"Yes, I want you to buy guns. A lot of them. And again, only private sale. But you have to be smart about it. Buy in different parts of town, never from the same guy more than once. Never at the gun shows. You don't talk to the sellers more than you need to, you don't give them any personal info. You don't become their fucking pal. You use a prepaid phone, and get a new one at least once a week. All you do is buy, buy, buy—but buy smart. And once a month or so you come down south with me and watch my back while we unload them. It's that easy. Very easy."

I think it over. It sounds like an easy thing to do. Arizona is gun crazy. People buy and sell guns all day in this town, but getting popped for a straw purchase or selling large volumes of guns for illicit purposes is serious prison time. Like anything, it comes down to money.

"How do I get paid?"

"Simple. You buy the guns, semi–autos only, rifles are the best, preferably AKs or ARs, but semi–auto pistols are good too. Shotguns are okay but don't pay as much. Stick to the semi–auto rifles as much as possible. You can buy with your cash or I can front you some. You Jew the seller down as much as possible, buy it, hold on to it until drop time, and we go down and sell them for three or maybe four times what we paid. It's always an easy transaction, not much haggling over price, all cash. Little to no bullshit. I get half of whatever we sell your guns for."

"How much are we talking about?"

"They'll buy whatever we have. Every time. You'll bring in ten grand a drop if you can hustle up enough units to sell. Take a look at this, for example."

He points to one of the ads.

"This guy is selling a shitty Romanian AK for four hundred dollars. You can talk him down to three twenty–five, no problem. Our clients will buy that same piece for twelve hundred. You multiply that by ten and you got nine grand. Easy."

"And the clients? What's stopping them from trying to rip you off?"

"Simple. It's easy, but not as easy as it sounds. I deliver every time. They have pretty much an unlimited demand, and your typical spic or eggplant gangbanger can't keep up without getting stupid and getting caught. I run a professional operation. They know that. They rob me and their best supplier is gone and they're back dealing with the fucking mutants."

The waitress drops off the check. I wait for her to walk away.

"So these guys are from across the border, I'm guessing? Cartel guys?"

"You could call them that. The big cartel guys, the big players, they get the military grade shit, full autos, explosives, all that shit, they get it from the South and Central Americans, from the Russians, shit, they get it from their own police forces and armies. The small to mid–level guys, the guys trying to fight their way up, they got the dope and the cash but they need firepower, and the easiest way for them to get it is from the States. And no matter how much you sell them, they'll always ask for more. I don't know if you've noticed, Nick, but there is full on war going on down there, and these crazy wetbacks are killing each other off by the thousands; fuck it, the tens of thousands. Now I've never much cared for these Mexican fucks, but if I can make a buck off of them wasting one another, fuck it, why not?"

He flashes that awkward grin of his. He has a weird vibe, sort of reminds me of my hard–ass high school gym coach that we were all convinced did some pretty strange shit during his time off.

"I have a few other guys working for me doing the same thing, so I suggest you jump on whatever you can get for now. The classifieds are good, but the internet is even better. Backpage.com is probably your best bet."

I nod. "Okay. I can do this."

"Yeah, I think you can. I wouldn't put my neck out like this if I didn't. I gotta remind you, kid; there is no room for mistakes here. You fuck up once and you're dead. It's a simple gig, with a simple ending for you if you fuck up. Got it?"

"Yes. I won't fuck up. Thanks for this, Tim. I really appreciate it."

He flips out a few bills for the check and I follow him outside. We go to his car where he digs underneath a seat and pulls out an envelope and hands it to me. I slip it into my belt.

"This is 5k, that lasts most of the other guys a week. When you're tapped out you bring the product to the storage lot where I store all the shit for the contracting business. Depending on when the next drop is, you either sit tight or I break off some more cash for you to work with. When you build up your own roll, the split is fifty–fifty. While you're working with my money you get a quarter of whatever the profit is. Got it?"

"Sure."

"Good. Take the day off from the crew tomorrow and get started with the guns. I'll see you bright and early the day after tomorrow, I'm gonna need you to swing a hammer. And, Nick, you drink up even a penny of that money and I'll have you digging your own grave. Got it?"

"Yes."

He slaps me on the shoulder and gets in and drives off. It dawns on me that I'm sweating, not just from the brutal fucking heat bouncing off the pavement…my nerves are kicking with a little excitement and little more fear. I know I can do this, no problem. It's an easy enough gig if I play it right. As long as I don't drink, this will be a breeze. I just hope that the possibility of a violent death is enough to keep me sober. I do this for just a few months and I should have more than enough cash to get set up and start living a normal, beautiful, boring life. I just gotta get there.

Chapter 9: HACK

THIS FARE IS A REAL PAIN IN THE ASS. I picked him up from
Axis Radius nightclub, stumbling drunk, and he's been shouting into
his cell phone ever since, slurring through a retarded argument with
someone whom I gather to be is his girlfriend. He wants to go to a strip
club in Tempe. It's not too long of a ride but the prick and his stupid
conversation are really grating. I grit my teeth and turn up the radio to
try and tune him out.

"Will you turn the fucking radio down? I'm on the phone!"

He shouts at me like I'm a fucking servant. I grin, turn down the
radio. I study him through the rearview mirror. What a fucking pig.
He's wearing a flashy, faggoty collared shirt with all sorts of stupid
designs all over it. It barely contains his gut; his double chin almost
hanging over its collar. He's wearing a tight pair of designer jeans,
expensive, the kind that come pre–ripped and cost hundreds of dollars.
A diamond–lined watch with an absurdly large face sits on his wrist.
He has a gold Star of David on his neck.

"Hey kid," I say. He doesn't acknowledge me. I say it again, louder.
He groans and presses his phone on his chest.

"What?"

"Are you Jewish?"

"What?"

"You're wearing a star of David," I say. "I assume you're Jewish?"

"Yes, I am. Why? Is that a fucking problem?"

"No, not at all. I just don't run across a lot of Jewish folks in this town."

He groans again. "Well that's just fascinating. Look buddy, why don't you focus on the road and stop interrupting my conversation, huh?" He goes back to his phone conversation, even louder, he's now shouting at whoever is on the line.

I wait a few seconds and I slam on the brakes. The cab skids and screeches and then comes to a full halt on the road. There are no other cars or people in sight.

The kid wasn't wearing his seatbelt; the sudden stop sends him slamming into the back of the front seat. He takes a second to gather himself and then starts yelling at me. "What the fuck is wrong with you? What the fuck, do you know how to fucking drive? I could have broken my fucking nose!"

"I saw a cat on the road," I say.

"I don't give a fuck! I could have your fucking license revoked for this shit! Now get me to the fucking club. And if you see another stupid fucking cat, run over it, okay?"

He picks up his cell phone up off the floor. He redials and gets back to his tirade, starting with a loud complaint about his "retarded cab driver and how he almost killed me."

I speed the cab up to fifty and count to 20. I check my mirrors then turn around toward him and grab the cell phone out of his hand and toss it out the window in one quick, fluid motion. I watch it bounce off the asphalt through the rearview mirror. I gun the car up to sixty. He's shocked, without words for a good thirty seconds. He lets it out.

"You motherfucker! I'm going to have you fucking arrested! That's a five hundred dollar phone! I want your name, you piece of shit!"

He goes on and on, shouting and cursing me. I take a turn off the road. We're stopped on an empty, dark side street.

"What the fuck? Why are we stopped? I'll kick your fucking ass! What the fuck is this—"

He shuts up when I reach under my seat and pull out the Colt 1911 I keep there. I casually turn around and press it to his forehead. I press the barrel into his forehead and he flinches back. The scent of warm urine fills the cab.

His voice rises several octaves: "Whoa, I'm sorry man, I'm sorry, I don't want trouble, just let me go, I won't tell anyone, I'm sorry," He starts to shake. "Look, I got money, man, I got this watch, this watch is worth over two grand, I'll give it to you, just let me go!"

He pleads.

"I don't want your money, Steven." I say, quietly. "I don't want your fucking watch."

"What *do* you want? And wait, how do you know my name? How do you know my fucking name?" He screeches.

"I want you to tell me something."

"What, what do you mean?" His lip quivers.

"I want you to tell me something."

"Sure, anything, please, whatever you want, just let me go!"

I turn the cab off with one hand; keep the pistol at his forehead with the other. I move the barrel back a few inches to give him a little room to talk.

"I want you to tell me about Lily McDaniels," I tell him.

His face goes pale with the mention of that name. His eyes widen. He was shaking before. Now he trembles.

"I don't know what you're talking about," he says.

"Lily McDaniels. Tell me about her."

He shakes his head. "I don't know who that is."

I push the barrel against his head again.

"I asked one simple thing of you; since you're not willing, I'm going to have to kill you."

I start to get out of the car.

"No, wait, stop!"

"Yes?"

"She was my neighbor. Lily McDaniels was my neighbor in high school. She lived next door."

"And?"

"What do you want? I told you who she is, but, but, but how do you know about her, why do you—what the fuck do you want?"

"I want you to tell me about Lily McDaniels."

"I did, I did, I don't know anything about her, she was just my neighbor! That was like, ten years ago, I don't know, she was just a kid that lived next door—"

I smack the barrel across his forehead, not too hard, just enough to get him to shut up.

"Okay, she was just a kid that lived next door I guess. But let me tell you something, Steven. I want to tell you about Lily McDaniels, what happened to her, what happened to Lilly McDaniels?"

He whimpers.

"You don't want to talk?"

He shakes his head again, pleads for me to let him go.

"Fine," I say. "You sit there and listen, and when I'm done I'll let you out of this cab and let you walk away, Okay, Steven?"

He nods. He's crying now. I start with the story.

"Lily McDaniels was a freshman at UC–Berkeley this last fall. She was very pretty, as you probably remember. She grew up to be a real pretty young lady. And smart too, brilliant even. She was a truly gifted student. She was pre–med and wanted to go on to be a pediatric neurosurgeon. She wanted to save little kid's lives. She had a lot of friends, her family adored her. She had a very bright future ahead of her. But you know what, Steven?"

He doesn't reply, so I jam the barrel into his forehead, hard.

"What," he whispers.

"Despite all that, her smarts, her beauty, her friends, her loving family, her brilliant future, despite all that, Lily McDaniels hated herself. She hated herself, Steven. She couldn't bear the way it felt to be her, to live inside her skin. And you know what she did, Steven? Do you know what she did in empty rooms and bathroom stalls and whenever she was alone, Steven? She cut herself. She'd drag a razor or a thumb tack, anything sharp, she'd drag it on her skin, just deep enough to bleed and leave a scar, always in a place where no one could see. So no one knew that Lily cut herself, she cut herself because for some odd reason that brief sensation of pain gave her a release from something, something inside that tortured her."

Steven moans and then sobs.

"What's that, Steven? Does that bother you? What, do you know what it was that tortured poor sweet Lily?"

He shakes his head back and forth, his eyes closed.

"This story doesn't have a happy ending, Steven. I'm sorry. About three months ago, Lily McDaniels used a credit card her parents gave her to rent a hotel room. She drew a bath, got in, and took three Xanax. She took Xanax, Steven, she took them because she had these awful panic attacks, Steven, awful, like the world was collapsing on her. She took the pills and when they started to kick in she took a razorblade and she dragged it deep across her arms, with the veins, not against them, the right way. She cut her arms open and she passed out from the Xanax and the blood loss, she fell asleep in that tub and she never woke up."

Steven sobs again. He starts to rock back and forth.

I give it a minute for it all to sink in. The cab is thick with silence and tension. I resume.

"The maid found her the next day, found this pretty little girl, all blue and dead in a bathtub deep red with blood. And you know what the worst part of it all was? No one knew why she did it. No one knew why someone as special as Lily would go and do such an awful thing like that, Steven."

I move my face close to his.

"But I know why, Steven. I know why Lily did it. I know why Lily did it, I know what tortured her, I know her secret, Steven, yes I do. I know what ruined poor Lily." I move my face right up against his ear, whisper to him: "And you know too, don't you, Steven?"

I pull back and grin at him. He starts to shake his head back and forth, violently.

"Oh yes you do, Steven, you know, don't you? Huh, buddy?"

He howls and starts to shout about not knowing what I'm talking about. He pushes on the side of the door and tries to get out. I slam the pistol onto his face, once, twice, and he falls back on the seat with his hands held to his bloody face. I get out of the car, open the back door, and drag him out by his feet. I let him fall down onto the pavement. He rolls over and tries to get up. I kick him back down and he starts to crawl away. I let him go for a few feet, then I slam my heel on his back to make him stop. I flip him around. I hover over him.

"I want you to tell me what it was that tortured Lily; I want you to tell me what made her do what she did."

He shakes his head.

I put the gun to his head.

"You have ten seconds to tell me or I'm going to kill you right here. Ten…nine…eight…"

"Okay, wait, wait," He sobs, does that sputtering lip thing as the snot and tears mix with the blood from his nose.

"Yes?"

"I know why."

"Why?"

"Because…" he starts and trails off.

I start the count down again. " Seven…six…five…four…"

He lets it out.

"Because I touched her!" He spits the words out between heavy sobs. "I touched her all over, I took her into the house when no one was home and I touched her and did other things and I did it more than once and, I, I, I told her that if she told anyone I'd kill her."

"How old were you when you first did that?"

"Fifteen."

"And how old was she?"

"Nine," he lets out a long, pitiful howl of a moan.

"And when did it stop?"

"When she moved, when, when, her family moved, when they moved two years later."

"How many times, Steven, how many times did you touch her, did you put your dick in her mouth, did you put your finger inside her, how many times did you use your tongue—"

"Stop," He moans. Please stop."

"Fifteen times, Steven," I say. "Fifteen times."

He rolls over and buries his hands in his face.

"Okay, bonus round. This is it, buddy. Just One more question, Steven. Here it is: Have you touched anyone since then, Steven? Have you molested any innocent little girls since then?"

"No!"

"I don't believe you, Steven. I don't believe you at all. In fact, I know for a fact you have a file hidden on your computer with pictures, Steven; wow, Steven, a lot of pictures. Wow, Steven, you're one sick fuck, aren't you?"

"Stop, please stop!"

"Answer the question and we're done, Steven. Have you touched a little girl since her?"

He makes a sound, barely audible.

I grab his hair and jam the pistol into his temple.

"Answer me, you sick fuck!"

"Yes."

I kick him in the side of the face, hard. It knocks him out cold. I drag him to the middle of the street and stretch his arms and limbs out. I get in the cab, start it up, pull out, and swerve around him. I drive off and leave him lying in the middle of the road, one pathetic mess of blood, fat, and feigned guilt. He has something coming and it's not good.

Chapter 10: NICK

THAT FIVE GRAND IS ALMOST GONE after three days. I guess I have a knack for this shit. I have a solid stash jammed behind the dresser in the apartment: two Glocks, a Mossberg 500, a Romanian AK, a shitty AR, a decent Colt AR, a Saiga AK, two SKSs and a Ruger 10–22.

Tim tells me to stop by the yard tonight—it's Friday—to drop the guns off and pick up some more cash. The drop is next week and he wants this to be the biggest sale yet. It's a competition amongst me and the other guys he has out there to see who can get the best of the best. Buying guns is easy, but we're all clambering to get the AKs and ARs; competition is steep for those. I've only had to use the phony ID Tim gave me once. Most of the sellers just want the cash, fast and easy. Some of them want to talk; I'm polite but make sure to get away as quick as I can. The gig itself is easy, but having an arsenal like this in my pay–by–the–week apartment is a little nerve–racking. I'm eager to unload the stuff tonight.

I have a couple of hours to kill before I meet up with Tim, so I take the time to check in with my AA sponsor Gary for my weekly reminder of how shitty I am at "working the program." We sit down for coffee at a shop in Tempe, surrounded by the fucking dimes that go to ASU.

The sun sets, and as I drink a couple of cups of motor–oil–strong coffee, I begin to feel a forgotten sensation, a nervous excitement–I guess it is enthusiasm. It's been awhile since I've been able to look past today or tomorrow and actually assume that things will get better. These years of constant relapse have kind of fucked up my sense of time; it's tough to plan and to hope when you're expect a whirling shit storm to pounce on you at any given moment.

Gary reads out of the Big Book in his monotone accountant voice, reads a chapter by the name of "We Agnostics." He is convinced I'm devoid of any spiritual understanding; it's tough to argue with that one.

My mind wanders to the tables of girls around me. I tune Gary out, but when he reads, *"We who have traveled this dubious path..."* I zone back in. I even jump up slightly in my chair.

He notices and laughs. "Something on your mind, Nick?"

Gary is one boring fucker, but I envy that. At one time he had nothing but a garbage bag, a ten–speed, and a couple domestic abuse charges. Ten years later he's a pillar of society, a hardworking family man. I'm certain he falls asleep with no worries or fears; he wakes up each day with no dread or apprehension. Normal.

"No," I answer. "Well, nothing new, just don't remember the last time I heard something that makes so much sense, you know, describes my life so well. Dubious path. I like that."

He reads on. My mind wanders and I tune him out again, start thinking about the guns in my Jeep, about how I only have to do this for a couple months or so and I'll have enough money to get my shit straight, not have to work at a night club or a titty bar—

"Some of us had already walked far over the Bridge of Reason toward the desired shore of faith. The outlines and the promise of the New Land had brought luster to tired eyes and courage to flagging spirits."

That snaps me back again.

Gary stops reading, tells me to reread the whole chapter on my own before we meet again to work on the second step. We shoot the shit for a while, talk about non–sobriety stuff. He tells me a strange story about how the police in Phoenix found a mangled body on a backstreet somewhere, literally torn to pieces, how they were baffled as to how it got that way—it was almost as if it had been ripped apart. The only identifiable item they found was a gold Star of David necklace found buried in the pulp of blood and tissue.

It's a strange thing for Gary to talk about, not really his typical topic of conversation. I point this out and he tells me that it was one his other sponsees who found the body, a UPS driver on his early a.m. route.

"The guy is pretty shook up about it. He thought it was road kill, maybe a dog or coyote or something," Gary says. "The cops think it was hit and run, maybe a semi or something."

He steers the conversation back to me, about what I'm doing with myself. I tell him about working for Tim the contractor, swinging a hammer and doing grunt work. He tells me that if I put some work in it and stay sober, better opportunities will present themselves.

"They always do," he says. "When you stay sober, that is."

I make a commitment to make the coffee at an AA meeting he runs after he insists I do so, just to keep me accountable. He reminds me to call him every day, no matter what. I agree and I take off. I smile at a few girls on my walk to the car.

Tim's storage lot is in the industrial area not far from the fairgrounds, toward the west side of town. I roll the windows down in the Jeep and I blast a Hendrix CD. Jimi and his guitar have me reminiscing about the good days of my drinking, back when it was all about partying; I drank beer and ate mushrooms and had a fantastic fucking time and still managed to operate as a normal human being most of the time. This was before the drinking became me instead of just being a part of me; shit obviously got pretty rough pretty fast. I didn't end up in rehab or living in a halfway house for six months by mistake. It got worse after I relapsed after five years of sobriety; that took me to lows I had never experienced, and yeah, I guess it fractured me a bit, changed me, and I suppose that's why I'm driving across town in a car loaded with guns bound for drug gangs in Mexico.

I get there. Tim's lot is surrounded by razor wire. I flash my brights. Someone comes out and unlocks the gate for me. I pull into the lot. Tim and a couple of guys are sitting outside a tool shack. I introduce myself, then realize they're the guys that showed up that day I shook down the guy in the Titan. They shake my hand but don't tell me their names. The lot is dark; a few floodlights hang from the fence around the perimeter, giving the area a faint yellow glow. Tim has me pull my Jeep into the aluminum garage and closes the shutter door behind me. I breathe deep when the door shuts; the garage is hot as fuck and near pitch black. The only light comes from a Maglite in Tim's hands. Tim and his two guys start to open metal footlockers. No one says anything to me for a few minutes.

"Take the guns out," Tim tells me.

I pull them out from underneath the seats and the spare tire, hand them to Tim and his guys one by one. They spread the guns out over the hood of the car and look them over.

"Not bad," Tim says. "They really don't want a fucking twenty–two though. They're looking to massacre people, not shoot squirrels or plink at tin cans. But not bad work nonetheless; a decent lot of guns, all in all."

"Get more AKs next time," the other guy says. "They fucking love AKs."

"Nick is coming with us on the next drop," Tim says.

"You sure about that?" the tall guy asks Tim.

"Yes," Tim replies. "And it's not your place to question it, is it?"

"I guess not."

"You don't guess shit," Tim barks. "You know. Got it? Anyway, you saw him the other day; he can handle himself just fine. We need more of us out there; it reassures these fucks that we have a strong operation going, not some fucking lone ranger shit. These fucks can't help themselves from preying on the weak, so we always show our strength. Don't forget that shit."

The guys start loading the guns into the footlockers. Tim motions for me to follow him outside.

"Good stuff, Nick. Good for your first buy. I assume you played it the way I told you to?"

"Of course. It was all very low key, all different sellers in different parts of town. I got rid of the prepaid and that phony ID you gave me."

"Good, I'll give you another on Monday. No work this weekend, okay? Not on the crew, and not with the guns. Take a couple of days off and relax. Good?"

"Sure, no problem," I say.

"You okay for money?"

"Well, the 5k is about gone."

"Yeah, I'll get you more cash on Monday. But what about in general, you got some cash for bills and stuff?"

"I'm a little low, to be honest. But I should be fine this weekend."

Tim nods. "Jordo's excited to see you again. He's setting up the next drop, that's why he's down in Tucson. He's pretty sharp when he's not chasing tail and putting that shit up his nose."

"Yeah, it'll be good to see him. He is, well, he *was* very entertaining in the tents. Always holding court and talking shit, telling stories—"

I stop midsentence; I notice Tim is giving me the "I don't give a fuck" look.

He talks. "So, yeah, about the money. I got something tonight, something a little unusual, and I think you could be of assistance. Be a nice payday for you. Should be pretty simple. Interested?"

"Sure," I say. "Mind if I ask what it is?"

Tim leads me back by the tool shed. We sit down. He opens a cooler and grabs two cans of beer, holds one out to me. I wave it off.

"Shit, I forgot you aren't drinking. That's good. Stay with that," he says.

He cracks open his beer and we sit down.

"So my business—my straight business, the contracting—I got a real nice set up with it, you see, a buddy of mine, good guy, he has a huge building business. He kicks down all the small jobs that aren't worth his time to me, and that alone gives me more than enough work for the crew to do. And as you know, I need that kosher income. Very important."

Tim's guys exit the garage with the footlockers, load them into their vehicle, and head out. Tim continues:

"We're meeting back up with them in a bit," he says, nodding at the departing vehicle. "So back to my buddy. Well, like I said, he's a good friend, so I look out for him, you know? Well, he got himself in a little jam. He's a married guy but he likes to step out a little bit, you know, real discreet; always call girls, always low key. Anyway, he fucks up and uses a new escort service, and these guys, these fucks that run this service, they figure out that he is big time here in the valley, that he has a lot of money and is a family man and all that. So they figure he's a good mark for a shakedown. He fucks one of their girls once, no problem, but the second time, the second time he bangs one of their broads, they threaten him, tell him they'll tell his family and shit, say they have a video of him fucking this whore. They make him pay double the price and demand another twenty grand in a week. Well, that 20k is due tomorrow, and he was going to pay them; he tells me this yesterday, asks me if I can drop the money off for him. He isn't too well versed in this kind of shit, and I tell him the truth: these fucks are going to squeeze every penny they can out of him. This isn't a one–time kind of thing. I remind him that I have his back, and no one fucks with me or my friends in this town. No one. So I told him I'll handle it, no problem. So tonight we handle it."

I get a lump in my throat. I'm not sure what Tim means by "handle it." I pray it doesn't involve killing these guys. I'm not going to do that, and Tim doesn't like being told no.

"So what's the plan?" I ask.

"I did some looking into these guys, and they're way out of their league. They run a smaller escort service, maybe six or seven girls. They're new in the business; I guess one of them used to manage a strip club and got it into his head that he could branch out and make some money in the escort game. Well, they fucked up, and tonight we're going to give them a lesson in customer relations. They rent a little office and warehouse over in Tempe. Friday being a booming night for their business, they're going to be there for sure. And we're going to pay them a little visit, set things straight. Cool?"

"Sounds good," I say. A drop of sweat falls over my eyebrow and stings my eye.

"You gotta know this about me Nick. I'm very loyal to friends and family, and when you work for me and do good by me, I take care of you. So tonight you get to see what happens when you fuck with my people."

I nod. He opens the door to the tool shack, rummages around, and comes out with two bags. He pulls out a black sweatshirt and throws it to me, followed by a black ski mask. The other bag has two bulletproof vests.

"Just in case. Like I said, these guys are bush league, they might have a piece, but I doubt they got the balls to use it. But better to be prepared."

We put on the vests and the sweatshirts over them. I start to sweat immediately; sweatshirts and six-pound vests are not ideal summer wear. We get into Tim's non-work car, a Mustang, and head out. He lets me know the play as we drive back to Tempe.

"Trevor and Saul, the guys you met earlier, they're going to meet us about a block away. We park and ride over in their Cherokee. They're geared up too. They're going in first. They have shotguns, but we don't plan on using them. I have a couple Sigs in the trunk, but you and me, we're gonna work with bats, have the pistols just in case. We go in fast, take control of it, make sure they don't get a chance to react. Then we teach them a lesson. Got it?"

"Yes."

We drive to a parking lot behind a dentist's office. It's dark and tucked back from the road. Trevor and Saul are waiting for us. Tim parks the car. We get the bats and the Sigs out of the trunk and get into the back of the Cherokee.

I follow their lead and put my ski mask on as we pull out of the lot. A block and a half later we turn into a little industrial–type parkway and follow it to the end, then park next to an eighteen–wheeler. Saul and Trevor get shotguns out of the truck and rack a round into the chambers. Tim hands out black rubber gloves. The lot is just like any other industrial lot on a Friday: empty, black, and quiet. A lone Mercedes is parked by an office. Furnace–like heat bounces off the asphalt.

"Third door," Tim says. "And don't forget, no names when we're inside."

We get to the third door and Tim motions Saul to move ahead. We line up against the wall. Saul knocks on the door and then moves back out of sight of the peephole. I hear nothing, then the sound of footsteps. Saul waits for the sound of the deadbolt unlocking. The door handle turns slowly, and *bam!* Saul kicks in the door and Tim and Trevor pile in after him. I rush in after them, adrenaline, it feels like I am in a fucking video game or something.

Everything phases out for a moment. There is shouting. A woman screams. I hear Tim shout "drop it!" and metal hits floor. A figure emerges off to my right, almost a blur; I instinctively raise my forearm and smash the upper part of it and my elbow into someone's face. There is this amazing sensation when you hit someone, when the hard part of your bone meets theirs, this instant connection, and the sensation travels down the bone, almost a vibration, resonates, and the force of energy hits the air around you, *snap*, then it all gets sucked right back in to the source and you either hit the guy again, marvel at your work, or flee.

I look down at this guy that came at me. My elbow caught him right below the eye. He's cut and bleeding. He clutches his face, hypnotized by the pain. It's pretty obvious that he hasn't been hit much before. I keep the end of the bat on his neck to keep him in check. He holds his face and cowers like a beaten dog.

I gotta hand it to Tim. He's a real pro at this shit. It's been thirty seconds since we came through the door and he has everything under control. Saul relocks the door while Tim takes Trevor's gun.

"Grab their wallets," says Tim.

I kneel down and pull the wallet from the back pocket of the guy beneath me. I get a good look at him for the first time: white guy, maybe twenty–three or –four, tall but not thick, graffiti tattoos on one of his arms. They're expensive, well–done tats, not the cheap shit you usually see on cons. He offers no resistance as I take the wallet. I toss it to Tim.

Saul and Trevor have the other two, a guy and girl, sat down in desk chairs with their hands held over their heads. Trevor orders them to give up their wallets and they do so.

Tim grabs the wallets and digs through them, taking out the licenses and whatever photos and other ID they have on them. I survey the room. It's a typical garage and office space, small and bland, two desks with phones and a computer. There are no decorations other than a bong on a desk. Cigs smolder in an ashtray.

"Hey, grab that piece off the floor, would you," Tim says to me, nodding to the area behind me.

I look over to the corner and see a pistol, the gun someone dropped when we made our grand entrance. I go over and pick it up. It's a crappy Hi–Point 9mm. A real piece of shit. I tuck it into my belt next to the Sig.

I study the two terrified people sitting in the desk chairs. The guy, a Hispanic, I think, looks a little more hardened than this pussy cowering at my feet, but he still doesn't look like much. He has a slight tremble to him. The girl next to him, she's trying to put a stone–cold face on, really gritting down on her teeth to stop her lip from shaking, but her excessive mascara is starting to run from her watery eyes.

"We don't have money here," the Mexican guy says.

"Not here for money," Tim says.

"Well, what do you want?" the girl says.

"I haven't decided yet," Tim says. He looks at one of the IDs and then back at the guy in the chair. "Eddie. You in charge of this little operation?"

Eddie doesn't say anything.

Tim stands still for a second and then hands the shotgun back to Saul in exchange for the bat. He backs up a few feet and then skips a few steps forward, using the momentum to slam the bat right above Eddie's knee. Eddie screams in pain and collapses on the floor. The girl gets off her chair to help him and Tim kicks her over.

"Hey, one of you two find something to tie these fucks up with," Tim says.

The guy beneath me, quiet until now, pukes all over the floor. Tim laughs at him. "I thought you guys were fucking gangsters? Real hardcore!"

Trevor finds some duct tape in a tool box in the corner and gets to work binding the hands and feet of Eddie and the girl. When done he moves on and does the same to the guy at my feet.

Tim says, "I won't tape your mouths shut if you don't speak unless spoken to. Or if you shout or scream. I'll tape your mouth then, for sure, and I'll most likely break something as well. So I'd keep your dumb fucking mouth shut if I were you."

"Hey, pukeboy," Tim says, he walks over and gives the kid a nudge with his foot. "Or should I say, Joseph Middleton of…" He reads his name and address off his ID card and then picks out a picture from the wallet. "Who is this?" He waves the picture, a picture of a young girl, in front of Joseph's face.

"Joseph, you have ten seconds to answer me before I have my friend here stomp on your balls. Who is this?"

"Sister," he whispers. "My little sister."

Tim looks at the picture. "Well, I gather from the picture that your sister plays basketball at Mesa High. And," he looks at the picture closely. "Class of 2015."

Joe whimpers. Tim moves back to Eddie. "Who is this, Eddie?" Tim asks, pointing to the girl tied up next to him. "This one of your bitches? This one of the girls you hardcore bangers have out there working the motels?"

"No," Eddie says through clenched teeth.

Tim looks at the IDs. "Hey, you two have the same last name. Do we have a husband–and–wife dynamic duo here?"

The girl shakes her head. The tears are flowing.

"What then? Brother and sister?"

"Yes," she says.

"Tory, shut your fucking mouth," Eddie says to her. Trevor kicks him in the stomach hard, punishment for speaking out of turn. Eddie lets out an "*oomph!*" The kick knocked the wind out him. Eddie spasms and struggles against the duct tape.

Tory cries out. The smell of urine fills the air. Joseph pissed himself.

"So I guess you're wondering why we're here. It seems there is a slight problem with your customer relations department. You have a very unsatisfied customer, and that can be bad news for a young business such as yours. A bad reputation can really kill a business, if you know what I mean. Once word gets out that you have bad customer service, well, it really spreads, you know, word of mouth. I'd hate to see such promising criminal entrepreneurs go out of business. By the way, do you have anyone coming by anytime soon? 'Cause if you do and you don't tell me, well, it is going to be pretty gory for all involved, to be honest. "

Eddie shakes his head no.

Tim in action is amazing. This shit really brings him out his shell.

"I probably should've asked you about that already, but I get so excited when I'm working, tend to forget the minor details. But there are certain details I won't forget, like your names, your addresses, and all the other info I have here in your wallets; names of kids, family members, you know."

"Just what the fuck do you want, please, tell us!" Tory pleads.

"You know what, Tory? I'm going to let that one slip and not break something of yours for speaking out of turn. Just this once, though. It's a fair enough question, I guess, and we should get going pretty soon. But let me ask you a question, Tory. Tory, have you ever heard the expression about a 'victimless crime?' I never understood that. I mean, isn't that the point of the crime, to victimize someone? Some people like to say that what you're doing here, this little escort business, is a victimless crime. I'm not so sure. I bet somewhere along the way you rip someone off or force one of your bitches to do something she doesn't want to do. Someone is always getting fucked in crime, even if it's you, right?"

Tim walks up to Eddie. "Can you relate to that, Eddie?"

"I, I don't know what…"

"Well that's the problem, Eddie. You don't know. You don't know because you and your sister and your crying buddy over there are fucking pussies, aren't you Eddie? That's why you couldn't get a shot off with that pistol when we came in. You ever killed someone, Eddie? Huh? Huh? You ever do someone in? Rub 'em out? Merc him? You ever fucking watch someone spit and shit and sputter and bleed and collapse because of an action you took? Eddie? No? I didn't think so."

Eddie closes his eyes. His lips move. He is praying now. Tim goes on, "So, anyway, the whole point I'm trying to make is this: You and your friends here start your little escort business, your little victimless crime, and I'm guessing you either aren't making as much you thought you would, or maybe you just got greedy, because at some point you decided that peddling pussy was not cutting it. Or maybe you just saw a chance, an opportunity, and you jumped on it. I don't know the specifics. I don't really give a shit, to be honest." Tim kneels down to meet Eddie face to face. "What do you know about blackmail, Eddie? Huh?" Eddie shakes his head. "Nothing? How about extortion? Nothing about that either?"

Tim laughs. "Good answer, Eddie, because it's true. You don't know shit. You don't know rule fucking one about it, you dumb fucking fuck.

Let me tell you something, next time you decide to run a scam on one of your customers, or anyone for that matter, make sure you don't pick someone..."

Tim trails off.

"Eddie, make sure you don't fuck with someone who has friends that are stone fucking cold killers, Eddie. The next time you and your cunt sister and your faggoty friend over there decide to try and rip off and smear a fucking customer for no good reason other than you are stupid fucking mutant scum, maybe you'll remember that you are fucking puppies trying to run with pitbulls."

All three are crying now.

"Look man, we fucked up, I know; we'll stop and we'll get you the money back and get whatever you want for you, just please let us—"

Tim puts the barrel of the shotgun on top of Eddie's head to shut him up. "This isn't about money, Eddie. This is just the way things are. You made a very poor decision, you picked a mark that wasn't going to let a few fucking piece of shit pussies like you three get away with it. And you offended me, Eddie. You offended me. No one in this town fucks with my friends and gets away with it. It offends me that anyone would even try."

Joseph, still cowering beneath me in his puke and piss, finally talks. "We got money in the trunk of the Mercedes outside and there's more, we can get more, I swear, I can get—"

Tim cuts him off. "This isn't about money. I mean, now that you mention it, we *are* going to take that money, but that isn't the point here. The point is punishment. You three aren't going to go unpunished for this. That wouldn't be fair to anyone involved, including you. If we don't teach you a serious lesson now, you're bound to repeat the same mistakes again. And you don't want that, do you?"

"Are you going to kill us? Please don't kill us, please, please!" The words tumble out of Eddie's mouth.

"I don't know," Tim says. "Do you need that severe of a lesson?"

Eddie shakes his head. "No, no, no, no, we'll leave Harwood alone, we'll—"

Tim flies into a fury, grabs the bat, and slams it over Eddie's ribcage repeatedly. Eddie howls, gurgles, twitches. Tory screams and Saul puts his shoe on her head to shut her up.

Tim unloads: "You don't say that fucking name, got it? You don't fucking say it! If you ever say it again, if you ever think about saying it, if you ever get within a fucking mile of him, if you ever do anything or say anything about him, I *will* kill you; I'll not only kill you in the worst possible way, but I'll kill your family, I don't give a fuck how old they are, I'll fucking kill them, I'll kill them all. Got it?"

"Yesh!" Eddie chokes out.

"That goes for all three of you: we know where to find you, and we can find you and your families whenever we want. And I have to be honest; I'm kind of letting my guys here down. They really wanted to kill all three of you, and they're going to be a little disappointed tonight that I didn't let them. So if you decide to go near our mutual friend or tell anyone about him or us, well, I'm going to have to let the leash off these sadistic fucks here and, Tory, your kids in your wallet, or Joseph, your sister, well–you get my point."

Tim whispers to Saul and Saul grabs the keys to their Mercedes and walks outside. I hear the car depart a minute later.

"Okay, Eddie, Tory, Joseph, let's get this over with, huh?"

Screams.

I follow Tim and Trevor's cue and bring my bat down on Joseph. I hit him repeatedly. I avoid hitting him in the head. I hear bones break. I hear swelling. I hear blood gurgle in his throat.

I wish I could say I feel bad about it, but I really don't. I just keep swinging; I think about all the stories I've heard from girls in AA, girls that were hooked on junk and crack or whatever, girls that ended up selling themselves to feed their habit, girls that ended up working for escort services like this, what this kind of people do to those girls, how they make them fuck guy after guy and give them just enough drugs to come back for the next shift, they make girls take it in the ass because it makes them more money, they come find the girls that are trying to get away, trying to get clean, and they find them and they get them hooked on dope again, they —

"That's enough. Let's head out." Tim stops me mid–thought, mid–swing.

We walk out. I get one last look at the three of them before Tim turns the lights out. They're still breathing, but that's about it.

Chapter 11: HACK

LUCKY ME. I GET A CALL TO PICK UP a young lady at a motel on the edge of Scottsdale and Tempe, and lo and behold, it's that same girl from a couple weeks ago, the stripper with the world–class body and acne–scarred face. She gets in the cab, slams the door behind her.

"Drive," she demands.

"Where?"

"Uh, fuck, hold on," she fumbles with her phone and then reads an address in Tempe. "Hey, do you mind if we stop at a Circle K or whatever so I can get a fucking drink? I really need one."

"Sure honey, no problem at all," I say.

I take her to a convenience store a couple blocks away. She storms inside; her miniskirt turns the heads of a few male customers. She comes out with a brown bag, pulls out a forty–ounce.

"You aren't gonna have a hissy fit if I drink this back here, are ya?"

"No doll. Do your thing."

She goes to work on the beer; the smell of shitty malt liquor fills the cab. I get on the 202 and head west.

"Thanks for letting me drink in here. Most cabbies are assholes about that."

"No problem. You having a rough night?"

"Fucking A. That cheap fuck back in the room didn't tip me and then my fucking ride doesn't show."

"Too bad."

"Yeah, too bad. Cocksuckers. They take sixty percent of what I make and they can't even pick me up? I mean, that guy was a total fucking pussy, but what if he wasn't, you know? What if he wasn't? The fucker could have chopped me into pieces if he wanted to. I mean, isn't the point of working for an escort service that they watch your back and take care of all that shit? Well, fuck these faggots. I'm done with this shit."

I hand her one of my cigs, light one for myself.

"I think I picked you up a couple of weeks ago," I say. "Don't you dance over at that club on Roosevelt?"

"Yeah."

"So what's the problem, dancing not paying the bills?"

She sighs and takes a long pull off the 40, exhales a cloud of cig smoke.

"I dunno, I guess. I got my second DUI and that pretty much cleaned me out, you know, and then my ex ripped me off and I had to do two weeks in the tents, and I was fucking broke and a friend of a friend told me about a private dancing gig, and I do it and these fucks want me to fuck strangers for money, and I, fuck, I don't know why I'm telling you this shit. Why do you care?"

She sneers and looks out the window. She's about halfway through the forty and I can already see a change in her; she's the type that gets mean from the sauce. I love it.

I smile. "I don't care, really. I mean, I don't like seeing a nice young lady like you having a rough go, but really, driving this cab all day and night is a fucking bore and it's nice to hear about someone else's problems I guess."

"You ever see that show, on HBO, I think it's called *Taxi Cab Confessions* or some shit?"

"No, can't say that I have," I answer.

She holds her hand out and snaps her fingers. I oblige her with another cig. She lights it off the spent butt and flicks the spent one out the window.

"It's like, it shows these cab drivers picking up people and shooting the shit, there's a camera and shit in the dashboard, and the cabbies get the people in the back to talk about all sorts of crazy shit. You should try and get on that show. I think you'd be good at it. Seems like you have a way of making people talk," she says.

"You have no idea." I say.

I turn off the 202 onto Priest and head south. She finishes the forty and drops it at her feet.

I ask her a question.

"You grew up Mormon, didn't you?"

She leans forward and folds her hands. Her head does that inquisitive–dog–tilt thing.

She says, "Yes, I did. Is it obvious or something?"

"No. Well, not really. I just have been doing this for so long, seen so many people. It becomes a pattern after a while, I guess. I can sort of figure things out just by looking at people."

"Yeah, well, what else?" She opens her purse and pulls out a weed pipe. "You mind if I smoke? I'll tip you extra."

"I don't mind at all."

She lights up. The smell of fairly high–grade marijuana fills the cab.

"So what else, cabbie, what else?"

"I'm thinking…" I trail off, study her through the rearview mirror; catch a glance at the full, authentic tits bursting out of her button–up shirt. I see it all. "Tell me about Colorado City," I tell her.

"Huh?"

"Colorado City. You lived there, didn't you?"

She puts the pipe down. "Are you fucking with me? I mean, do you know me from someplace else?" She exhales a cloud of thick pot smoke, her words haggard with it.

"No. I don't even know your name. But I'm pretty sure—well, positive, actually—that you grew up Mormon, Fundamentalist, and that you lived in Colorado City, Arizona."

"I..." She starts, then shakes her head and holds a hand up. She takes a huge pull of her pipe, coughs, then resumes. "Yeah, that's true. Holy shit. Listen, this is kind of freaking me out, I don't want to—"

I cut her off. "We're here," I say.

We pull into a small industrial lot. She perks up and looks around the lot, which is empty except for a parked eighteen–wheeler.

"Motherfucker! They aren't even here. They're supposed to fucking be here. I need to get paid, what the fuck. Park over there, next to the third door."

I do so. She tells me to wait and exits the cab. She bangs on the office door a few times, then jiggles the door handle. She waits a few moments, then bangs on the door again. Next she presses her ear up to the door, hops a step back, and puts her ear back to the door again. She hustles back to the cab.

"Mister, I know you're gonna think I'm just high and shit, but I'm pretty sure someone in there is yelling for help."

I get out of the cab and walk to the door, put my ear against it. Nothing at first, but now I definitely hear a faint voice, a faint voice trying to shout, trying to shout something.

"Yeah, I think you're right, I hear something, too." I say. I start to walk back to the cab. "So you want me to take you home?"

She holds up her arms. "What? We have to call someone. What about, what if someone is hurt in there?"

I shrug. "Do you really care? I thought these people treat you like shit?"

"Yeah they do, but, I mean, it sounds like someone needs help and, I mean, we can't just not do anything."

"Nonsense," I say. "Doing nothing is always an option."

I grin at her, her all distressed and sexy under the halogen bulb glow from above. She shakes her head back and forth, then stomps a foot on the ground. She wipes a slick of sweat off her brow. Her makeup smears with it.

"Okay, honey, your call," I say.

I pull out my cell phone and dial 9–1–1. I tell the operator the address and the situation.

"Tempe cops are pretty quick," I tell her. "You might want to stash that weed and whatever else you have before they get here, you know, just in case."

She scurries over behind a dumpster and unloads her purse, stashes a few things underneath a wooden pallet.

She comes back and sits on the hood of the cab next to me. Her chest glistens with sweat. I watch it drip. Fuck, it's hot out here.

"I have a really bad feeling about this," she says. "I think something is seriously fucked here."

"Well, Ashley, it's sort of par for the course. This shouldn't be much of a surprise."

She looks at me with this blankness, and for the first time I notice that despite her quite mediocre face, she has a gorgeous set of big blue eyes, eyes just a tad bloodshot from the grass she smoked. What a cruel joke, I think, for a girl to have such an amazing body and amazing eyes, all framed by a face that's worse than ordinary, scarred, maybe even ugly to some.

"What I mean, doll, is when you associate in this kind of world, with this kind of people, well, you're going to stumble into things that are, as you said, seriously fucked."

She takes a cig out of my pack and lights it, grinning that mean grin.

"You don't know shit, cabbie. You don't know shit about me, and you don't know shit about the world I live in, okay? So shut the fuck up."

I smile at her sudden defensiveness, and that irritates her even more. "You're a dumb fucking cab driver. And who are you to lecture someone about what they do, with your life, you fucking loser?"

"So you don't want to talk anymore," I ask her.

"No, I don't," she says.

"Well, the cops should be here in a minute. You mind if I pass the time, tell a story?"

She shrugs and rolls her eyes.

I tell a story. I tell it slowly.

"I know a good one. It's about this little girl, a precious little girl; her mother was the sweetest thing on earth, dumb as a fucking rock, but sweet nonetheless. Her dad, well, he was smarter than her mother, I guess, but he really had no personality, you know, he was just a real blank kind of guy. Not much shine there. You see, his parents really drilled the Bible into his head at a very young age; they never really let him get much else in terms of education and stimulation. This girl was an only child, her parents only had sex once, and even though everyone around them, their church, their neighbors, they all told them they needed to have more kids, well, they lied and said she was now infertile, but the truth was that the father had come once and was so confused by that brief, insane and intense foreign sensation that he was plain terrified to do it again. Imagine eating nothing but white rice your whole life, and one day someone hands you a candy bar. That's what it was like."

"Will you shut the fuck up?"

"No, I think you'll actually appreciate this story if you just let me finish. Sorry, I got sidetracked, I guess, this story really isn't about these people and their fear of fucking, as fascinating as that is. This story is about their daughter, about how much she loved her parents, her loving mother, and the odd but consistent presence of her father. She loved them both very much. She had no idea how strange the little world she lived in was, she had no idea that the town she lived in, the people there, the things they did, the way they lived their lives, she had no idea that ninety–nine–point–nine percent of the rest of the nation thought they were all bat–shit fucking crazy. She thought the whole world lived that way, the way her people did, because, at the age of eleven, she had never stepped foot outside of Colorado City, Arizona."

At that Ashley hops off the front of the car and backs up a few paces, her mouth wide open. I follow her. I keep talking.

"Tell me something, Ashley: how did it feel to be betrayed by the very people you adored so much? How did it feel when they pushed you into the arms of that old man when you were just eleven–years–old? How did it feel when they walked out that door and left, and you went from being a sweet little daughter to a fifty–year–old man's wife?"

She shakes her head back and forth, holds a hand up to me, chokes, she mouths, "stop."

"And just four months later, when the state took you away, and you started on that journey from foster home to foster home, you loved your parents for a while, didn't you? But as you got older, that love turned to something, didn't it, and you didn't even hate them as much as pity them, pity people that could be so fucking warped, so fucking empty, that they could literally hand over their own eleven–year–old child to a fifty–year–old man and think they were doing the Lord's work? That pure pity you've felt these years, its toxic isn't it? It's why you drink and do the things you do for money, its why—"

I stop. Two police cars pull into the lot. It's a welcome break for her; she runs toward the cars and points toward the door. She follows behind them as the three cops walk to the door. They knock. They knock again. They call out "Police!" An officer puts his ear to the door.

"There's someone in there, I can definitely hear something. Check it out," the officer says to the other. One of the other officers puts his ear to the door, listens, and then nods. They discuss the situation for a moment; one officer returns to the car and gets on the radio while the other goes to the trunk of his squad car. They bring Ashley back to me. They tell us to sit on the car and not move, ask me to make sure she stays put.

"Ashley, I didn't mean to scare you with that story. I just wanted to let you know that you are an incredible human being; I mean, the durability and resilience you had at just eleven–years–old to endure that time you spent with that horrible man, you are truly an amazing person. Your potential is limitless, you have a calling, and you need to see to it."

She stares straight ahead, her eyes blurry with forming tears. Her hands tremble as she smokes.

The officers return to the door. One has a crowbar. They remind us to stay put.

The officer struggles with the crowbar. He twists it into the doorframe, grimacing. He stops, covered in sweat and panting. One of the other officer tries for a good minute or so until the third officer gets impatient, says fuck it, backs up, and kicks the door open.

The door opens. The unit is dark, the officer calls out "hello?" and a feeble voice responds with "help." The officers shine their flashlights into the room.

"Holy shit," one officer says.

"Oh my God…"

The third officer gets on his chest radio and calls for medical personnel to come to the scene. I can't hear exactly what he's saying, only that there're three people inside that are in very bad shape.

The cops find the light switches inside the unit and flick them on.

"Check for a pulse, check for a pulse on those two," an officer shouts.

Ashley stands up and moves toward the open door. I'm supposed to stop her, but she needs to see what's in that room. She peers inside the room and screams.

"Jesus Christ, get her out of here!"

One of the cops takes her by the arm and leads her back to me.

"Will you please not let her get off this car again; can you handle that for like a fucking minute or so?"

I smile and nod.

Ashley is shaking. Whatever she saw is so fucked up that she actually digs her face into my chest. I put an arm around her to comfort her.

We hear sirens, and within a few minutes more cop cars arrive, followed by an ambulance, then two more ambulances, then a fire truck. Within ten minutes the entire parking lot is lit up with flashing lights and hectic cops and paramedics. They whisk Ashley and me off to the corner of the lot, into the back of a squad car. We're left alone. We don't speak. I want to give her some time to absorb it all. We watch as they bring three bodies out on stretchers; we don't have that great a view from the backseat, but it's obvious that the people on those stretchers are in very bad shape. The grim look on the cops' faces says it all. The ambulances screech away.

"You should've seen all the fucking blood," Ashley says quietly. "I've never seen so much blood."

The cops talk to us for the next hour or so, ask us a million questions. Ashley is very honest about why she was here, what she does, the kind of work she does for the people they just carted away in that ambulance.

They don't pay too much attention to me. I'm just a run–of–the–mill cabbie that happened upon a pretty strange night. They want to take Ashley back to the precinct to answer more questions. I object. "She's told you all she knows, I think. This poor girl is exhausted. Let her get some rest."

The cops shrug. They're probably not too worried about the case now that they know it's likely a case of scumbags robbing fellow scumbags. They tell her it's fine, they'll take her home.

"If its okay, I want him to take me home," she tells them, pointing at me.

"Okay, that's fine. That okay with you?" they ask me.

"Sure. I'll take her home. No charge."

We get into my cab. We pull out of the lot and onto the road in silence. I remember where she lives from the last time I took her home. She stares out the window the whole ride. We get off the highway and head toward downtown Mesa where her apartment building is. I swerve to miss a drunken bum that wanders into traffic. Two cop cars fly by us. Feral cats are everywhere. Fucking Mesa. Ashley sighs.

We arrive. She looks out the window, then back at me. She doesn't get out.

I dig underneath my seat, pull out the watch I got off that shithead kid the other day.

"Here," I say. "I want you to have this. Some drunken brat left it in my car the other day. It's worth quite a bit, a few grand. Sell it; use the money to take care of yourself, okay?"

She takes the watch, looks it over. She gently runs her fingers over its diamonds. "I don't know what to do," she says. "I have no idea what to do. Will you tell me what to do? Please? Will you tell me what to do?"

That sneering, weed–smoking, hard–drinking, escort stripper has turned into a troubled angel before my very eyes. Her eyes, so massive and anxious, they look to me for some sense of it all. *I'm sorry little girl, that's not my department.*

I shake my head. "I can't tell you what to do, doll. You have to figure that out yourself. But I will tell you this: that man is still there in Colorado City, still doing the same thing. Nothing has changed. And your mother and father, they're still there, too, and I can also tell you this: the only regret they have is that you were taken away, not from them, but from him. Nothing has changed, nothing, after all these years. The whole fucking scene, it's all still stuck in time, just the way you left it."

She stares ahead of her, trance–like.

"I told you earlier that I'm in awe of you, right? I told you how amazing you are, the resilience you have, and I told you, yes, I told you, that you have so much potential, so much, so please don't forget that, and don't ever settle, don't settle, don't you ever settle as a victim, okay?"

"I don't understand." She wipes tears off of her cheek.

"You're always going to be a victim until you make things right, Ashley. Right now there's a huge fucking chasm in your world, that, well, here you are, all fucked up, with all those horrible things done to you, and you suffer still while the people who did this have never once felt an ounce of guilt or remorse for what they did. I can't tell you what to do, Ashley, but I can tell you what I think you should do. I think you should sell that watch, take that money, get a car or a bus ticket, whatever, you go up to that miserable fucking city you come from, you go up there and you close the fucking chasm, Ashley. You go up there and you realize your potential. You go up there and you make things right."

"I…I don't understand."

I reach into the back of the cab; run my hand through her hair, as gracefully as a man like me can.

"Think about what you saw tonight in that office. Do you think that was all a coincidence, this whole night? Three bodies, Ashley. Two men, one woman. Think about it, Ashley, think about it. I know you screamed when you saw those bodies, Ashley, even though you hated those fucks, you screamed at the sight, that brutal sight, all that blood... But I'll tell you something, Ashley: not long after that, when we were back in the car, I watched you, I studied you, I *read* you, and you know what I saw? Peace. I saw peace, incredible peace. Three bodies Ashley, two men, one woman. Think about it. So you go, Ashley. You go close that chasm, sweet girl."

I let her think for a moment. "You should get some rest, doll; it's been a long day. You take care of yourself."

She actually smiles. She leans forward, kisses me on the cheek, whispers "thank you."

She gets out of the cab and goes inside. I get back on the clock. Still a long night ahead.

CHAPTER 12: NICK

"WHAT DOES IT MEAN TO YOU, when it says 'we came to believe'?"

"I don't know, Gary. I've been telling you that. I don't fucking know."

Gary looks at me, arms folded. My answer is not good enough.

"Look," I say," I told you I don't believe in a Judeo–Christian God, I just don't, and I told you that I accept the fact that there are things or forces or whatever the fuck you want to call them that are greater than me, but, honestly, I don't see how I can believe or come to believe in something that is so incredibly abstract that it actually makes my fucking brain hurt to even try and think about it."

"So don't think about it then," Gary says. "Just do it. Fuck it, just try to do it."

I toss my hands up and then shake my head.

"You think too much," Gary says. "And remember, the dumbest fucking guy on the planet can still have the bad habit of thinking too much. You need to realize you aren't as smart as you think you are, and learn how to turn your head off and just be. Just be. Just do. Don't analyze everything like whatever goes on in your mind is that fucking important."

I chuckle. "I've actually been doing a fair amount of that lately, you know, just doing it, going with the flow, whatever you want to call it."

"Really."

"Yeah."

"Where?"

"Uhh...work," I say.

"Okay," Gary says. "So when you're swinging a hammer, smashing something—"

Or someone, I think.

"—your mind shuts off, right?"

"Yes, in a way."

"Well, there you go. Take that approach to step two. Just keep swinging and hammering on it. Eventually it will just make sense."

"Okay," I say. "So are we done with step two? Can we move on?"

Gary smiles. "No, there is still a cloud in your mind, I can see that. A lot of people just fly past step two because step one is pretty black and white and step three is really the big one, you know, but I need to see a light kind of go on with you for step two, I need to ask you, 'do you now believe, or are you even willing to believe, that there is a power greater than yourself,' and have you answer without that cloud still lingering over the whole thing."

I shrug, take a sip of my coffee, and stare at the legs of a girl sitting nearby. She reminds me of Sarah, has the same Midwest style: perfect blond hair and Nordic features, athletic body. I miss Sarah. I haven't thought about her much lately, but I know that some part of me misses her. Maybe when I get this stuff with Tim done and I get my shit straight I can get her back somehow. Maybe.

Gary goes on: "Yeah Nick, you know this quite well, but this isn't busy work, the steps. This isn't a formality. We're not gonna go through the motions on this one, not with the way you drink, the places you're headed; we're going to treat this as a life or death thing, because it is."

"I know that."

"Do you? Do you really?"

"Yes."

"Well, fear doesn't keep us sober, not for long, you know that. Remember that."

He gets up, slaps me on my knee. He reminds me to pray every day, go to a meeting every day, read the book every day, and call him every day. I finish my coffee, get another for the road. Long night ahead. I call Tim and let him know I'm on my way.

It's one hundred and twelve degrees, even with the sun almost all the way down. I have the windows down. I sweat that coffee sweat. My entire body is pleasantly sore from hauling rocks and grit for the last two days. I haven't been this lean and mean in some time, all the hard work in the dangerously hot Arizona sun is showing its effects on my body. Fuck joining a gym, I haven't felt or looked this good in some time. I suppose not lounging around drunk day and night probably helps. The way I am when I drink, sloth–like, I get enough drinks in me and I start to lose all skeletal structure, a giant worthless mess stuck to the floor or the couch, staring at the TV for hours. Some fucking life.

Any life is better than that, even what I'm doing now. There is no disputing that.

I get a little nervous as I near the Nineteenth Avenue exit on the 10, a highway patrol car switches into my lane and follows me for about a quarter mile. I keep my speed the same, right at the speed limit. I have five AKs, three ARs, an M1, and three other semi–auto rifles in the back. I didn't fuck around with shotguns and pistols this time.

I take the Nineteenth Ave exit. The patrol car doesn't follow me. In the clear. Tim opens the gate to the storage yard. I pull the car into the garage and we unload the rifles into the hollow stash area under the bed of his work truck.

"Is this it?" I ask, looking around. It's just me and Tim. "Where are the others?"

"I sent Saul and Trevor and a couple other guys down there over the last couple of days," Tim says. "They're with Jordo, setting up the meeting spot and getting shit straight. You ready to go?"

We pull out of the lot, lock up, and head out. Tim opens a pill bottle, pops two, and hands them to me.

"You know how I feel about drugs and junkies, but it's gonna be a long night and we need to stay on our toes, so if you want, take a couple Dexedrine's."

I shake my head. "I can't fuck with that stuff; it'll just make me want to drink."

He nods. "Good. I don't need you falling apart on me. This is a big fucking drop tonight, and we're gonna grind every penny we can out of these fucks, so if negotiations get tense, I need to know you're watching my back. Like I said, I've never had a problem with these guys before, but at the end of the day they are what they are, fucking maniac third–world drug runners, and there're no guarantees with people like this. You catch 'em on the wrong day and they'll kill you out of boredom, you know. Life doesn't mean shit to these fucks." We take the 10 out of Phoenix, through the suburbs, past Casa Grande and into the desert. Tim pays attention to the road, no stereo. We ride in silence for a half hour, just smoking. The engine hums hot on the highway. The truck has the workingman's scent of cheap gas station fragrance and a decade of spilt coffee and cig ash. I watch the sky open up with stars as we get farther and farther out, away from the lights and the pollution of the great valley.

"The thing about it is," Tim says, continuing our last conversation as if the last half hour of silence were a mere pause to catch a breath, "yes these guys are unpredictable, fucking violent animals, really, but what they don't have is brains, and that's the way we keep them honest. I mean, the guys at the top, the bigwigs in the cartel, the shot callers, they are smart as fuck, and ruthless too, a terrifying combination really, and that's how they stay on top when there are a million shitheads looking to take their places, a million fucks with guns and no conscience, nothing to lose; it requires an equal balance of high intelligence and sheer ruthlessness to stay on top of that shit heap. That's the reason one guy can manage to stay atop of one of these cartels for so long, with so much competition from outside their operation and within–he is one wicked smart and mean motherfucker, no doubt. Of course, the guys we deal with, they're small time, just runners and errand boys, not much in the way of brains. Now the guy behind them, whoever is calling the shots back in Mexico or wherever, the shot caller, he's probably bright enough to know that we provide a valuable and professional service, and if his boys try to fuck us he's probably going to lose money over it, and that's all these fucks care about."

Tim coughs and spits out the window. "They're simple fucking animals, the most of them. They won't ever even get a chance to really enjoy the money they make. I mean, even if you have a pocketful of cash, if you're in shithole Mexico, does it really matter? Most of these guys have a life expectancy of another year or so, tops. I mean, we could run dope for these guys up to Phoenix, make millions, millions, but we'd end up dead or in the joint within a year or two, guaranteed, no matter how smart or careful we are. That's just the way it is. I'd rather make less and live to enjoy it. At the end of the day, I'm not a greedy man. Not at all."

He stops talking, turns on the radio. We catch a faint signal of a rock station, sixties stuff.

"Have you ever been to Three Points?" Tim asks.

"No. Is that where we're going?"

"Yeah. Around there."

Ten minutes pass.

"We have about two hours to go," Tim says. "We'll stop and grab you a couple of those fucking Blue Bulls or whatever the fuck they are called, keep you up and running. Yeah, it's going to be a long night."

He lets out a rare smile and turns up the stereo; the signal is stronger, and "Roadhouse Blues" by The Doors is perfect right now.

Chapter 13: HACK

I'VE BEEN DRIVING FOR FOURTEEN hours straight. I ache everywhere, but I'm nowhere near done. I go into a dirty bathroom at a c–store, lock the door, and peel my clothes off. I splash water on my face, wash my hands, take out a travel–size of menthol body powder and rub it in from neck to toes. I step out feeling like a new man. There was a time, years ago, that I would pop Dexies or over–the–counter uppers like ephedrine, but I burnt out on that shit. Now I just sort of will myself into prolonged periods of alertness. A cup of shitty, burnt, gas station coffee every couple hours helps, too.

But most of all, the conversations keep me awake. Most people I drive are fucking boring and dumb, but just one or two interesting souls a night is all I require. This shift, though, this last fourteen hours, has been pretty fucking dull, mostly non–talkers, drunks, out–of–towners. I see nothing in them. Nothing.

When it gets slow and not a lot of calls are coming through, I like to drive around the residential side streets. I drive nice and slow, with the windows down. If I drive slow enough I can smell the individual scent of each house, usually whatever they're cooking, or the smell of fabric softener, of dust, the smell of dogs, marijuana, sometimes the overpowering stench of clutter and garbage. I make a game out of counting how many consecutive houses have the TV on, have that distinct blue glow through the window or closed blinds. It never ceases to amaze me how many houses have the TV on, often every house on the block, people tuned out and killing time and living vicariously through the pixels and sound. It bothers me. Maybe I'm just jealous that I seem to be immune to such simple comforts.

I get a call for a pick–up at the hospital. I drive the eleven blocks, then sit and wait for about ten minutes until an overweight black lady comes out. She struggles as she walks, limping badly. I get out of the cab and open the door for her, hold her hand to help her as she sits down.

"Where to, ma'am?"

She gives me an address. We pull out and I study her through the mirror, see if I can get a read on her. Nothing much. Maybe I'm just off tonight.

"I think you picked me up a couple of weeks ago," she says.

"Did I? I pick so many people up; it's tough to remember sometimes."

She smiles politely. "I might need to go back to the hospital tomorrow. I might need to stay for a while."

She's a talker. There's an incredible loneliness in her. There's also something unpleasant about her; well, maybe not about her, but around her. I see it.

"I'm sorry to hear that, hopefully they're taking good care of you at that hospital."

She smiles. "Yes, they're taking good care of me, I suppose. They say I'm not taking good care of myself; you see, I do what they say, I eat right and I take the medicines, but they don't believe me because I keep getting worse when I'm supposed to be getting better."

I don't know what to say to that. I offer a canned response. "I'm sure things will get better."

"I can't find my daughter, you see."

I don't fully understand her. "Excuse me, ma'am?"

"My daughter is missing."

I know.

"Oh, I'm really sorry to hear that, I'm sure she'll turn up," I say, trying on my best concerned–citizen voice.

"I'm not so sure," she says. "I think that's why I'm not getting better. This worry, this stress, it's keeping me sick. I don't think I'll get better until they find her."

"I'm sure they will, ma'am, the Phoenix PD is good at what they do."

"Well, I don't think they much care."

I don't know what to say.

"My daughter had a problem with drugs, just like her father and her brother. But she got off them, and she was doing so well, then—"

She starts to tear up. I grip the steering wheel until my knuckles whiten. No. Not this. Not this.

"She was doing so well, and then these people came to my house, and they convinced her to go out with them, even though I told her not to, and they gave her drugs and got her all sorts of messed up, and my niece tells me these people ran an escort service, and they got her hooked on the drugs and made her work, to do the awful things…"

Bile pushes up against the back of my throat. I didn't ask for this, I didn't. There is nothing I can do. There is nothing I can do about this. I curse a nameless and faceless entity in absence of anyone or anything else to curse—perhaps chance, or fate, or whatever the fuck you want to call it.

"They told her she was supposed to just dance for men at these parties, but some of these men hurt her, they hit her and they held her down and they raped her, over and over. And the people she worked for, the ones that gave her the drugs and made her go to that party, they just dumped her off on the street like she was trash."

I swallow. I remember her now. I remember this lady. I remember the whole story, the way it made me feel, the same way I feel now, this incredible urge to vomit and scream. I can't handle this; this is not on my terms. This is not under my control. This is not me. This is not what I do.

"She was in the hospital and then she came home with me. She slept for days; she walked around the house like a zombie, so quiet, not at peace, not at all. But so quiet. And then one day she slipped out and I haven't seen her since. The police think she's probably off getting high somewhere, but I don't know. I worry so much. She was the sweetest girl, she is the sweetest girl, you should have seen the way she was when she—"

"We're here ma'am."

I park in front of her little run–down house with its cracked paint and meager lawn.

"Oh, okay."

"Do you need help getting to your door?"

"No, sir, thank you. How much do I owe you?"

"Nothing ma'am. This one is on me."

"Well, thank you. I guess there are some decent people left, huh?"

"I don't know," I say.

She gets out of the car and I head straight home.

CHAPTER 14: NICK

GETTING OUT OF THE VALLEY MAKES you really appreciate how inhospitable and stark the desert really is; these battered little towns and homesteads show how much of a battle it is to carve out civilization on a land so naturally opposed to it. We pass by depressing little towns and highway stop–offs with their dilapidated buildings and abandoned homes, dirt lots, fuck, it looks like the great depression pictures they showed in school. Much of southern Arizona is a series of tiny dots on a map, specks of civilization surrounded by thousands of miles of raw desert wilderness, rock, and mountain. It's a wonder we even bother trying to patrol the area for smugglers and border hoppers. We pass through trash heap Tucson and turn onto the 86. We pass by open lots, ranch and farm land for about twenty minutes until we make an abrupt left onto a barely visible ranch road.

Tim taps his hands on the stereo. The uppers are doing their job. His speech is fast and clipped as we bounce on the rough road, stopping occasionally to slowly roll over some rock gardens.

"You wouldn't believe all the roads out here," he says. "Most of them aren't even on any map, old rancher routes, smuggler routes, 4x4 trails. Makes it easy to go to the middle of nowhere, but just be sure to remember the way back. Everything starts to look the same after a while, and if you get lost out here, you might be alone for quite some time."

We follow this snaking trail over hills and over a dry riverbed, through a sea of cholla and barrel cactus; we come across a faint marker on a boulder and take a right. We then turn onto an even worse trail for about fifteen minutes, the truck gets a workout from the rock ruts as ocotillos hit the side of the ride and scratch like nails on a chalkboard. At one point it looks as if we're not even on a trail or road anymore, there doesn't seem to be any discernible difference between our route and the desert around us. Towering saguaros loom everywhere. We pass over another hill and the truck's wheels skid against a long, smooth rock bed. We get to the top of a hill. I look out the window to a faint circle of light down in the valley beneath us. It gets really fucking dark out here.

We follow a narrow creek bed for about two hundred yards until it opens up to a cluster of mesquite trees. We veer right past a watering tub for cattle and park next to other vehicles. Tim cuts the lights and we get out. He whistles and a voice calls out. Tim shines a flashlight ahead of us and we take a short path to an old tin storage shack about thirty yards away. Jordo, Saul, and a stranger are seated around a small fire, holding beers and talking quietly. Jordo sees us and jumps up to greet me. We do that grasp–hands–and–back–slap half–hug thing.

Words spew out of Jordo's mouth. Coke talk.

"Fucking A, man, good to see you. From the tents to this, huh? We're going to make some serious cash, man; I can't believe how well you did, all those fucking guns, man! I knew you'd be good, I told Uncle Tim I had a good feeling about you, and man, I heard about the work you did with those stupid fucks at the escort—"

"Jordo, shut the fuck up," Tim says. "And what did I tell you morons about drinking before the meet–up? Are you fucking deaf or just dumb? Pour that shit out."

They lower their heads like scolded children and pour their beer out.

"And if I find out any of you morons have been blowing coke tonight, I'm going to leave you out here with nothing but a black eye and the clothes on your back."

"No coke tonight, Uncle, don't worry," says Jordo.

"Ok, good. I do have Dexies if you guys are tired, but don't get all tweaked out on me. Let's make this quick and smooth, just like all the others. And put out that fucking fire for Christsake. You shitheads think we're camping? Huh? Gonna roast some fucking marshmallows and sing songs? It may seem like we're out in the middle of nowhere, but the border patrol does get around here once in a while. I swear, whenever I leave you guys alone you turn retarded on me. Fuck."

Jordo ribs me in the side, makes a jack–off motion, and grins.

"Okay, is Trevor in place?"

"Yes," says Jordo. He holds up a walkie and speaks into it. Trevor responds.

"And Jake and Dante, they have everything in place?"

Jordo checks in with them on the radio.

"Good. Saul, pack up the guns in the back of the truck and take them up to Jake and Dante." He throws Saul his keys. "Tick, I'm assuming you remembered to bring the heavy locker?"

This Tick guy flips open the back door of a Jeep Rubicon, a damned nice one too, with a lift kit, big wheels, metal bumpers, and a wench, a very nice off–road ride. He's a big guy, almost as big as me, six–two and a solid two–forty. He lifts the crate up and out. Tim opens it with a key off his keychain. The crate is full of bullet–proof vests, the same type we wore on the job at the escort service. We each put one on. After the vests are out, Tim pulls out five gun cases and hands them out. I open mine and find a MAC–10 submachine gun.

"Damn, is it full auto?" I ask, mesmerized by the gun.

"Yes, and entirely rebuilt so it doesn't jam like the shitty street models, too. Be careful with it, these fuckers weren't cheap," says Tim.

I readjust the sling to fit and throw it over my shoulder. The box has two full extra mags. I tuck them into the cargo pockets on my shorts.

"Okay," Tim says. We have an hour and a half until our friends arrive, so let's head up there. Jordo, you take Tick's Rubicon since you can't ride a quad for shit. Don't worry, Tick, if he fucks it up it'll come out of his share. Tick and I are taking the ATVs to do a little recon of the area. Saul, you stay here until I tell you to move. Nick, you go with Jordo. We all understand?"

We disperse. I get in the passenger side of the Rubicon. Jordo takes the wheel and we creep out of the trees and up a very steep rock face, barely a trail. The Rubicon handles it with ease. "This fucking Jeep is a beast, man," Jordo says.

We climb out of the valley and back up to the flats. Jordo cuts the lights and climbs halfway out the window, looks around in all directions, then flips the lights back on and we proceed on another rugged trail.

"Trevor is up on a hill about a football field away from the drop spot with one of those fucking military–grade night vision scopes, I got it off a private contractor that was over in Iraq and came back with buckets of stolen shit. You should see this fucking thing, you can see for fucking ever in the middle of the night. We have the scope on top of a pretty nice .50 cal, with a silencer on it I might add. Uncle Tim's got this whole process down pat, I mean he was in 'Nam in shit, but I'm the one who got us all this gear. You know Tim, he's kind of a dick, right, but he's pretty good at this shit, but I'm not exactly a scrub either; like I said, I took this whole operation up a notch with the new gear."

He stops talking to light a cig, then slaps me on the shoulder. "You excited, you big fucker? Out in this fucking desert, make some easy cash off of these fucking Mexican gangsters, strapped with a fucking MAC 10? I love it!"

I smile and say, "Fuck yeah!"

If Tim wasn't a little tweaked out on the Dexedrine himself, he might have noticed that his nephew is indeed pretty wired on coke.

"So what happened with that girl you were always talking about, you work that out or what?"

"Nah, like I told you," I say. "She kicked me out. Probably for the better."

He nods and we speed it up a little. We hit a rut and the Jeep bounces violently and then rights itself. Jordo laughs. "Tick would kill me if he saw that, but fuck it; it's what this thing is built for."

We reach a fork and veer left, down a gradual slope and through a field of giant looming saguaros.

"Can I ask something, Jordo? Why're we selling these guys the civilian semi–auto shit when we have these sick Mac 10s and that other shit you were talking about? I mean, if they pay that much for a semi–auto AK, I can imagine they'll pay pretty damn well for one of these."

I pat the Mac on my shoulder.

"Fuck yes they will, but Uncle Tim wants us to have the ability to spread some serious firepower fast in the rare case that we get in a jam and have to shoot it out. Plus, all of us having matching SMGs makes us look that much more professional. Like I said, I know a former PMC guy that has a shit ton of high quality stuff he wants to move, but Uncle Tim says that the military–grade stuff attracts too much attention, even if it fetches much more cash; when the low– to mid–level Mexican gangbangers and cartel guys start spraying one another with the military stuff, right across the border, the Fed's take notice, you know? We can move thousands of these semi–auto's, no problem, but the Feds have a real hard–on whenever they find out about US military weapons ending up across the border. Uncle Tim's been doing work for a long time, never spent a night in jail either. So you have to go with what he says, I guess—even if he is an ornery bastard. Here, take the wheel a sec."

I do so. Jordo digs his hands in his pockets and pulls out a vial of coke, dabs a little on the back of his hand, and snorts it up. He rubs his nose and takes back the wheel.

"You want a bump?"

"Nah, that shit just makes me want to drink," I say.

"I hear that," he says. "So, yeah, please don't let my uncle know I did a few small bumps to keep on my toes, right?"

"Don't worry man, you got me in on this thing, I got your back no matter what."

"That's right, brother." He pounds me on the shoulder. "Look, we do this gig tonight, easy money, and I'm going to convince Tim to let you come down to Tucson soon and help me out. I got some things going and I could really use you, and it'll be a lot better than having to work like a fucking day laborer for Uncle Tim's crew."

We take a tight turn into a narrow passage of sorts, just barely scraping through two sides of massive rock walls into a circle of land, a clearing cut out between the very beginnings of what is either a tall hill or a mountain; I can't tell in this dark. One tall tree rests in the middle of the clearing; two mounds of rocks sit next to it beside a makeshift table made out of tires and what looks to be the rusted–out hood of a car.

He parks and cuts off the engine and lights.

"You like our little cover here? And wear pants next time, dude, this area is crawling with fucking scorpions. Don't sit down without checking. And you hear a rattler rattling, well, don't make any sudden movements," Jordo says, laughing.

We lean against the car.

"So what now," I ask.

"We wait. Uncle Tim and Tick will be here on the ATVs soon." He picks up his walkie. "Trevor?"

"Yeah," Trevor responds.

"You see us?"

"Yep. I have a bead right on your fucking head, douche bag," Trevor says.

"Good to know, stay awake up there."

I look above at the high peaks of the hills around us, imminent like towers on a castle. My eyes adjust to the dark. I scan the small area around us.

"What's with those rock piles?"

"Graves."

"No shit?"

"Yep. Border crossers that didn't make it, most likely. This area is probably littered with bones. They come over the border and their guide ditches 'em half the time; they're left wandering around lost in the middle of nowhere. You need like three gallons of water a day to survive out here in the summer, and most of them don't have much more than the clothes on their back. Fucking brutal."

"So what's the deal with the buyers, how do they haul it back across the border?"

"Plane."

"Really?"

"Yep. You'd be amazed at all the makeshift runways they have out here. They time every gun buy with a drug drop, so they take a plane in under the radar, land, and unload dope. Two crews meet the plane. One crew grabs the dope and runs it to Tucson or the valley, wherever, the other crew meets us, buys the guns, fills the plane with them, and then heads out. They have a pretty tight system."

"You trust these guys?"

"I guess. It's like Tim says, at the end of the day, the guys calling the shots are smart enough to know not to fuck with a good deal, and we provide consistently, so my only worry is one of these errand boys gets a big head and decides to make a move of his own and try and keep the guns and the cash. But we're prepared for that. It probably will never happen; you see, these guys, the runners, they know damn well if they fuck up in any way, if they go against their orders, they're as good as dead, and the guys they work for, they don't stop there. You fuck them over and it's not just you that's getting your head chopped off, it's your family, friends, anyone remotely close to you. That tends to keep people pretty honest."

We shoot the shit for a few minutes until we hear the sound of a vehicle approaching. A pickup with an extended cab pulls in and parks next to us. Its bed is packed with six footlockers. Two guys get out and introduce themselves: Dante and Jake. Jake looks to be at least sixty, a cowboy type, with the boots and hat and all. In contrast, Dante is a black guy, wearing jeans and a wife–beater with a vest on top, a backward hat, and a thick gold chain with a big cross that sparkles in the moonlight. We help them unload the crates and spread them apart on the ground. Jake has a big revolver of some sort in a hip holster. Dante has a sawed–off Mossberg in a sling.

"So, kid, you know the drill?" Jake asks me.

"Hang back and keep my eyes open."

"That's about it. Tim does all the talking. They show up in a pickup or two, take a look at the guns, pay us, and take off. It's a simple process. Keep your hands off your piece, and don't make any sudden movements. If shit goes wrong, you'll know it. Otherwise, just hang tight."

Tim and Tick show up on the ATVs.

"We all set?" Tim asks.

"Yep," says Dante.

"Okay, go grab a spot behind the Jeep. Stay out of sight," Tim tells Dante.

"These guys don't trust brothers, so Dante has to stay out of site," Jordo tells me and chuckles. "Luckily it's easy for Dante to hide out, all he has to do is close his eyes and hands, isn't that right, brother darkness?"

Dante ignores Jordo.

"Jordo, shut the fuck up," Tim says. "We have a half hour till the meet. No talking till then, Trevor'll let us know when he sees them. Everyone just sit tight, and remember, let me do the talking and stay relaxed. Don't spook these guys; they're already wired too tight."

With that we all lapse into a long period of silence. The desert gets so quiet. There's no wind tonight. The only sounds are a few insects, our breathing, and slight, fidgety movements—sounds amplified in this little cove. The temperature has dipped considerably, but I'm still sweating from the added weight of the jacket. The sweat runs off my forehead and down my face. I wipe my face off with my shirt constantly. Jordo passes me a bottle of water and I take it down. I hope I don't look as fucking nervous as I feel.

The waiting gets my mind wandering. I wonder if this spot is such a smart choice; we're all but trapped in here if they wanted to hole us in and take us out. I know Trevor is up there watching with the big gun, but if we have to shoot it out, our backs are literally up against the wall. We have plenty of firepower, that's for sure, but who knows what the fuck these guys bring to the table. I chain–smoke, nervously; I do my best to hide the slight tremor in my hands. I know I have it in me to shoot it out if I have to, but it's not something I want to do. I guess if I had to kill someone, this is the place to do it. You kill someone out here, you bury them out here, shit, they'll never find the body—needle in a fucking haystack. *But what about border patrol?* I think. Tim said they do come around here sometime; what if tonight's that time? Fuck, you get caught in this situation, with a truckload of guns and illegal machineguns strapped on your shoulder, you catch a case like that and you're going away for a long, long time. And worse yet, if someone decides to shoot it out with the Feds, fuck, that's death penalty stuff right there. I imagine it, a helicopter comes out of nowhere, shines that bright light on us, Fed's swarm in like a cloud of locusts, I swear I can hear the sound of a distant helicopter, like it *is* hovering just out of sight, waiting.

"Okay, two sets of lights, about a half mile out," Trevor calls out from the radio.

"Roger, keep an eye open," Tim tells him. "Everyone sit tight."

I take deep, durable breaths and manage to stop shaking. My heart still pounds through my chest. My throat is raw from all the smokes.

Lights appear. I watch them get closer and closer until they shine over us. Two vehicles park just short of the opening to the cove. The cars shut off. The lights go out. All is dark and still for a moment, a long fucking moment. Tim picks up a flashlight lantern and turns it on, waves it back and forth three times. Four Mexicans walk toward the light, into the cove, all wearing Mexican cowboy wear: jeans, plaid shirts, boots, big belt buckles. Two have AK pistols on straps.

Tim walks up to them and shakes hands with one of the Mexicans. I can't understand what they're saying, but the guy speaks perfect English. Tim walks him back to the foot lockers while the other three stay behind. They stare straight at us through the dark.

Tim opens the foot lockers and the Mexican spends about fifteen minutes inspecting the guns.

"You happy?" Tim asks him when he finishes going through the last case.

"Very," he replies.

Tim walks with him to their vehicle. They talk for another minute or so, and then one of them backs their pickup back toward us. They load the gun crates while Tim looks through a duffel bag and counts the cash. Once the truck is loaded up, Tim shakes hands with the talker and they leave. It's all over just like that. After all the nervousness, all the sweat, the heart pounding, the constant worries of "what if's," the whole thing is as quick and smooth as any other daily business transaction.

Tim walks back to us. "It's that simple, guys. Hang tight for a few." He gets on the walkie.

"Trevor, keep an eye on them until they're out of sight, then keep a watch for another fifteen minutes or so to make sure no one doubles back. Watch our backs once we leave and then come meet us back at the camp."

Tim sits down on the makeshift table, puts the bag down, and pats it. "Two hundred grand," he says. "Excellent work everyone."

Jordo comes out of the dark. "Those fucking spics better not have paid us in pesos."

Everyone laughs.

"They had to be happy with the buy," says Jordo. "That was the best lot yet."

"Yes they were. But they want more," Tim says. He chuckles. "They want more. And they'll always want more."

Chapter 15: HACK

I WAKE UP AROUND TWO OR THREE in the morning. It's Friday or Saturday; the days blur together. I worked for a couple of days straight, then slept for a couple. I feel all right. The air in my apartment is frigid, just the way I like it. I have few luxuries in life, few are possible with the income of a cab driver, but AC is one of them. It takes three shifts of driving to cover my AC bill, but it's well worth it. I get out of bed and flip the lights on, survey my one bedroom apartment. It's spotless and sparsely decorated; the walls are bare, with the exception of a single cross and a tackboard with my military stuff on it. I like simplicity and order in my living space. I spend so much time in the mess out there, driving that fucking cab through the shit storm all these days and nights; I have to come home to a rigid, almost sterile environment. I shower, put on pressed slacks and a Dickie's work shirt. I put my pistol in my waistband, feed my pet fish, and I head out.

I'm going to work the DUI beat. This time of night is perfect for that. I head over to a parking lot where they take the night's DUI offenders for portable intake and processing. The cops usually cut the offenders loose after four or five hours, and there's no shortage of bleary–eyed, half–drunk fools in need of a ride home. They don't tip for shit but the work is steady. I arrive to find about three other cabs ahead of me in line, but that's nothing. We'll all have fares in fifteen minutes or so. I wait, drink coffee, and smoke.

I flip on the local news channel, listen to the overnight guy burn time talking about UFOs and aliens and shit. The news break comes in with a breaking story about three brutal murders up in Colorado City. I smile and turn the volume up. Three murders, two crime scenes. A husband and wife were found shot dead execution–style in their bedroom. A couple of miles away, a prominent local figure in the Fundamentalist Church was found dead in his home with more than fifty stab wounds. The reporter uses the familiar terms they use to grab attention…grisly scene…shocking…quiet community…

They have no potential suspects at this time. I smile and slap my hand on the steering wheel and flip the radio off. The two cabs in front of me are gone in minutes. A tearful young lady opens the door and gets in my cab.

"Can you please take me home?"

"Of course I can, darling," I look at her again in the mirror. "Might be a detour on the way, though," I add.

Chapter 16: NICK

"WE COULD WISH TO BE MORAL, we could wish to be philosophically comforted, in fact, we could will these things with all our might, but the needed power wasn't there. Our human resources, as marshaled by the will, were not sufficient; they failed utterly."

I'm trying to pay attention to what Gary is reading, trying to absorb at least something out of it, but my mind is stuck on that thick wad of cash I have locked in the glove compartment of my Jeep. Fifteen Grand. Tim gave me a hundred and fifty Ben Franklins earlier today, at the tail end of a particularly grueling day spent tearing down walls in a trashed foreclosure property. The day started poorly. Apparently the owners—well, former owners, I guess—of this property were upset at the fact that the bank was foreclosing on their property. They made their point by shitting on the floors, and with no electricity and who knows how many consecutive days of over a hundred and five degree temperatures, well, the house reeked like death. We worked right through it, seven straight hours of demo work in a sauna of an outhouse.

Tim wanted me to keep the five grand he had loaned me, to let it ride a bit, but when sober, I make a point of avoiding debt as much as possible. I now have my own money to play with, and every penny that doesn't go to necessities like food, rent, and gas will go toward buying more guns for the next drop.

"Nick, are you listening?"

Gary jolts me out of my day dream.

"I'm trying man, it's been a long day, you know, swinging a hammer in the heat; I'm pretty spent," I say.

"Oh yeah? Well which is tougher: swinging that hammer or dragging yourself out of a three–day drunk with your hands shaking and that terrible doom creeping in?"

I laugh. "You know the answer to that."

"Well listen up then. I'm not reading this shit for my own amusement. I mean yeah, trying to get this stuff to fill your dumb head is fun and all, but I have a wife and cold house to go home to that's a lot more fun after a day of work. So listen up or don't waste my time. Matter of fact, why don't you read a bit."

He points to where we are in the book and I start to read: "We look upon this world of warring individuals, warring theological systems, and inexplicable calamity, with deep skepticisms. We looked askance at many individuals who claimed to be godly. How could a supreme being have anything to do with it all? And who could comprehend a Supreme Being anyhow? Yet, in other moments, we found ourselves thinking, when enchanted by a starlit night, (I instantly think of the other night in the desert as I read this) 'Who, then, made all of this?' There was a feeling of awe and wonder, but it was fleeting and soon lost."

"Tell me about that," Gary says.

"About what?"

"That part of you that has this internal debate. Every alcoholic, before and after they get in the program, does. It's normal to question, provided you're at least trying to figure it out."

I light a cig to buy me a few seconds and stare at a cute tattooed chick sitting nearby, look at the tattoo all over her chest. It frames her tits perfectly. Fuck, my sex drive is coming back, finally. I turn my attention back to Gary and I let it out.

"My mother was a lapsed Catholic and my father avoided the subject of God or religion or spirituality entirely. It didn't really fit in with the way he saw the world, which was a strict balance of excessive work and excessive partying. There isn't much room for ruminating on God, or whatever you want to call it, in that equation. So I really have made it a point to not think about it, either. I mean, maybe I have on some subconscious level, but it does kind of fuck me up to think about how little thought I've put into it."

"Well what about before, when you had that period of sobriety before, those five years or whatever it was, you worked the steps, you did the deal, surely you had to think about it somewhat?"

I shrug my shoulders and take another glance at the tattooed broad nearby. She catches me looking and smiles. I smile back. I page through the book to find this quote, which I read aloud:

"Most of our experiences are what the psychologist William James calls the "educational variety" because they develop slowly over a period of time. Quite often friends of the newcomer are aware of a difference before he is himself. He finally realizes that he has undergone a profound alteration in his reaction to life; that such change could hardly have been brought about by himself alone."

Gary nods. "That's good, and it's true for most. I don't know many people that experienced the burning–bush sort of event that led them to their spiritual path. Most of us figure it out along the way, just by going through the motions, the physical act of praying in the morning and at night, going to meetings and saying the serenity prayer, sharing and listening to one another, these are all things we can just do that will most likely educate us into a state of spiritual growth. Fake it till you make it, right? But some people are too good at faking it, and I think you fall into that category. When I talk to you, when you talk, it's like there are two parts of you, one that is spitting out something that has some relevance to the subject at hand, and the other part, the part that worries me, is that little gleam I see in you that suggests that the other half of you is far, far away. You know what that means?"

"Huh?"

"It means you're a bullshit artist."

We stare at one another in a mini standoff for maybe thirty seconds and then we burst into laughter.

"You do read me pretty well, Gary, I'll give you that."

"Yes, I do. And you know why? Because you aren't nearly as unique as you think you are. There are thousands of shitheads just like you in the program, and tens of thousands just like you outside of it, just drinking and living miserable fucking existences. There's just a slight difference between those inside the program and those outside, and you know what that is?"

I shrug.

"Step two. The people that make it 'come to believe.' "

"In what?"

Gary shakes his head. "Don't be a smart ass. You know damn well that's a question only they, or you, can answer." He grabs his key off the table and gets up to leave.

"So are we done with step two?"

"No, not even close. But you never answered my question, about what you believed in the last time you were sober, those five years."

I start to talk, try and answer the question. He cuts me off.

"Save it for next time. I want you to think about it. And I want you to write it down. In great detail. Don't leave out a thing, no matter how trivial it seems. Just get it down on paper. And remember, Nick, you can't do this thing with one foot in and one foot out. You either do it or you don't."

We bump fists and he walks away. I'm relieved to not have to answer that question right now. I don't know the answer; or maybe I do, but explaining it to someone sounds almost impossible. I drain the last bit of my

coffee and light another cig, stare off into space. I think about the hows
and whys of how I got sober those years ago, at the relatively young age
of nineteen. That little private college I went to up in Washington gave
me two options: expulsion from school or enter an inpatient substance
abuse program as suggested by the campus counseling office. I got
blacked–out drunk and belligerent one too many times, and despite
my good grades–I could study like a motherfucker with the help of
Ritalin or Adderall—the school wasn't thrilled about me redecorating
the hallway walls of my dorm with my fists. The fact that I wrestled and
pinned the security guard that came to calm me down didn't go over
well, either. It took four guys to pull me off. I didn't hurt him; luckily
I didn't deem it necessary to punch him while I had him pinned to the
floor. I guess in my blacked–out state, the act of thoroughly dominating
the supposed authority figure was good enough.

So I went to treatment, in the Midwest, in the bitter fucking cold. I
was on a flight the same day the school gave me the ultimatum; they
had been in touch with Mom (Dad was dead by then) and had the whole
thing planned out. I was, to be perfectly honest, horrified by the events
of the previous night. I woke from that blackout in the local detox, a
depressed building with brown walls and the smell of puke, piss, and
aerosol cleaner. I had no idea where I was or what had happened. I
figured it for jail at first. I came to, still drunk, in a small room with five
or six cots. Only one other bed was occupied, and when I stood up and
stumbled a bit, panicked and confused, a voice called from the other
side of the room to let me know that the cops had brought me in a few
hours earlier, in cuffs, struggling, and they gave me a shot and put me
to bed. I was in detox, he said, and neither of us were going anywhere
anytime soon, so you either sleep or you talk—only way to pass the
time.

I had no recollection of the last six or seven hours. The last thing I
remembered was having a drinking contest in my dorm room, vodka
shots with a dash of lemon juice and sugar, one after another at a

reckless pace. That's all I could remember, the taste of cheap vodka made syrupy sweet with lemon juice and cubes of sugar.

I started to shake, wondering what the hell had happened, what got met here.

A nurse came and peered in the open door to the room, asked me if I was okay and if I could understand what she was saying. I nodded yes, and she asked me if I was going to be calm. I said yes. She took my blood pressure and temperature and gave me a glass of water. I asked her what happened. All she told me was that I had drunk too much, and no, I couldn't use the phone, not yet. She left and I curled back up on the bed. I felt more and more sober with every passing minute, and with that growing sobriety came a fear unlike anything I'd ever felt. I'd blacked out before plenty of times. I had done plenty of dumb and bizarre stuff while blacked out: made embarrassing phone calls, fell asleep in strange rooms, hooked up with less–than–attractive girls, got into fights, thrown up often, even pissed the bed once or twice, shit like that. But whatever I had done that night must have been really fucking stupid or I wouldn't have ended up in that room. At that point I finally noticed the bandages on my hands and the pain that pulsed beneath them. *Oh fuck, fuck, fuck, I must have beaten someone up. What did I do?* At that point, the post blackout, the partial recollection period, you start to assume the worst, which at the time was that I had gotten drunk and beaten someone to death and the rest of my life was over as I knew it.

I barely made it to the trash can in the corner where I threw up, not from being drunk, but at the pure fucking terror that gripped me and clenched my stomach in a vise. I threw up twice, felt those knife–stab convulsions in my stomach. A thick, cold sweat spread across me. I don't know why, but I could not take my eyes from the puke I just left in the trash can, the warmth emanating off it, its bright and noxious yellow hue. Pure liquid. I started to remember just how many vodka shots I'd taken before I blacked out. It was plenty. *Oh fuck. My poor mother is going to be so broken by this, by the horrible things her only child did…*

"Hey, kid," a voice from the other bed called out.

"Whu?" I turned around, frightened. I'd totally forgotten there was someone else here.

"Stop worrying," the voice said.

"What? What do you mean?"

"I know what you're doing," the stranger said. "You're thinking of all the things you might have done in that blackout, all the depraved and horrible things you could have done to get you here."

I sat down on my bed. I couldn't see his face. That side of the room was all shadow. He had a sheet pulled up all the way to his lips.

"How do you know what I'm thinking?"

"Because I'm psychic," he said.

Great, stuck in a room with a fucking lunatic, I thought.

He laughed. "I'm kidding, kid. I know what you're thinking, what you're going through, because I've been there, been there more times than I'd like to admit. I'm somewhat of an expert in that area."

"So why do I not have to worry?"

"I was having a smoke in the day room when they brought you in, and I overheard it all. You had a few too many and decided to punch a few holes in the walls over at your college. Then you wrestled a security guard to the floor, big feller that you are, and they had a hell of a time getting you off of him." He laughs. "But you didn't hurt him, not physically at least, but you probably hurt his ego a little bit. Big bad rent-a-cop gets pinned like a baby by some punk college kid. I bet he goes home and takes it out on his wife, what do you think? You know what? I'm almost certain he does."

"Oh fuck," I moaned." I am so fucked."

"Not really. You might get kicked out of your little school or whatever, but in the long run that doesn't mean much. It's not that big of a game changer, kid. It might seem like it now, but trust me, in the grand scheme of things, it doesn't mean shit."

This guy, he talked most of the night. I never caught his name. I was too scared or ashamed or whatever to sleep, all I could think about was how embarrassing it was going to be when I had to go back to school to pack up my stuff, how all those people I lived with all semester were going to look at me like I was some sort of monster. I was certain that even my friends would see me in an entirely new light. No one would ever look at me the same. I was sure that I was going to be kicked out of school, so it came as some surprise when the counselor from the school showed up the next morning. He told me that he had talked to people in my dorm about me, how they said I drank so much so often, and the school understood that I had a problem, and that if I was willing to get some help I'd be allowed to return to school, on a probationary status, after I had completed an inpatient treatment program of sorts. He told me that he had spoken to my mother, and they had found a bed open for me at a treatment center in Minnesota, and that he would escort me back to school to pack and then take me to the airport.

I agreed to it with no hesitation. I was so frightened by my behavior that I was willing to do pretty much whatever I could to get as far away from the situation as possible, and Minnesota in the winter fit that bill. I had only one request, and that was that I didn't want to return to the campus before the flight under any circumstances. "Just take me straight to the airport," I told him. "I'll pay to have my stuff shipped to me." I knew at that point that I was never going to return to that school. I would go to the rehab, I would do whatever they wanted, but there was no way I would ever return to that school to face my shame head on.

And I never did.

I got on that flight, and to make a long story short, I actually liked being in treatment. It dawned on me, two days into treatment, that it was the longest I had gone without a drink or a drug in three years; I knew it was the right place for me. I was more fucked up than I had realized, and once the shakes and the sweats and the headaches were over I rather enjoyed being sober once again. When I was done with the twenty–eight days they insisted I go to a halfway house, and Arizona had one with an open bed that was the perfect place for me. That's how I ended up here, seven years ago—a long fucking seven years. I had five years of awesome sobriety and I had to go and fuck it up. I've spent two years being drunk for months and then sober for a week, maybe a month, repeat, and finally I'm here, optimistic that I might finally be back on track to staying sober for real. At some point toward the end of those five years of sobriety, I guess I forgot what I felt like that night in detox, that incredible shame, the seething dread, me puking and shaking with fear, sure that I had killed someone and that my life was all but over. I forgot that fear, forgot the place that alcohol puts me in, and I conned myself into believing that I could drink like a normal person. And I picked up right where I left off. I blacked out the second day of my relapse, and I woke up again with that fear, not in detox this time, but in my apartment, my head spinning, not sure of what happened but certain that it wasn't good. The problem was that I never ended up doing anything too bad in my blackouts, maybe a fight or two, or I'd fall asleep somewhere strange, but after a while, when I came to from blackouts there was little fear or shame. It became so matter of a fact, so routine, and just a drink or two always erased any unpleasantness or delayed it at the least.

And that drunk, the guy in the detox—I never got his name, and come to think of it, I don't recall ever seeing his face—he told me this would happen if I kept drinking, kept on the way I was.

"Eventually you'll come to from a blackout, and it's not that there won't be any fear, because there will be, there will always ways be, at least some, but you'll get to a point where you just don't give a shit about what you did or didn't do when you were blacked out. You won't give a fuck. It becomes a part of your life, your routine; it becomes a part of you, of who you are. I wake up in places like this, and you know what I do? I yawn and go back to sleep. Not a worry in the world. I'm not saying it's a good thing, because nothing about this is, but it's just the way it is for people like me. There is a certain point you cross, kid, and it's tough to return after that. So tread lightly, huh? You ever get a spot to make something of yourself, you take it."

I think about that talkative drunk all the time. I catch myself wondering what ever happened to that man; I guess I don't even know him as a man, just a voice that came out of the shaded side of a room. I try to guess what happened to him, if he is still out there doing the same thing, if he died the drunkard's miserable death, or maybe he's like all the fortunate souls I've met who shed years of drunken horror to rejoin society, to rejoin normalcy, and its dull and consistent splendor. I would like to think so, that that is the case, hope he is sitting outside of an AA meeting somewhere, shooting the shit—laughing even. I suppose over the years he has reached an almost mythological status in my memories, this voice coming out of the darkness, the bum that was clueless and lost in every part of life but one; he was a master of the art of embracing a lifelong love affair with alcohol–tragic, fucking pathetic even, but fascinating nonetheless. I think about him. I wonder if he's alive still, if he happened to be one of those rare, bottom–of–the–barrel drunks who skirted the odds and actually got sober. It happens, not often, but it does. Even the worst cases sometimes find a way to come back. There's hope for us all, I guess.

As much as I cling to memories of that drunk and his prophetic wisdom of alcoholism and life, it was the conversation we had right around dawn that I remember clearest. It happened right before I finally caught an hour of two of sleep. I guess he'd worn tired of talking about drinking so much, hell, it probably just made him crave his next drink that much more. He steered the conversation, well it was more of a lecture to be accurate, he started in about his time in Vietnam, his best years in some ways, he said, the last part of his life that was not entirely consumed by alcohol. His tone changed when he spoke about the war and his experiences there, he spoke faster, a little louder. There was a noticeable urgency to his words. I tuned him out a bit as I drifted closer and closer to sleep, but a story he told just before I fell asleep has for some reason stuck with me ever since, and it is a strange story, disturbing even, a story about how he and his friends or other soldiers or something killed a couple of Vietnamese hookers and put them in oil barrels and left them on the doorsteps of the whorehouse where they worked, as a warning or punishment of some sort, I can't remember the particulars of the story. It had something to do with the hookers giving information to the enemy. The story has stuck with me, well maybe not the story as much as the way he told it with so much pride, how proud he was to have been a part of those whores getting chopped up and jammed into barrels, and the way he told it was like it was the greatest story of justice ever told.

Chapter 17: HACK

I TRY TO MAKE A HABIT OF GIVING FREE rides for the VA hospital in central Phoenix when I can. It used to be a lot of guys from my era, Vietnam, maybe Korea, some World War II vets that didn't have family or much else. Nowadays it's a lot of these younger guys fresh back from Afghanistan and Iraq, and whether it's a curse or a blessing, most of these guys survived shit that would have killed a soldier in any other war. Lots of brain trauma, missing limbs from IEDs, PTSD, poverty, drugs, and drunkenness. One look at these guys and you know they don't sleep well. Some came back without as much as a scratch on the outside, but you know that they're not right and maybe never will be. To make it worse, they came back smack in the middle of a shit economy and a government more concerned about building new hospitals and schools for towelheads than taking care of the guys they paid to do their bidding. I listen to the news and talk radio, to these military experts and talking heads talking about how important it is we win over the "hearts and minds" of the citizens of these shithole countries we've been bombing to oblivion for the last decade–the same shit the brass spewed back in my war.

Then I see these broken guys, fuck, some of them are kids, and I don't see jack shit being done for their hearts and minds.

I guess I was a rare case. I came home from Vietnam and didn't give a shit if the hippy fucks called us baby killers or spat at our feet. I was in good health. I caught minor shrapnel once, but I was the rare infantry soldier that came home in fine health. I had no nightmares, no lingering effects from the war other than a couple of newfound obsessions that would prove to shape the rest of my life, namely alcohol and fire. I didn't give a flying fuck about what people thought of me and what I had done in Vietnam, what I had been forced to do. I was drafted, but I did whatever they said and more, and I never complained, not once. So when I came back, I was back for maybe a week or two when I walked out of a bar and I came across a group of college kids, comfortable hippy types, shit spawns of the middle class, know–it–alls. I ignored them when they followed me down that street in Cleveland. They called me every name in the book twice. I didn't give them as much as a glance in response. And the more I ignored them the angrier they got, till they circled me and shouted hoarse, shouted about murder and pigs and Nixon and all sorts of other bullshit. They yelled themselves tired and I didn't say shit, and they gave up and walked the other way. Part of me wanted them to put their hands on me; I had a gorgeous bowie knife tucked in my belt, and they had no idea how ready I was to use it. The second they touched me might have been their last. They were fucking pussies, of course, all bark and no bite, and I'm sure they never knew how close I was to slicing them all up, no problem. If one of them had put a single finger on me, they would have gotten it and gotten it good.

One of them did end up learning a lesson. About a week later I was wandering through the city, probably aimlessly, I had nothing to do with my life, no ideas, no plans, no inspiration, so I either walked or I drank. Sometimes I played with fire in alleys or woods. That was about it. I spent my days walking for miles, paying no attention to anything but the rhythm of my steps. I stared at the ground and watched my feet move. I had spent all those months humping klick after rotten klick overseas, and being back home was strange. Standing still was even stranger. So I walked.

I was on one of my walks, trudging along, when I happened to look up from my feet and right in front of me, not even ten feet away, was one of those fucking college pricks that had made a show of harassing me the week before. Our eyes met. We recognized one another instantly. He started to back up, slowly, and when I grinned at him he made this squeaky noise like a dog does when you step on it. He turned around and tried to run, but he didn't make it more than a few yards before he stumbled and fell. His sandals or moccasins or whatever they were didn't make for good running shoes. I was on top of him in a flash. I had boots on and I let him have it good. I kicked and kicked and kicked; I felt and I heard his ribs snap from the impact. He moaned and pleaded at first but he soon accepted his fate. I gave him a world–class ass kicking that left him a bloodied, bruised, and gasping mess. He cried, he shivered, and he sobbed. And I left him there. I ran away, cackling, I ran and ran until I hit a forest on the edge of the city. I entered the dim mess of trees and I collapsed against a tree, panting, laughing hysterically as I struggled to catch my breath.

The next morning I boarded a Greyhound bus with sixty–eight dollars and a canvas bag, headed for Denver, Colorado. I like to think back to that fucking hippy, hope he appreciated the lesson I gave him, a lesson that there are consequences for our actions, and we don't get the liberty of knowing when those consequences will make their grand entrance into our lives. So stay on your toes, fuckwad. You never know where you're gonna be when the past comes back to give you the ass whipping you're due.

Chapter 18: NICK

I GET BACK TO WORK ON THE GUNS. There's a gun show over at the fairgrounds today and there are going to be a lot of guys doing private sales, but Tim's right, there are too many eyes there. I know for a fact the ATF is usually there, milling around, wasting everyone's time. As Tim says, you last in this game by keeping a low profile.

Thanks to Backpage, I happen upon a guy in Gilbert that's having a fire sale of all his toys. His ads show a room full of stuff that has to go, today: two ATVs, a pool table, a huge flat–screen TV, and all other sorts of shit that men buy when times are good. But times are not good for this guy, not anymore, and he needs to pay his backed–up mortgage payments today or the house is gone. His loss is my gain. I meet him in a box store parking lot. I almost feel bad for the guy when I peel off three grand for a Bushmaster AR–15, an Arsenal AK, a top of the line LMT AR–15, a Colt M4, a Sig 5.56, and a Springfield XD 9mm. He knows he's getting fucked, but there isn't much he can do about it. I almost feel bad for the guy.

"It's just stuff, man," I tell him. "Nothing you can't have again."

He doesn't ask for an ID or a bill of sale or anything. He gets the cash and peels out. I have a slight moment of panic, thinking this deal was too good to be true. I look around; I almost expect cars to screech up, and cops to pile out with guns, and badges to get pointed my way. Nothing happens. I bring the guns home and disassemble and wipe them down to remove any fingerprints. I then pack them in bubble wrap. The Colt M–4 is a beautiful gun and I need a good gun to keep in my truck, something to have besides the Glock that I now carry twenty–four/seven.

Tim calls me, wants to talk. I tell him to meet me at that coffee shop in Tempe I go to with Gary. I've been going there a lot, trying to run into that tatted girl with perfect tits and smile. My life is getting better by the day. I think I need a good woman to top it off. I haven't thought about Sarah much, not at all, and when I do I think about how maybe I wasn't really that much into her at all, in fact, until I left, I spent more time caring about whether or not she was fucking someone behind my back than I did actually caring about her.

I head over to the coffee house and find Tim in a corner, smoking and drinking coffee.

"What the fuck, Nicky, what's with you having me meet you at this street trash beatnik joint? A fucking diner is just fine next time, okay?"

I laugh and tell him that I like the eye candy. He smiles and shrugs, tells me I have a point. He's been a lot chiller with me lately, actually showing some personality. Much remains to be seen, I'm sure of that. He has a lot of layers to him, I'm sure of that, too, but I don't know if I care to stick around long enough to really figure it out. As good as this gig has been, you don't see too many retired successful guys in this game. I have to remember that. I look around, make sure there's no one sitting nearby, and quietly tell him about all the guns I got today.

"Good. You keep this up and I'm going to up your take to sixty/forty. But honestly, Nicky, I don't know how much longer we're going to do this."

"What do you mean? I thought we had a great drop?"

"Oh, we did. But my sources tell me that the guys we're selling to are in the beginning stages of a civil war of sorts in their organization, which is barely organized as it is, and things are getting blurry; and as usual, everyone wants to be the top dog. I don't know how long the guys at the top can keep it going, and from what I hear, the guys that're gunning for the top are real fucking maniacs, not the sort that make good business partners. There's too much money down there right now; they're moving so much fucking dope they don't even know what to do with the cash. They have houses with rooms full of piles of cash, too much to ever spend. After a while it becomes more of a game to them, the money comes after the violence and power and shit. They are fucking savages; these guys don't give a fuck about tomorrow. But we do. So when the day comes that the current head of their organization gets rubbed out, we're done as well. The Russians in town are looking to get in the business either way, so I'll gladly hand it off to them when needed. Besides, as good as it's been, it's still a lot of work for a modest gain. A lot of risk, too."

"So then what? "

Tim smiles. "I like that about you, Nicky, you're always willing to jump right in. The first day I met you I worked you like a slave and you didn't say a word, and then that same day you beat on some guy for no reason other than I asked you to. But I like that you got limits too, kid, and you aren't afraid to make them known. You had no problem telling me you don't off people. That's a good thing. I don't trust guys that can kill someone without batting an eye, and that's the exact reason why I don't trust those savages south of the border."

He looks around us for a moment and then leans closer.

"As you probably figured, we have our hands in some other stuff. The gun stuff is just a piece of it. That's why Jordo is down in Tucson. He might be a bit of a pain in the ass, but the kid is smart, and he ferrets out information better than anyone—as long as we can keep him away from the coke and the girls. He's putting together some good stuff. But like I said, the kid is a pain in the ass, especially when he gets to partying. That's another thing I like about you, you don't fuck around with the blow and all that bullshit. So I know Jordo wants you down there to help watch his back. I'm gonna send you down there soon, maybe a week or two to do just that, watch his back. I need eyes and ears down there. I need you to make sure he isn't fucking off too much. So I just want to let you know that's what's going on, want to give you a heads up that I might send you down there soon. Cool?"

I nod. I turn to my right to shield myself from a breeze while I light a smoke and there she is, finally. I've been stopping by the shop every day with the hope that she might be here. Today is my lucky day. We catch eyes. She smiles. I smile back and my stomach does that little nervous–twitch thing. She's got a short skirt on, a baby tee; her hair is dyed a hint of red. Knee–high socks frame her perfect legs. A friend comes and sits down across from her and she looks away. I turn back to Tim. He grins at me.

"You come here to look or you actually going to shop?"

"What do you mean?"

"That broad with all the tats and shit, the legs and tits. I'm a happily married man and well out of the game, but I'm telling you, you don't make a stab at that then you are one stupid son–of–a–bitch. Life isn't all about work, Nicky. I know you like the cash, but you gotta enjoy yourself, too. Why do you think I do all this shit? When I hit my goal I'm done; I'm going to retire and buy a big fucking house and travel and all that shit. You gotta have goals, son. And your most urgent goal right now should be getting that girl in the sack."

He slaps me on my back as he gets up.

"Hey, Tim, before you leave—one thing, do you mind if I ask you what Jordo is working on? I mean, I kind of want to know what's going on if I'm gonna be heading down there."

He sits back down. "Sure, I don't have many details for you, but let me ask you this, what is the common denominator in all the jobs you've done for me?"

I think for a moment then shrug.

Tim talks. "I'll tell you this: everything we do, it always involves other people in the game. We sell guns to drug runners. I had you beat up and shake down that guy because he stole from us. We put an ass whipping on those morons running the escort service and robbed them. Everything we do, it never involves the common folk. We don't rip off civilians. We don't push junk. We don't scam or con normal people. Everything we do, it is either with or against scumbags. And you know why? Well, you think the police gave a fuck–all that those fuckers at the escort service got beaten like that, and robbed? I doubt they spent a single day investigating it. That's how you stay under the radar—you don't fuck with the normals. The beauty of what we do is that there are always going to be people around that are in way over their heads, just asking to be taken down, fast and easy, the sort that can't do a fucking thing about it when we do. And honestly, no one gives a fuck when a dope crew gets jacked or a monkey pimp gets beaten down and cleaned out. And the best thing of all is that my conscience is clean, I have no problem falling asleep every night. Do you?"

"No, not anymore," I say. It's the truth. Maybe it's being sober, maybe not, but whatever is going on, I haven't felt this good in years.

"Now don't be a pussy, use that brain of yours to talk your way into that girl's skirt, right?"

He chuckles and walks off. I watch him walk away. My stomach does that flip thing again when he stops at the tatted girl's table, leans down next to her, and speaks to her. She listens, then smiles and laughs. He points back to me, smiles, and walks off.

I don't have time to be embarrassed. She smiles and waves me over.

Chapter 19: HACK

THE AC IN THIS CAB IS NOT WORKING well. It's a hundred and nine out, and I honestly don't know if there's a difference between the temperature inside or outside, even with the AC going full blast. My fare, a rigid–looking business guy in a suit, is making a show of fidgeting and wiping his brow, even though we're only going a total of eight blocks in all. It's not that hot, you fucking pussy.

"Sorry sir, the AC is not cooperating. We're almost there," I tell him.

"Yeah well, it's probably not too smart to be without AC on a day like this. It puts people in a bad mood, and people in bad moods don't tip. Trust me."

I get it, fucko, you aren't going to tip me. I fucking hate passive–aggressive fucks like this guy. Just say what's on your mind, you pussy.

"Sir, are you implying that you're not going to tip me? Because I don't know if I can go on living without that one dollar you were probably going to lay on me. Poor little Susie might not get that organ transplant."

We stop at a red light.

Mr. Businessman laughs. "Smart ass cabbie, I love it. Look buddy, you probably aren't the brightest guy in the world, that's why you're driving a fucking cab, so I'm just telling you I think you should get your AC fixed, its—"

I cut him off. "You know what I think?"

He smiles. "No, enlighten me. What do you think?"

"I think you shouldn't have stolen that money from your grandmother, you greedy fuck."

His smile drops. "What the fuck are you talking about?"

"C'mon buddy, don't play dumb with me. You know what you did. You forged your own grandmother's signature and altered her will, didn't you? You pocketed that 35k that was supposed to go to her church's charity. Not only did you steal from your own grandmother, who was too far gone with Alzheimer's to catch on, that money was supposed to help feed third–world famine victims. You stole from your own grandmother, and the worst part was, you didn't even need the money, did you? You do pretty well, don't you? But you are such a greedy, self–absorbed soulless fuck that you couldn't believe your granny would leave that money to anyone but you, especially not some starving peasants halfway around the world. Isn't that right Paul?"

His face contorts from an open mouth of shock to a sickened sneer.

"You are fucking crazy; I don't know what you're talking about. Let me out, right now," he says.

"Hold on a sec, we're almost there, just two blocks away. But is this really bothering you that much? Do I sense some guilt? Well, that's a good thing, Paul; at least you have some sort of a conscience. I mean, it takes a pretty twisted person to steal from their own grandmother and to literally take the food off of starving children's plates. That is some pretty cold stuff. I wonder what else you've done. I bet there's something; no, I'm sure of it, Paul. Paul, you have done some pretty bad things, haven't you? You've got dirty little hands, don't you, my friend?"

He fumbles with the door. "Let me out. Let me the fuck out right here!" He shouts.

I pull over to let him out. He struggles with the locked door. "At least be man enough to admit that everything I said was the truth. You have that in you, Paul?"

I unlock the door. He steps halfway out of the car and then turns back to me. "It wasn't a charity that feeds starving kids," he says. "They provide malaria vaccines or something like that. They waste money helping a whole giant lot of doomed people. They might as well take that money and set it on fire. It's all a big gigantic waste; it won't make a fucking difference. Those people will just continue to shit out more and more kids that will die of disease or starve to death. And you know what? I don't feel the least bit sorry about what I did, so fuck you."

He flicks me off then slams the door. In a rush, he forgets that he's getting out on the driver side of the car. He steps right into oncoming traffic. A mid–sized sedan slams into him. He does a full flip in the air and lands on the pavement, hard; the sound his body makes is like that of a sack of potatoes dropped onto the floor. He isn't dead, but it's not going to be a pleasant recovery, that's for sure. I step out of the cab. Our eyes meet right before he loses consciousness. I wink at him. Someone screams in the background, a real shrill female scream, probably at the sight of the bone sticking out from his leg.

There's a burst of activity. A crowd gathers. I can't move. I'm stunned that I was wrong about the charity, thinking it was for famine when it had something to do with vaccinations. I'm almost never wrong. It's usually pretty black or white. I see it all, I see it in great detail, or I see nothing. But this, getting a detail wrong, this is new. Maybe I'm just having an off day. I hope. They cart poor little Paul off and I'm in a pretty damn good mood after that.

CHAPTER 20: NICK

A WEEK HAS PASSED. With the exception of a couple of days spent smashing rocks for a new subdivision, I've spent almost all of my time with her, with Rebecca. She waved me over to her table that day, after Tim said something to her. I joined her, so nervous, and I asked her right away what Tim said. She told me that he said he was my boss, and I wasn't paying attention to him because I couldn't get over her, that he was going to work me extra hard the next day for not paying attention to him so the least she could do was flirt with me a bit.

I'd never seen Tim with women before really, had no idea he had such charm, the ability to walk up to a young lady and get her to smile like that. I don't know if I've ever known someone with a confidence like that. So Tim worked his magic and she waved me over. I sat down, nervous as all fuck. I was a little shy at first, intimidated even; she has that rare kind of energy. I spent ten minutes with her and I was already craving more, craving not unlike the way I feel when I have just one drink and the second doesn't just sound good, it's necessary, and to be deprived of it is torture. She and her friend had to leave after those wonderful ten minutes. Before she left she pulled a permanent marker out of her purse and wrote her phone number in between the tattoos along my arm. She had me do the same around the tattoo on the upper part of her thigh. My hand shook as I drew the sloppy numbers for my cell around a large tattoo of a bird of some sort, all vivid color and perfect lines, the beauty of the tattoo enhanced more by my sloppy writing. She giggled and got up, tousled my hair, and walked away.

After she left I sat there, in awe of this girl, ruminating over what is the proper amount of time to wait until I called her. *At least a day or so. Or should I wait for her to call me? Or maybe she was just fucking with me because Tim told her to do so,* I thought. I left the coffee shop and headed home, and not five minutes on the road my phone rang and it was her. She invited me to some dive bar on the edge of Scottsdale and Tempe. We listened to some shitty punk band play and had a conversation by shouting into each other's ears. She told me about herself. She works for a group home for foster kids, transitional living stuff. She asked what I did, and I told her the truth, that I do whatever Tim tells me, and I told her I was going to go back to ASU next semester to get my Master's in social work. We left that bar and I followed her to a parking lot by Tempe Town Lake. We parked and walked by the lake. She showed me her favorite spot, next to the light–rail bridge; the bridge has this line of bright lights that alternate in color and glow off of the water. We sat and talked for hours. I told her about my struggles with drinking. Turns out she is clean too and has been off Oxycontin for a year. I open up to her, not too much, just enough, I tell her about how much my Dad's heart attack fucked me up, how I dreamed about alcohol as a child, long before I tried it for the first time, how the first time I drank I looked at the liquid in the glass like it was some amazing gift, how I kept that same love for so long until that love became ordinary, then necessary, and finally horrifying. I told her about how I managed to sabotage a perfect life by drinking again. I told her about the tents, how I passed the days doing push–ups and reading dog–eared, stolen library books and listening to people lie their way through great stories. I told her about how for the first time in years I am finally starting to feel comfortable in my skin.

She paints. That's what she does. She loves working with the damaged kids, but her real passion is art. She showed me cell phone pictures of her paintings. When she told me she painted I figured she painted pop art tattoo kind of stuff, but quite the opposite; she is an oil painter, plein air style, she paints magnificent paintings of the desert and forests and other outdoor stuff. She is gorgeous and smart and funny and she has just the right amount of a troubled past and beautiful flaws that makes her that much more perfect. She gave me a quick goodnight kiss that night. The moment her lips touched mine I knew that everything had changed now; whether I liked it or not, Rebecca now rented quite a bit of space in my head.

We spent the next three days together. Four days after that first kiss we slept together for the first time. It was perfect. When we finished we collapsed on the sheets, sweat soaked, with the AC rattling full blast in my bland little rental. I had a sudden and nervous reminder about alcoholics and relationships, how when it comes to our love lives we like to throw it into high gear as soon as possible, desperately forcing the relationship to mature at an obscene pace that is not sustainable at all and leads to an inevitable sudden explosion and collapse. I decided there and then that I will do whatever I can to try and keep this thing realistic. There is no need to rush. If it's meant to be it's meant to be. There is a part of every alcoholic that truly believes that nothing good lasts. Our natural inclination is to jam as much of whatever it is we are hooked on or interested in into ourselves, desperately even, as if it might be taken away without notice at any given moment, so we need it now, now, now.

I wake up next to her. The light from the parking lot comes through the blinds and orients itself right upon the perfect curve of her back. She sleeps soundly. I like that. Before bed she takes off her makeup and lets her hair down, and even with the tats and the piercing she still has that girl–next–door kind of beauty, so effortless.

The phone rings. It's five a.m.

"Yeah."

"Hey, Nick, we have a problem. I need to talk to you. Meet me at the job site. And bring a bag. I need you to go down to Tucson, today."

"For how long?"

"As long as needed. Why do you ask?"

"No reason."

"Okay, well, get over here then."

I hang up the phone. Rebecca runs her fingers over my back. I look back at her and smile.

"Lucky me," I say. "I get to go down to Tucson today."

"For how long?" She makes that cute, pouty face. Fucking adorable.

"I don't know. A day or two. Maybe longer."

She yawns. "Well, if it's longer, I have some time off this weekend and there are some great spots to paint down there."

I kiss her. "That sounds great."

I start to get dressed, tell her she can sleep in; there's an extra key on the table.

She smiles and goes right back to sleep. I throw a few things in a bag and head out. I'm not thrilled about going to Tucson, but I suppose it's good for us to have a couple of days apart. We can't spend every day together, not this fast. Or maybe we can. Either way, I have to go.

I get to the worksite. Tim waves me over and we sit on the back of his truck. He hands me a thick envelope full of cash.

"Don't give Jordo a fucking penny of that money. That's for you, expenses and such. Jordo and a couple of guys are staying in some trailers on a piece of land I own about ten minutes outside of town. It's not much, so if you can get things under control you can stay in town at a hotel or whatever. I don't know how long you're going to be down there, but I need someone to get down there and take control of the situation, and I can't do it."

"Fine, fine, so what do you need me to do?"

Tim spits in the dirt. One of the workers walks up to say hi but Tim waves him off.

"A local guy down in Tucson has built a little operation smuggling illegals over the border. Well, it's not a small business, it's grown quite a bit; this guy is making some decent cash, and like an amateur, he has no idea how to wash the cash. It's actually pretty easy to smuggle Mexicans over the border, you know, its wide fucking open. The tough part is what to do with all the cash. Washing cash isn't a simple thing these days. So this fuck, Packridge is his name, he figures out that he can't just make huge cash deposits in his savings account without raising some suspicion, and he doesn't have a business or anything set up to wash it. He starts asking around, asking every shithead and con he can find. Eventually, word gets to Jordo; you know I had him down there setting up the gun stuff. Jordo gets a buddy of his to make contact with this Packridge guy, convinces him that he owns a couple bars in Phoenix, but what he really does is wash cash. This moron Packridge tells him about how he has a lot of cash holed up, he won't say how much, but he does let it slip that we're talking about over 500k in bills. Packridge is sold on the money washing, but he's smart enough to only commit to handing over 50k at a time. We were going to try and convince him to hand over the 500k and then we walk away, but in retrospect, very few people are dumb enough to do something like that. So Jordo and I decide to just do it the old fashion way and rob this fucker blind. So I have Jordo and his guys keeping an eye on this fuck while we set it up, but Jordo has been dragging his ass. I send old man Jake down there and check on him, and turns out that fucking Jordo has been doing nothing but partying and chasing broads since that last drop we did. He's down there blowing coke and drawing a lot of attention to himself. To be honest with you, Nicky, I don't want to go down there because I am afraid of what I might do. If he was anyone else, well, I would just handle it, but being that he's my kid sister's son, I have to be a little more reserved in the situation. Plus I need him for this job, he has all the details, and like I said before, he might be a fuckup and he puts that shit up his nose and goes haywire, but the kid is fucking smart, and he has a good habit of making us all a lot of money. But the problem is this: Jordo has dragged his ass on this thing so much that this Packridge fuck got cold feet about the bogus money–laundering guy we set him up with, and he went and somehow found some prick that owns a used car lot to wash the cash for him, and from what we've gathered he's going to start any day now. So the window is closing on our chance to nab the cash, and with Jordo the way he is, he's going to get busted for something stupid and end up locked up again. So I need you to go down there, Nick. First things first, you put an end to the partying. I don't care if you have to literally knock some sense into him. You get him to sleep it off for a day or two, and when he sobers up, you do the job. He has all the details, but you're running the show now, you call the shots. He's demoted, this is your gig now, and if you do it right you get a flat thirty percent of whatever the take is."

I take a moment to absorb it all. I don't like it. I'm new to this whole operation and am sure Jordo and the guys won't appreciate me coming in and taking their thing over. Plus, trying to get someone to stop getting fucked up is tricky. The only surefire way to do that is to literally tie them down. Plus, I don't know Tucson at all. I don't know how things work down there. I'm not sure if I can do this. And Tim won't take no for answer. Plus, thirty percent of this take could be fucking huge, enough to be done with this shit.

Tim goes on, "I'm sending Tick down there today to back you up. He knows the scene pretty well. He knows that you're calling the shots. He'll do whatever you tell him to. His loyalty is with me, and he knows his role. I know this all sounds like a pain in the ass, but all you have to do is get Jordo's head straight, the rest will be a breeze. So lock him in a room, knock him the fuck out, do what you gotta do. Just get him to sleep it off. I'll deal with Jordo once this is all over. For now we gotta keep him in play. This thing is too good to pass up."

He walks me to my car.

"And Nick, no bodies on this one. You do what it takes; you have to rough this guy up, no problem. But no bodies, we don't need that kind of attention. Be surgical."

He hands me an unopened prepaid cell and a piece of paper with two phone numbers written on it.

"Use that burner while you're down there. That second number on there is Tick's burner, the first one is mine. I want updates. Often. Only call me on that number I gave you, and when you're done, don't forget to smash that burner, huh? Do your thing, Nick, I know you'll do just fine."

Chapter 21: HACK

I HAVE THREE GOOFY TEENAGERS in my backseat. They're stoned and drunk, good kids having a good time. I don't see anything in them, nothing dark. They are decent people. It's nice for a change. I watch the remnants of a monsoon season storm trickle lightning over South Mountain. The streets have that post–storm energy, a collective finger in the socket; they flood with the pursuit of vice. These young men are along for the ride, looking to indulge themselves while they still can.

"Hey Cabbie, what's your name?" one of them asks me.

"Cabbie," I answer.

"Huh?"

"Cabbie. That's what people call me."

They chuckle.

"So what's the plan tonight guys, you out chasing tail?"

"Maybe. What we really want to do is go milf hunting, you know, cougar hunting. We want some broads with some mileage, some experience. Show us some new tricks. Broaden our horizons."

"I like it," I say. "A little tread on the tires can be a good thing."

"Hey cabbie," one of them says. "Can I ask you a personal question?"

"Sure, shoot."

"What's the strangest place or time you got a hard–on?"

One of his buddies cracks up; the other punches him in the arm and tells him to shut up.

I smile. "Don't worry guys, I've been asked much stranger things. But why do you want to know?"

"I'm compiling a master list for my blog; I write about weird sexual stuff. I'm going to write the great American sex book someday!"

"Is that right?"

"Yep. Well, my mom and dad think I'm going to be an aviation engineer, but what fun is that, right?"

"So what is the strangest place you ever got a hard–on," his buddy asks me. He flips up his phone. "You mind if we record this?"

I yawn and crack open the window, a gust of humid post–storm wind sweeps across my face, reminding me of the place where this little story takes place, that wretched fucking country that tore me down to shreds and built me right back up. I talk:

"Well, I don't know if it's that great of a story, one that needs to be remembered or whatever. But when I was not much older than you guys, shit, same age maybe, I got drafted into the war, infantry, I was in–country right around the time of the Tet Offensive. You guys study that shit in school? Probably not. It's not a particularly popular part of American history. Anyway, long story short, we were backing up some Navy craft on the Mekong Delta; you see, the dinks were masters at using the rivers to sneak around and attack the south, so the navy had these boats, ZIPPO boats, they used them to clear out the areas around the river so the dinks couldn't sneak around as easy. We were on patrol of a patch of the river, a hot patch, making our way to help out some of our guys that were bogged down. So it was night, and we were across the river from this fucking village, and I guess our guard was down, and the VC let us have it, straight ambush, they were sniping out from that village, and, thing was, it was always tough to tell who was who, and the VC were entrenched right in that little fishing village so we were hesitant to return much fire, seeing that there were kids and old folk, you know, so we tried have some fucking restraint, tried to pick our shots and avoid just hammering the whole village indiscriminately. We lost two guys right away and our radio operator screamed for help over the gunfire. About ten minutes into the fight we lost another man, and at that point we said fuck it and started to spray the whole village, not even bothering to aim. It was a helluva fight, but we were outgunned, who knows how many of those fucks there were; they saw us just fine but they might as well have been fucking ghosts to us. We started to run low on ammo, so we smashed our faces into the ground and prayed for it to end, prayed for the gooks to do their usual shoot–and–run routine, but the bullets zipped by, and thank God, the RPGs were just a few feet shy of us, and minutes turned into eternity, and just when it looked like we were toast, this ZIPPO boat arrives and they had the big guns roaring and tearing the shit out of this village, but the dinks kept shooting, they had the bunkers and tunnels and shit in this village. Well, the boat's .50 cal and the 40mm were just not cutting it, so the boys in the ZIPPO fired up the napalm thrower and covered the area until the whole village was one gigantic glowing orb of white, yellow flames soared up, and the whole village then turned orange until it was all a haze of smoke and fire like a gigantic clenched fist. The shooting stopped, and for a moment everything went dead silent, quiet enough to hear the sound of the river rocking against the boat. Then the screams started. Napalm isn't your ordinary kind of fire. It burns longer. The shit burns right through muscle. The pain is so intense you can die from that alone. So the napalm burned right through the village, down into the bunkers and tunnels, and the dinks had no option but to flee from the smoke and the heat or die from smoke inhalation, so they ran out, and if they weren't on fire by then, they were the moment they stepped out. We didn't even have to shoot them. The screams were incredible, with all of these people flopping around, covered in this amber orange glow, the heat of it, fuck, even across the river we had to shield our faces from the heat. We stood in silence and watched the enemy drop one by one as the napalm torched everything to the ground. Napalm burns forever."

The boys in the back of the cab sit in silence. The grins are gone. *Sorry boys, you get what you ask for.*

"We watched the fire consume the village and the jungle around it. I watched in awe as the flame consumed and consumed—flaming debris floated in the air and settled on the river and drifted downstream; I watched the floating flames stay alight until they travelled beyond my sight, and the whole world was so amazing and fierce in that moment, the fire even sucked out the jungle's incredible humidity, it sucked out every last bit of moisture and the air we breathed was as hot and dry as a sauna, as dry and deadly as the hottest day in Bullhead City. I watched the village go down. It dawned on me that I was hard, that my cock was as stiff as it ever had been, painful almost, something about watching the napalm so effortlessly consume everything in its path: buildings, vegetation, people—something about being privy to watch such a God–like force at work made me harder than I'd ever been before."

My story ends as we pull up to their destination, a bar in old town Scottsdale. They fumble with some cash, pay me, and file out of the cab without saying a word. I guess it wasn't the story they were expecting to hear.

CHAPTER 22: NICK

I PULL INTO A TRUCK STOP ON THE edge of Tucson and get ahold of Tick. He tells me he is about twenty minutes behind me. I wait for him. I lean against my Jeep and smoke. I watch hints of a summer storm come rolling in from the mountain ranges in the distance. I grew up staring at the sky. Dad liked to take me out on the boat. We rode in silence for hours sometimes, and Dad always had this stern look about him, his gaze not just on what was in front of us but seemingly beyond, all the way to the very edge of the horizon. Dad loved nothing more than being on the boat, but he had this look on his face in those quiet hours we spent together on the water; I always thought it had just a hint of dread, as if he always expected something to appear in the distance that would ruin everything. Eleven years later, I look out as far as I can, and I am certain Dad's grim look is now my own.

Tick pulls up in that beauty of a four–door Jeep Rubicon. I stop reminiscing about those summer days on the boat. Tick gets out of the car and we shake hands. I don't know much about him other than Tim says he's solid. That's good enough for me. We stand in an open parking space and talk.

"So what do you think about this shit," he asks.

I shrug. "I don't know. We'll do what we have to do. Hopefully Jordo has settled down and we can wrap this thing up quick. If not, we deal with it."

"Jordo will be easy. I brought some Xanax and Ambien. We get him to sleep a bit; he'll wake up like new. This other thing, you know, this Packridge guy, that's the part I'm not so sure about. I know Jordo has Tim convinced it's an easy in–and–out on a soft mark, but I call bullshit—that's rare. I mean, you don't get too far in the smuggling game without getting some people behind you. Don't get me wrong, if we can get this guy at the right time, no problem, but I bet he has friends and connects that we don't know about. Jordo can be a little too much of a cowboy. And he likes to leave out details, especially when he thinks they'll bother Tim. So we catch this Packridge guy off guard, we get him to give up his cash, and you ask me, we should waste the guy. We can't have this shit back to us, man, and the way Jordo's been acting up down here; he's put himself on the map. This isn't Tim's show. Tim operates under anonymity; Jordo, he does not, he can't help but make a scene. So this might get ugly. I just want to air that out. It's never as simple as Jordo makes it."

"Tim doesn't want any bodies," I say.

"I know. I'm just bringing it up for the sake of discussion. Look, I'm usually the last guy that wants to see anyone get offed, but these fucking smugglers, man, they're scum, they leave those poor saps out in the desert to die, they starve 'em, they beat 'em, and when they get 'em to the safe house, shit, half the time they hold 'em hostage until they can come up with more money. So I'm just saying, if it seems like leaving this guy alive might somehow come back to bite us in the ass, I got no problem dealing with it. And trust me, man, no bodies turn up."

I study him for a moment. I can't figure this guy out.

"Let's handle one thing at a time, man, not get too far ahead of ourselves. You know where we're going?"

He nods.

"Lead the way then."

I follow him onto the highway. The road cuts through Tucson, painting a very unflattering picture of the city, all dust brown, industrial, and dull. We exit onto a two lane road, follow it outside the city for four or five miles, where the world gets desert and desolate again. We pass a few abandoned or soon to be abandoned home sites then cut onto an old ranch road. The road curves down a decline for about a half mile then settles into a vast flat, with nothing around but sparse desert hills as far as the eye can see. Hints of heat lightning flicker in the distance. The sun bounces off of rocks and sends shimmers of light throughout the desert, an oasis–like appearance of diamonds in the sand. Three battered trailers sit in an L–shape bordered by a wooden fence and an old horse pasture. The trailers surround a smoldering fire pit surrounded by empty bottles and a million spent butts.

Jordo's car, a newer BMW, is parked behind the trailers. I motion to Tick and we park our cars in front of Jordo's car, blocking it in.

"If we have to slap some sense into these guys, you ready for that, right?"

"I actually look forward to it," Tick says with a grin. "I'll follow your lead, man."

This odd assortment of land and dilapidated mobile homes is like the most depressing vacation property in the world. I suspect it is more than a hideout—I see it as the entrance to a great burial ground beyond. Who knows how many people Tim and his guys have lain to rest out there.

We walk up to the first trailer, an elder model with faux wood panel and rusted trim. Chips of ancient paint flake from the sides. A generator hums behind it. A door swings open and a figure stumbles out with a double–barreled shotgun in his hands. He raises it up toward us, then recognizes Tick and stops.

"What the fuck do you guys want? And who the fuck are you?" he asks. He points the barrel toward my knees. He's pale and unsteady on his legs. He has a slight weave in his stance. He looks at me with huge raccoon eyes and blinks rapidly.

"This is Nick, Grey." Tick says "Tim sent him to take over, and I'm here to help."

Grey's mouth opens with an exaggerated gape. "But this is Jordo's thing, you can't just come in here and—"

I walk up to this Grey character and put my hand out to shake his. At the last second I reach out and yank the shotgun from his hands, then flip it around and slam the butt into his stomach. He collapses on the ground, gripping his stomach and coughing for air. I put my shoe on his chest.

"I don't like guns pointed at me. Got it?"

The door to the second trailer opens and another guy steps out, a short fucker but built like an anvil.

"What the fuck, man, get off of him!" He hollers and charges toward me. He's pretty fucked up too, with crazed, sleepless eyes and bright red skin. His nostrils are caked with blood. He walks right into my fist; I knock him over with a straight right. He falls to the ground and scrambles to get back up. Tick pins him down.

"Fucking time–out for you, Sean," Tick says to him. "You dumb fucks need to know the score. This little butt–fucking coke party, or whatever it is you got going on out here, is over. Tim sent Nick down to clean up your mess and take over, and I'll do whatever it takes to make sure that happens. So if you guys want to act like little bitches, we'll treat you like so. Got it?"

The door to the third trailer opens. Jordo walks out. He looks like a year of hangovers. His flashy designer jeans are wrinkled and soiled with dust and ash. A torn and stained unbuttoned dress shirt hangs off of him. He has the raccoon eyes too, that sleepless–zombie–look of drunken sleep deprivation. He's sporting a decent–sized shiner around his left eye. He walks toward us, casually.

"Relax guys," Jordo says.

"Don't tell us to fucking relax," Tick says. "Your boys gave us attitude and we had to sit 'em down. They keep up with it and I'm going to tie them to that fence there and horsewhip them. Got it? So don't tell us to relax, motherfucker."

This Tick cat is one intimidating fucker. I can see why Tim sent him to help me out.

"I wasn't talking to you. I was talking to them," Jordo says. He points toward his two friends on the ground. "Let them go. They're just high strung. It's been a rough couple of days."

Tick looks to me for permission and I signal that it's okay to let them up.

"Into that trailer," I say, pointing toward Sean and Grey. "Tick, sit these guys down and tell them what's what, okay?"

"Roger," he responds.

I glare at Jordo. He smiles back at me. "Let's talk," I say.

"Come on into my palace," he replies, motioning to the third trailer, a wretched, sun–beaten mess of plastic and wood.

I follow him into the trailer. The smell of overflowing ashtrays and mildew greets me. The trailer is a real shit show. There are bottles everywhere. Clothes are strewn. I step over a few condom wrappers on the floor. Jordo sits down at the kitchen table and cracks open a beer. I sit down; notice a plate on the table with a small mountain of coke on it. I swat it off the table. The coke flurries in the air. The plate breaks.

"Aw come on, man, what the fuck?"

I ignore him; notice a glass bong on the table, the hand blown kind, about two feet tall. It's an expensive one. I pick it up and hurl it against the wall. It shatters.

"Okay, you've made your point," he says.

"Look Jordo, I don't give a shit about what you want to do with your spare time, but I have a job to do, and first things first Tim wants me to get your head straight. So the coke, the weed, the drinking, whatever the fuck else you're doing, it stops now. You can pick back up when the job is over, but until then you'll stay off it all. Ok?"

He grins and shrugs then take a pull on his beer. I snatch it out of his hand and throw it in the sink.

"Jesus," he says. "That ornery bastard really has you on a leash, huh? Do you like being my uncle's little doggie? Fucking relax. You don't want to end up like him, wound too tight. I know what I'm doing. So take it down a notch. Everything is under control."

"Oh yeah?"

"Yeah."

"Well from the looks of it, you and your buddies are having a fucking frat party. You're supposed to be working."

"The work is done," Jordo says. "We have it under control. The day after tomorrow is game time. Easy. Easy gig."

He fumbles with a few pieces of the broken bong. "You know what, Nicky, with some TLC and some super glue, maybe we can put this baby back together. What do you say, bro?"

He giggles.

I shake my head. "You aren't in control of shit. You and those two fucks can barely walk straight. You couldn't pull off a fucking purse snatching in your condition. You're too strung out to think straight." He responds by rolling his eyes and making a jack–off motion.

"And what's the story with the black eye," I ask.

"I got sucker punched by a bouncer, no big deal."

"How did that happen?"

"Yeah, we were at that titty bar, and this bitch gave me an attitude so I gave her a little shove. Next thing you know the bouncers are giving us shit, so we say, yeah, we'll leave, and on the way out one slugs me from behind. We're about to handle business but they called the cops so we left."

"That's it, that's all that happened?"

He smiles that vampire smile of his. "Well, no, not really. We came back when the joint was closing, followed that fuck home and gave him a little beating."

I slam my hand on the table. "Did Tim tell you to keep a low profile, yes or no?"

"Sure, but I'm not about to let some fuck think he can sucker punch me and pay no consequences. Don't give me the parent act, Nicky. You would have done the same thing."

He's right about that. "That's beside the point, Jordo. What's done is done. But this is the way it is; you fucked up and Tim sent me down here to deal with it. I'm running the show now. I didn't ask for this, it was ordered, so don't give me a hard time. You got a problem with it, take it up with him."

I take my phone out and offer it to him.

"No, I get it. Tim calls the shots, and if he wants you to take over, that's fine."

"Good. Please don't be mad at me, man. This was Tim's call, not mine."

The generator gives out for a moment and the lights flicker on and off. A gust of wind rocks the trailer. I continue.

"Tick brought some Ambien and Xanax. You take whatever you need to sleep it off. Same goes with your boys. You guys get some rest and we do this job, nice and clean, quick. We get the cash and we all head back up to the valley. It's that simple. You got it?"

"Sure. I'm not exactly having a blast here you know, in this shit hole town, sleeping in a fucking trailer. I want this be over as much as anyone."

"Good. So get your fucking head straight, Jordo. I don't like having to come down here and play big brother, you know? I just want to make some cash, easy, low profile. I didn't get in this to play politics. Remember that. And I know you got me in, so I'll always thank you for that, and my loyalty will stay with you. I wouldn't be doing you any favors by letting you keep up like this. You gotta see that."

He nods. I go grab the pills from Tick, who has already played doctor and administrated them to Grey and Sean. I watch Jordo take them down with a glass of water. I force him drink two more large glasses of water; the fucker is probably dehydrated.

He gets drowsy fast. "Nick, that bouncer I was telling you about, I talked to one of the dancers at the club, and I guess this guy and his shit–kicker friends are looking for us, and some of the girls at the club have been here partying you know, so he might know where we're at and come by. I just thought you should know."

"What the fuck, Jordo! Are you serious?"

He barely makes it to the mattress in back before passing out. He took a big dose of downers and should be out for some time.

I meet up with Tick outside. Sean and Grey are now passed out as well. We lean against the trailer and I update him on the situation.

"Fuck, man, we can't have a bunch of locals coming out here looking to mix it up," Tick says. "This is bad man, bad. We have to do something. They come out here someone is going to end up dead, guaranteed."

"I know. You stay here and babysit the sleeping beauties. I'm going to go handle this situation with the bouncer. If any of these pricks wake up while I'm gone, make them take more pills. I want them to sleep this shit off. Good?"

"Good."

I get the address for the titty bar off of my phone and use the GPS to find my way there. I drive the seven miles cursing myself for ever getting involved in all of this, wondering what the fuck has happened to me. The decisions I've been making and the actions that have resulted, when I stop and take a moment to think about them, fuck, it is downright disturbing…almost as disturbing as how natural and instinctive it all feels, plunging into this crazy fucking scene of guns and beatings and piles of cash and fuck, part of me is entirely comfortable with it. *What the fuck happened to me? What happened to the big momma's boy that wanted to save the world and help the needy; where is the guy that spoke at AA meetings about serenity and peace of mind?*

I have no fucking idea which version of me is authentic. No fucking clue. I crank up the stereo and Led Zeppelin helps drone out my little existential crisis.

I arrive at the strip club. The parking lot is packed. The lunch rush is in full swing. I pay my way in. Some shitty rap song blares from the speakers. A meth–skinny broad with comically sized fake tits works the stage. The room reeks of beer and cheap fruit–scented body spray. I give my eyes a moment to adjust to the black lights. I know this scene well, having worked off and on for clubs like this for years. A girl leans up next to me and I politely decline her offer for a dance. I scan the patrons of the club, looking for the staff. I spot a big mean–looking fucker standing near the bar, clad in a suit. He has a bandage over his left eyebrow and a nasty bruise on the right side of his face. This has to be the guy that Jordo and his guys worked over. I walk over to him. He looks me up and down.

"You need something?" he asks.

"Yeah, I need to smooth some stuff over with you on behalf of a friend. Is there somewhere we can talk a minute? I'll make it worth your while." I flash a wad of bills.

He looks me over again.

"This about those fucks that jumped me like a pack of niggers?"

"Yes. Like I said, I'm here to smooth it over, try to make it right. Can we talk it over?"

"There's an office in back," he says.

I shake my head. "No offense, man, I know you're pissed, you have every right to be, but I can't go back there with you. I got to watch my ass, too, you know? Let's just step outside for a minute."

He snorts. "Yeah right, fucko. You think I'm going to go outside with you? What, you got your boys out there again for round two?"

I shout over the music. "No it's just me. And I stick to my word, I'm here to make things right. They fucked up, and I have to clean up their mess." I can barely hear myself over this fucking music. Let's just go outside, around back. You can have one of your boys check outside first, shit, you can have them come too if you want."

He thinks about it for a second. "Okay. I suppose you and your buddies aren't dumb enough to try and pull that shit in the middle of the day. Wait here a moment."

He flags over another bouncer and whispers into his ear. The other bouncer leaves the club and comes back a minute later and gives him the thumbs up. We walk outside. A slight dust storm is building up. Rain is on its way. We walk around to the back of the club.

"Okay, talk," he says.

"Okay, well, first things first, did you file a police report after you got jumped?"

He smiles and shakes his head. He pulls back his shirt to reveal a tattoo on his wrist, the logo of a notorious motorcycle club. Fuck. That is not good.

"I'm a one–percenter, fully patched in. We don't call the police. We handle business, and we're going to handle your friends. They picked the wrong guy to fuck with," he says.

"I got it. And like I said, I agree with you, they fucked up. They got hammered and acted like morons. He shouldn't have been harassing your girls, and he sure as fuck shouldn't have jumped you like that for giving him a shot he probably deserved."

He shakes his head. "Harass my girls? The motherfuckers beat on one of them pretty good. Your shithead friends get them over to that little trailer park of theirs to party—these bitches can't say no to coke, you know—and your friends end up slapping Sasha around. She won't dance for a week, not with that swollen lip. So listen asshole, don't come here and pussyfoot and say they harassed one of the girls. They did more than that. And then they had the nerve to come back to the club the next night, and when we didn't let them in they got mouthy so I sat the mouthiest one down. Then the fucking idiot goes to his car and gets his piece and starts waving it around. Lucky for him his friends dragged him away. I never thought they'd be dumb enough to jump me like that, though. So your friends have it coming, and it's not going to be pretty. I suggest you get out of town too, because if you're around, you got the same thing coming."

Motherfucker. Jordo didn't even give me the straight story. Having those girls coming over to the ranch was dumb enough. Tim would fucking blow his lid if he knew they had people over to what is supposed to be a discreet location, and I shudder to think about what Tim would do if he knew they slapped around a girl and were dumb enough to go back to the club the next night. I saw what happened to the last guy Tim was pissed off at, that guy I worked over in that parking lot. I don't know where Trevor and Saul took that guy, but wherever it was he probably didn't walk away from it.

I tell the bouncer, "Okay, so I guess I didn't have the full story, I apologize. And I agree, the whole thing is fucked, real fucked, and I promise you I'll get those guys out of town in a day or two and you'll never see them down here. Their Tucson privileges are revoked, I'll see to that."

He snorts again. "It doesn't matter where they go, man; I think you know that my crew is everywhere. You don't get to just walk away from this shit. There is no hiding. That's just the way it is. Apologies don't mean dick."

"I understand, and trust me; we got nothing but respect for your crew. I know a few of your guys up in the valley and we're on good terms, and I'd like to keep it that way. I'm not here to apologize. I'm here to make it up to you."

"How?"

"Money. I'm here to pay a fine, a hefty one. I figure why risk gunplay when we can work out a situation that is more agreeable to you? I know you guys have a lot of heat on you right now with the Feds around, and the last thing anyone needs is a shootout over some dumb fucking drunks acting the way they did. I came down here to put a leash on these guys. They fucked up, and they'll pay the price with us, no doubt. We don't allow that kind of behavior to go unchecked, it looks bad on us, and we're professionals, you know? But if I just leave town without smoothing this thing over, if I leave town without them, and you guys have another run in, man, those guys are going to shoot it out, I'm sure of it. And I know this is your town, you got the firepower, but this kind of thing is going to bring too much attention on all of us."

I pull out a wad of cash, 5K in 100's, and hand it to him. He counts it and puts it in his pocket.

"That's a start," he says. "I can't guarantee anything. If I run into those guys I might not be able to control myself. You understand that?"

"Of course. Like I said, I'm down here to make sure they leave town and never come back. We don't have a lot of business down here, so we just have to settle a couple things and then we're out in a couple of days. That cool?"

He takes a step closer to me. I instinctively clench my right fist.

"About that," he says. "You know you can't just come into our town and do business without clearing it with us right? It doesn't work like that."

The wind spits dirt in my eye. I swipe it away.

"I understand, but like I said, we have some common friends. We aren't here to cut in on your turf or your business. I know you're busy enough with all the cartel guys flooding this town. We're not here on anything big. A guy owed us some money, so we had to come down here and make sure he signed over some deeds to some property. It's minor, a one—time thing."

I've always been a good liar.

The bouncer doesn't budge. "Well, like I said, this 5k, it's a start. I don't know you or your buddies, if you want to have some of our so—called common friends vouch for you, if they really exist, that's fine. But I'm going to need something more to let you and your friends off this one time."

Fuck. We both a have a number, what he wants and what I'm willing to pay. I'm sure they're not close.

"Okay, let's negotiate. Throw out a number."

He takes a step closer to me, gauging my comfort as he gets into my personal space. I don't move or remove my gaze on him. He leans back.

"No negotiating here, buddy," he says. "I tell you what I want and how it is. No wiggle room. So one of the ladies that went out to your trailer park, she says one of your guys was showing of a pretty nice rifle, something he said came straight from Iraq. Sounds like you guys have a line on some decent hardware."

Motherfucker. Fucking Jordo. I think about those full auto Iraqi AKs Jordo told me about. The idiot must have gone ahead and picked them up behind Tim's back. The bouncer goes on:

"You give us what you got, and this whole thing is done. I don't want to see any of those fuckers back in Tucson ever. And if you come back, next time, you check in with us first before doing any business, you get our approval, and you pay our fee. Got it?"

This fucking cocksucker. I know for a fact that only small–timer meth peddlers and pimps are paying these guys tributes down here anymore. The drug cartels have taken over this town and they have way more people and firepower than his crew does. But for now, I gotta get this thing over with. Jordo wasn't supposed to pick up any of that shit anyway, so we're going to have to unload them fast either way.

"Deal," I say. "I don't know much about the guns, that's a side job of theirs, one they should not be fucking around with, honestly. So, yeah, whatever they're holding on to is yours. It's probably not a ton, probably two or three AKs, full autos. They're not easy to come by, so they're quite valuable. You got my word; whatever they have right now is yours."

"Good," he says. He takes a step backward and relaxes a bit. "Your friends are lucky they have someone with half a brain to clean up their mess." He pulls out a business card and hands it to me. "You call me the day after tomorrow, and I'll tell you the when and where. Like I said, you come through on this and you and your guys leave town with no problems, guaranteed. You don't and, well, you don't leave town. Ever. You understand?"

"Completely. Talk to you soon."

We jockey for position for a moment, waiting to see who is going to turn his back to the other first. I let him think he won this one. I walk back to the car, shielding my face from the wind and the dust. A bolt of lightning cracks. The rain starts with big warm drops. I curse that dumb fucking biker for leaning on me so heavy. I don't like motherfuckers that try to intimidate me. I fight the urge to turn around and mix it up with him, just the two of us. Instead I pick up the phone and call Tim to fill him in on the situation. He's not going to be happy.

Chapter 23: HACK

I GET A CALL TO AN ADDRESS that seems familiar. It is tough to keep all the numbers straight, you drive in this city long enough and you've been everywhere twice.

I pull up to the house and my stomach drops. No. Not this, again. My life is supposed to be wonderfully random, chaotic even. But this, *this* is becoming a pattern, and frankly, nothing scares me more than patterns. Patterns bring expectations. There's a reason why I'm edging toward sixty and have no wife, no kids, no family, and a small, rented apartment. I don't do well with expectations and commitments. A pet fish is about all I can handle.

She walks out of the house; she's using a cane now. She smiles and waves. I get out to open the door for her; I hold her hand while she manages her bloated frame into the backseat.

"Hello again," she says. "You drove me before, remember?"

"Yes ma'am." I manage a smile. "How is your health?"

"Stable. But stable is not as good as it sounds. I could be worse, but I'm not getting better, either. I'm kind of stuck, I guess."

I get back behind the wheel and turn off the meter. This ride is on me.

"I'm sorry, I'm sure things will get better soon. Where are we going today? The hospital again?"

"No sir. I need to go to the police headquarters," she says, sighing.

"The police headquarters?"

"Yes. I keep calling them about my daughter, and they either blow me off or take a message, and if I do get to talk to someone they tell me there is nothing more they can do. And I don't believe that. I watch these programs on the television where they find lost people all the time. How hard can it be to track down one girl? But I call them and they blow me off. And I'm sick of calling. I figured I'll go down there and not leave until someone talks to me, someone real, a detective maybe. Someone who cares." She pauses for a moment and dabs her eye. "There has to be someone who cares," she adds.

I start the car. It's a two–mile ride to the downtown Phoenix Police Headquarters. I don't know if I can take much more than two miles with her. This lady, she is a good soul, sweet and warm to the point of fragility, but her sad story is getting familiar, and I can't do that. I can't do familiar. I don't read anything about this lady, there is no darkness in her; she's a perfect example of a person that has always done right. But with every moment I spend with her I start to see this image of her daughter, an image like pixels slowly coming into focus. The picture is of a beautiful, smiling young lady. And it fucking terrifies me.

"Okay, Phoenix PD it is," I say. "I hope they show you some respect, ma'am. You deserve that."

"You seem like a kind soul," the lady says.

I smile. "I'm not so sure about that, but thank you. That is very kind of you."

"Will you help me?" she asks. "I can pay you. I'll pay you whatever you make on a usual shift, or by the hour, whatever."

"You need some more rides? Of course ma'am, I can take you wherever you need to go, no problem."

"I need you to take me to some neighborhoods, to drive around, places I think my daughter might be, maybe some places she used to go."

She lists off some names of streets and neighborhoods. I take a long deep breath. My forehead starts to sweat. I roll down the window to let some air in.

"Ma'am, those are bad, well, I mean, those areas are a little rough sometimes; I don't think you should go there, even if it's with me. It's not, well–I don't think it is a good idea."

"Someone has to," she says. "I know the police aren't going to spend any time doing that. They're too busy I guess, too busy to look for a lost girl, not one they dismiss as just a junkie and a whore."

She starts to cry softly. I grip my wheel until the tendons and little bones in my hands ache.

"Ma'am, I'm sure the police are doing what they can do. Have you ever thought of hiring a private detective? They are usually very good at this kind of thing."

"I don't know," she sniffles, "That sounds great, but I'm on a fixed income, and they're probably pretty expensive. I just have to do something. I can't sit around and wait and think. It hurts too much, and I think it's going to kill me. They say I'm high risk of having a stroke."

We reach our destination. She wipes her face and gathers herself.

"I'm sorry for laying this sadness upon you, it isn't right," she says.

"Most of my fares are very rude, ma'am, always angry and impatient. You're a wonderful break from that, so please, no apologies," I lie.

"You're a kind soul, don't ever question that," she says.

I help her out of the car. She reaches for her purse but I refuse to take any money. She smiles and pats me on the shoulder.

"Do you want me to wait for you, ma'am? I can wait."

"No sir, that's quite all right. You've done more than enough."

"Okay, well, you just call our dispatch and let them know when you need to be picked up. There are always a lot of cabs around here."

She smiles and starts to walk away. I start to get in the cab, but decide I can't just leave it at that, no matter how much I want to.

"Ma'am?"

She turns around.

"I'll tell you what, when I'm around those areas you were talking about, I'll keep an eye out, maybe ask around. People have a way of opening up to me."

She smiles and goes into her purse, pulls out a small photo and hands it to me. "Thank you, thank you so much." She walks into the police station. I get back in the cab and look at the photo. It's her. It's the exact same image that's been building in my mind, but in full clarity. It's there to stay now, I guess.

Chapter 24: NICK

I DRIVE BACK TO THE RANCH THROUGH the dust storm's chaotic wind. Huge clouds of brown dust dredge up trash and debris all over the roads. Visibility is poor. I call Tim, get his machine, and leave a message to let him know that he needs to get back to me ASAP.

I park and find Tick next to a trailer, underneath a flapping canvas awning; he's smoking a cigar and reading a paperback. A very nice tricked–out Bravo Company AR–15 sits at his feet.

He looks up at me and grins. "Your knuckles aren't bruised. I guess it went really well or not at all, then," he says.

I sit down next to him. The wind does not let up. It howls and spits specks in my eyes, and flips the pages of Tick's paperback. I spot a small dust devil dancing around at the far end of the old horse pasture. The rickety old wooden fence shakes.

"Let's go inside, things just got more complicated," I say.

"If you don't mind, I'd rather stay here. Those trailers, man, I can't stand the fucking smell."

I yell over the wind to fill him in on the latest developments. He takes a moment to digest it all.

"You played it right," he says. "I don't know about the gun hand–off though, not like that, on their terms. I don't trust those guys, not with the heat they always have on them. ATF has a real hard–on for those cats, wouldn't be surprised if they got them under surveillance for something right now. It's too risky to hand off those guns like that. You ask me, we leave the guns somewhere remote, bury 'em or whatever, grab the GPS coordinates, and when they call we just tell them where to go, and that's that. If they want the guns that's what they gotta do. On our terms. When we get back to the valley, we sort it out with the guys up there if we need to. Tim's got a buddy pretty high up in the Phoenix chapter."

"Good thinking. If they want the guns, they can go get them. Now let's go take a look around and see if we can find them while those cocksuckers are asleep."

"I tell you, man, I think this is the last gig in Tucson I'm up for. Shit just doesn't feel right down here," he says, looking at the sad trailers and the dirty storm air. "Something about this place makes me fucking miserable."

We search the trailers one by one. We don't spare an inch. We find one AK next to the mattress Jordo's sleeping on, buried under a pile of dirty clothes and bedding. I take the AK outside to look it over. It's the real deal all right, a genuine Iraqi National Guard AK. We find a few other guns, their personal pieces: a Glock, a Kimber 1911, a Taurus Raging Bull .44, that double–barreled shotgun, a Yugo AK, and a Savage bolt–action with a decent scope. We find three bottles of booze and three cases of beer and pour it all out. Jordo has a bag of coke in his pants pocket. That goes out with the wind. We grab the keys to the cars and search them, too; we find a bag of grass, at least an ounce, a Ruger .380, and a bag of pills that look to be ecstasy.

"I tell you, man, Tim is going to flip his shit. Jordo really fucked up here. I wouldn't be surprised if he says fuck the job and has us bring these shitheads back up to the valley. I can't say I'd disagree with that decision," Tick says. I try Tim again, get the voicemail.

Tick and I lock up all the guns in his Jeep and sit back down under the awning.

"I gotta tell you, Nick, I know you and Jordo are friends but—"

I interrupt him. "We passed some time together in the tents. I guess you don't really get to know someone like that."

"No, you don't. I have to tell you, man, that Jordo, he's a ticking time bomb. I told Tim a couple months ago what I think, but he doesn't want to hear it. He thinks he can control Jordo. It doesn't look that way, does it?"

"No, it doesn't."

"I mean yeah, Jordo is smart and all, but smarts don't mean shit when you have no self–control, right? I'm no fucking saint, but I play it smart enough to stay out of trouble for the most part. Jordo, he walks right into it, and he never learns his lesson. The fuck really thinks he's invincible. He thinks he's so damn smart that he's never gonna get pinched for anything big. He sees his uncle, how Tim has never caught a case, and Jordo figures he's smarter than him so he ain't going to get pinched either." Tim pauses to relight his cigar. "Jordo is going to get people killed, Nick. It's just a matter of time. I know this is Tim's call, but the time will come; Tim is going to have to address this situation. If he doesn't, I will. I'm not gonna let that fuck Jordo get me locked up or killed. I don't care how much cash is at stake. You know what I think we should do, not saying we should, but what I'd do if it was my call?"

"Huh?"

Tick picks up his AR and aims it at Jordo's trailer. "I'd go in there right now, drag him out, and put a bullet in his head. The other guys too. No hesitation, I'd off them and bury them out there somewhere, nice and deep, where they'd never be found." He points off into the distance.

I stare at him for a moment. "This is Tim's call. He'll take care of it."

"I know," he says, putting the AR back at his feet. "I'm just saying, at some point self–preservation might come into play. And I want to know if you're ready for that. I don't know that much about you, Nick, but I gather you—"

My burner rings, I hold my hand up to Tick and answer the phone. It's Tim. I can barely hear him so I hop into the Jeep to take the call.

"What's going on down there, Nick?" Tim asks in that rigid calm of his.

I fill him in. I don't spare any details. When I'm done talking he takes a good half minute before he responds, long enough for me to think we lost a connection.

"Tim, you there?"

"Listen to me carefully, Nick. You do what I say, no discussion. You get Jordo up and you make him tell you where those guns are. I don't care if you have to break his fingers. You get those guns, you break them down to pieces, take them out on the land, take them far out, and you bury them. Don't let Jordo or his dumb fucking friends see you. I don't need those pricks sneaking back and digging them up. I'm going to see a friend and get this thing with the bikers worked out."

"What about the job? What's the plan with that?"

"No job. Jordo fucked it up. We can't do shit down there with all the attention Jordo brought upon himself. You get rid of the guns and then you deal with the guys. Take their keys, their phones, and their wallets. Take their money and their guns. Take everything. Leave his fucking car there. You bring them up here for me to deal with. If they give you any shit, you beat them down. Shit, if you have to, have Tick deal with Sean and Grey. For good if he has to. If you have to beat Jordo down, I don't give a fuck, if you have to hog tie him and put him in the trunk, I don't give a fuck, you do so. Just bring him back still breathing. You let those boys know I want them up here, and now, and it is not up to discussion. You do whatever it takes, but do it. You got it?"

"Absolutely. Tick and I'll take care of it."

"Good. Leave your car down there, too; we'll go grab it in a day or two. Pile everyone in Tick's Jeep. I need you to do just as I say, all right? Call me when you're on the road."

"Got it."

"Good. You run into any problems, you call me right away. Now get going."

Tim hangs up.

I get out of the Jeep. The wind is relentless. Spots of sun break through the clouds and dust; the rain starts and stops and again. I tell Tick what Tim wants and then we go inside to wake Jordo up.

Chapter 25: HACK

I DON'T DREAM MUCH. Not when I'm asleep, at least. Sometimes I'll be sitting in traffic or parked and waiting for a ride and my head starts to wander and it always goes back to this night I had when I was a teenager. I grew up poor white trash and we didn't have shit except resentments for those who had more...but there are some things in life that the filthy rich and the filthy poor enjoy just the same. Fire is one of those things. We didn't have money but we had plenty of land, well, access to land at least; land was the one thing in abundance and the prairies stretched on and on, all but worthless to us but for the sensation they gave that this world stretched on and on forever, one ream of hypnotic dullness that only reinforced the common belief of the poor that it was a dead end every which way, so why bother venturing too far out. The land was good for one thing, though. We had bonfires, big towering bonfires made of stolen wood pallets and scrap lumber and sometimes even spent tires that sent up greasy black clouds of toxins as we drank cheap beer and coughed and watched the trash fires burn into big beds of devil–red coals only to throw more on and watch the process repeat again.

I sit in the cab in idle and I find myself thinking back about the frequent nights when I drank too much—I always drank too much—I was a wandering drunk from the get–go. I'd leave the people and the fire and wander away, often passing out only to come to hours later with dry grass itching my skin and big horseflies buzzing. It'd be late night and the sky that prairie summer purple, but everything else below would be pitch black given the lack of contrast or change in the landscape, and always there would be one guiding light back to sensibility, that bonfire in whatever state it was. All I had to do was walk toward that glow to find my way back.

I got older, and things get more complicated no matter how much of a broke, drunken loser you are and as the years go on; still now I daydream and think about how nice it would be to have just one fucking guiding light back to sensibility, something to bring me back to a state of reasonable equilibrium. I daydream about watching volcanoes and forest fires and napalm drops, I dream about them, watching them from a reasonable distance, far enough away to be safe from harm but close enough to feel the heat, to smell the smoke, to have it sting my eyes and make each breathe hurt just a little. I dream about having a great fire nearby at all times as my own personal compass, an orderly direction to comfort me and help me maintain.

When I snap out of my daydreams I remember that every fire either burns out of control or it fades slowly…what kind of fucking guiding light is that, anyway? You can only sit around wishing and waiting for so long until you really start hating yourself. That's why I always start it up and get back to work. No one ever dreamed up any of this anyway. Everything was simply done.

CHAPTER 26: NICK

"TICK, GO CHECK ON THE OTHERS. I'm going to wake this
dumb motherfucker up."

I nudge Jordo—wake up fucker—he murmurs and slaps my hand
away. I grab ahold of his shoulder and shake him hard. He rolls over.
I do it again. No luck. I go into the kitchen, grab some ice out of the
freezer, and mix up a nice batch of ice water in an empty cooler. I
bring it back and dump it over his head. He thrashes on the mattress,
flinging water all over the room. His eyes flutter open and then shut.
He mumbles incoherently and rolls over to go back to sleep. I slap the
side of his head. "Wake the fuck up." I reach back to slap him again and
he sits up and looks at me with blurry red shot eyes. "Wha…"

"Wake up, Jordo."

He scans the room around him, unsure of where he is. He clumsily
rubs a hand over his wet face and studies it. He looks up at me with big
dope–heavy eyes. He is all pilled out.

"Huh. Why am I wet?"

"I dumped ice water on you," I tell him.

"Why?"

"To wake you up."

"How long was I out?"

"Three, maybe four hours."

"Whu…let me go back to sleep."

"Not an option."

I grab his arm and pull him off the mattress. He protests. I drag him into the kitchen and pull him up onto a chair. His head rolls around like a drunk's. I smack him again to wake him up. He took two Ambiens and two Xanax just six hours ago. Getting him fully conscious isn't going to be easy. Out of options, I pick up the shards of the plate I smashed earlier; the pieces of broken plate still have some coke left on them. I sweep up as much coke as I can off the pieces into a glass, then fill it with soda from the fridge. It's a decent amount of coke mixed in with a shot or two of soda, enough for a jolt.

I pull his head back and make him drink. It hits him pretty fast. He comes to.

"What the fuck is going on?"

"Where are the guns, Jordo?" I ask him.

"Huh?"

"The guns, Jordo. The AKs. Where did you stash them?"

He rubs his face and fumbles a cig out of a pack on the table, puts the cig in his mouth the wrong way. I stop him before he lights it. I flip the cig around and light it for him. The smell of the trailer is getting to me. It smells like a small animal died on a bed of old potpourri.

"Did you just give me coke?" Jordo asks.

"Yes," I say. "To wake you the fuck up, because you are in deep shit and I have to deal with it. So tell me, right fucking now, where are the fucking AKs?"

"The Yugo? In the other trailer."

I grab him by the collar, pull him up out of the chair, and push him against the wall.

"Don't fuck with me. The AKs, the Iraqis, where are they?"

He smiles. "I…don't remember."

I cock back my hand to slap him.

"I'm serious, man. My head is like a fucking wave machine, man, you can't just take a handful of Ambien and Xanax and snap out of it, dude. My brain is fucking, I, you gotta get me some more blow to wake me up. It's the only way."

I shake my head. "All gone. I threw your stash out."

"Behind the fridge." He points to the fridge. I release my hold on him and he sits back down. I go to the fridge and pull it back from the wall. It has a package duct–taped to the back. I rip the package off the back and hold it up to the light. A smell of faint rubber and lighter fluid hits me. Holy fuck, its coke, and a fuckload at that, a fucking kilo at least. This motherfucker is dealing, too, on top of all this shit. I hold it in front of his face.

"Are you serious, Jordo? What the fuck?"

"Give me a bump and I'll explain," he says.

I grab a kitchen knife, stab it into the wrapping, and then pour out a pile of blow on the kitchen table.

"I'm holding onto this until Tim says what to do with it," I say, waving the package, causing coke to spill out onto the floor.

He grins and takes a huge snort of the table, then another. He leans his head back, lets out a deep breath, then sits up straight.

"Much better," he says. "Now, what were we talking about?"

"Tell me where the AKs are. Tim's orders."

He chuckles. "You're a good little soldier, aren't you?"

I drop the kilo on the floor and grab him by the throat. He giggles as I push his head back against the wall.

"Listen, motherfucker, Tim gave me the word—hell, he even encouraged me—to beat the living fuck out of you. And your friends, well, I say the word and Tick puts a bullet in both of them. You tell me where the rest of the AKs are, now. I'm trying to help you get out of this shit. You really fucked up and I have to clean up the mess and bring you back up to the valley, tonight, so let me know where the guns are so we can get the fuck out of here. I know this is all a joke to you, but you're going to get us all killed with this shit. So get your fucking head straight."

I let his throat go. He sniffs. "There's only one AK, my connect only had one on him. The rest are on their way."

"Bullshit. You're lying."

"Am I?"

"Yes. You told me the guy had crates of them, and you expect me to believe you just bought one? Horseshit."

"Don't worry about the guns. We do this job, then I take care of the guns. Tim gets his cut, you get your cut, everyone is happy. Fucking A, Nick. Those guns are going to go for 10k apiece, at least. There's no sense in walking away from that kind of cash. It's the way it is, man."

"No, that's not how it is. Not at all. There is no job. You fucked it up. You had to go running around blowing coke and beating up strippers. And then you were dumb enough to go to the club and pull a piece on the bouncer, the same bouncer who you jumped that night, the same bouncer who happens to be a patched–in club member of the Tucson chapter. You get it, Jordo? You fucked up. So there is no job, not now, not ever, not in Tucson. We're going home. Your uncle's orders. And trust me, it's for the best. For you."

"Bullshit."

I throw my phone onto the table.

"Don't believe me? Call your uncle. He'd love to have a chat with you."

He pushes the phone back toward me.

"Don't need to talk to him. We're going to do this job, and then I'm going to sell my guns. You go with me or not, I don't give a fuck. But you aren't stopping me."

I lean up real close to him.

"Your uncle told me to beat you unconscious if I have to. He told me to hog tie you if I have to. Get it through your head, Jordo. You aren't calling the shots here, not anymore. I'm doing you a favor here. You are out of fucking control and you're going to get yourself killed."

"Is that right?"

"Yes, and you have only yourself to blame. This isn't my call, its Tim's, so don't give me shit. We're going back home to straighten this out."

He studies me for a second. "Fine, whatever. What a fucking waste." He gets up. "Can I at least take a shit before we go?"

"Fine, I'll be waiting right here." I take my pistol out of my waistband and put it on my lap just to make my point. He goes in to the bathroom and closes the door.

"Hey Nick?"

"Huh?"

"We got any reading material out there?"

"Very funny. Hurry the fuck up."

"Christ Nick, I thought we're friends."

"We are friends. If we weren't I would've beaten you unconscious by now. And if you want to save your ass I suggest you tell me where the guns are."

The toilet flushes. He steps out, buttoning up his pants. "I don't know where the guns are. But you know what I found in the bathroom?"

"What?"

"A Taser."

I try to get my gun up in time. I'm too slow. This incredible jolt of electricity smothers every square inch me, screaming pain, and I am on the floor, twitching and bouncing. It only lasts a matter of seconds, but if feels like forever. Everything goes black.

V

Chapter 27: HACK

I FLIP OFF THE METER AND THE dispatch computer. I'm taking a few hours off. I turn left onto Van Buren off of Central. Van Buren used to be a jewel of Phoenix, a bustling and prosperous line of car dealerships and hotels. Somewhere along the line, the chief commerce of the street switched from cars and hotels to crack and blowjobs. A couple of years ago this stretch of Van Buren Avenue was pure urban mayhem, another sprinkle of third world on the American dream. The city got a bug up its ass one day and decided to clean the area up. I suppose they succeeded. At least a little. They strong–armed the cheap motels to stop renting rooms by the hour. They harassed enough whores and Johns to move them elsewhere. The young blacks and Mexicans that sold crack and junk on the corners, they ended up on another street corner or in prison or dead, I suppose. Van Buren got better, not good, but better. Of course, the world itself hadn't changed at all, not one fucking bit, and all the crackheads and junkies and whores and Johns and dope dealers just moved a few miles away and set up shop again. And the cops and the city keep playing Whac–A–Mole.

I drive down Van Buren. It's slowly returning to its old ways. Bums with grocery carts shout into the night. Crackheads scurry around.

Dull and vicious looking young men sit on stairs in comically oversized white tee shirts. A haggard, end–of–the–line whore looks for a date. Some things can't be changed, no matter how hard we try. Good luck fighting the most primal urges of man, Mr. Mayor.

The real activity is now on the side streets of Van Buren, almost as if the city decided that cleaning up the street with the big name under the lights was enough; the shit show could and would travel toward the darkness of the side streets.

I drive a few blocks. Groups of street dealers try to wave me over to peddle their wares. A crackhead or two tries to wave me down for a fare, but I know their ride and dash game. Crackheads, junkies, drunks, and bums pay up front or they don't ride. I spot a young lady with a pretty face. She's in a wheelchair, sipping from a forty of King Cobra. I pull up to her. She says, "I didn't call no cab," after I roll the window down, and in instant I see her on this very street two years ago; it was a November night, I watch the trajectory of an errant bullet miss its mark; it pierces her spine and she collapses. She's not a bad person. There are no major dark clouds in her past, nothing that peaks. She just got dealt a shitty hand, I guess.

I hold up the picture. "You know her?"

She wheels herself closer to the cab and inspects the picture. She has a squeaky voice, childlike even.

"Maybe, I dunno," she says. "She a street girl? They all look the same after a while, ain't many girls working this area anymore. Check Twenty–seventh Ave, or Maryvale. Fortieth Street and Broadway. Fuck, man, you're looking for a needle in a haystack."

"Okay, thanks. You just look like you know the area, figured it was worth a shot. Take it easy, doll."

I start to pull away. She puts her hand on my arm to stop me.

"Hey, how about giving me a few bucks? My brother stole my fucking Oxys and a couple of these beers is about all that's gonna keep me pain–free enough to stop that needle jones. I'll be goddamned if I end up a cripple and have the HIV. Know what I mean? I'm just trying to stay off the junk."

I dig through my pockets and find a ten spot, hand it to her. "Stay away from that needle."

"I'll try," she says.

I drive off. I stop at a light to get back on Van Buren. I guess I forgot to lock my doors; a bearded and wild-haired man jumps in my back seat. A rotten scent of piss and sweat grime fills the car.

"Need a ride to South Phoenix, Central and Broadway," he says.

I look at him through the rearview.

"Crackheads pay up front," I tell him.

"I ain't no crackhead."

"No? So why are your fingers all are blistered like that?"

He looks down at his hands. "I really need a ride, man."

"And I really need to pay for three-eighty-five-a-gallon gas. Show some cash or get the fuck out, it's that simple."

He slams his hands on the seat and shouts. "Can't you be a decent fucking person and give a guy a ride? I'm fucking homeless, man. I walk all goddamn day and night. Just a ride, man, that's all I'm asking."

"You want to me to be a decent person," I ask him.

"Yeah. Is that so hard?"

"Are you a decent person?" He doesn't respond. "So are you? Are you a decent person?"

"Yes," he says. "I get nothing but shit on and you don't see me bothering no one about it."

"Really?"

"Yeah. Can we go now please?"

"Sure. Let me ask you something, though." The light changes and I pull ahead. I offer him a cig and he lights up.

I ask him a question. "Would a decent person stab a person in their sleep?"

The cab gets church quiet. He fidgets in the back seat and runs his hands through his greasy hair. "Answer the question," I say.

He shakes his head and peers out the window.

"What the fuck are you talking about, man?" he asks softly, meekly even.

"I asked you a question. Does a decent person jimmy a door open and stab a person in their sleep just to rob their purse of a measly twenty–seven dollars in cash? Maybe you and I have different opinions as to what 'decent' means. I think most would agree that stabbing someone in their sleep isn't an action a so–called 'decent' person would take. But what the fuck do I know. Maybe you have a real twisted view of things. You're entitled to that, I guess. But you still haven't answered my question."

He fidgets for a moment before slamming his hand on the back of my seat. "You're fucking crazy, man," he tells me. "Fuck the ride. Pull over here and let me out. Cocksucker." He raps his hand against the window. "Let me the fuck out."

I pull over into the parking lot of a boarded–up Mexican restaurant. I pull my pistol out and point it at his face before he can get out of the car.

He holds his hands up. "Fuck, man, I'm sorry, I didn't mean anything; I just had a bad day. I'm sorry."

"I don't want your apologies," I tell him.

"I don't have money, man, I got a five–dollar rock, you can have it. Just let me go." He digs through his pockets and pulls out a tiny cellophane wrapper; he offers me the pathetic, tiny little yellow crack rock as if it were some great offering. I put the gun a couple inches closer to his face.

"I don't want your fucking crack rock, shithead. All I want is for you to answer my question. Does a decent person stab a person in their sleep? Rather, does a decent person stab someone at all? Huh?"

"I, uh, I don't—"

"She didn't die, the woman you stabbed. Your blade wasn't that sharp. But it was dirty, yes it was, a dirty and rusted piece of metal. She got a pretty nasty blood infection that almost killed her. Did you know that? Did you know that your filthy little knife poisoned her blood? That was probably the worst of it. Well, that and the fact that she'll be on dialysis for the rest of her life. She crawled to the phone and an ambulance got her to the hospital just in time. She was lucky. She's lucky to be alive. Not for your lack of trying though, huh?"

He buries his face in his hands and shakes his head back and forth.

"The worst thing about it is you didn't have a reason to do what you did. You had the money already. She was asleep, wasn't she? She never saw you. She never saw you. You could have just walked right out of that house with those twenty–seven dollars. So why did you stab her? Why?"

I prod him with the gun, one tap to his face for each word: "Huh? Why? Why did you it?"

"I, I was high, I didn't know what I was doing. I swear, I didn't mean to—" He does that stutter that men do when they're on the business end of a loaded gun. I reach over with my free hand and flick him on the forehead.

"Does it matter? No, it doesn't. It doesn't matter what you *meant*. You did it. That's all that matters," I tell him. "I suppose in the end it doesn't matter what reason you had to stab that woman in her sleep. Though I suppose part of you had some reason, some urge—some part of you had to have a reason. Maybe you just wanted to know what it felt like to kill someone. Maybe it makes your dick hard. Shit, it doesn't matter. You did it. What's done is done."

"How do you know about that? I never told anyone! I never told *anyone*. Just tell me what you want, I'll do anything, just let me go. I'll do anything."

I lean over the seat so my face is right in front of his. His bum stench is sickening being this close to him but I don't give a fuck. What I have to say is too important:

"I don't want anything from you. You're a piece of fucking shit and you always will be. You and your miserable, selfish life contribute nothing to this world, never have, and never will. I could blow your brains out right now, but that would be doing you a favor. I would rather let you out of this car so you can continue to live your miserable existence and suffer every single moment, hopefully for a very long time. Just do me a favor—don't ever claim to be anything even close to decent again. If anyone ever asks what you are, you tell them this; tell them that you are the lowest form of life on this earth, worse than any bug or parasite. At least they contribute something to the world. You tell them that. You tell them that you're on the lowest rung of life. You tell them that you're worthless. Tell them the fucking truth, no one gives a fuck about you and no one ever will."

He looks at me with his big empty crackhead eyes.

I wave with the pistol. "Now get the fuck out. Get the fuck out and run down that dark street."

He fumbles with the handle for a moment and then bursts out of the car, his feet hit the ground and he sprints away, past the closed business, out of the parking lot, and off to the black streets beyond. I let him go, yes I did, but nothing can prevent what's coming for him soon. Very soon.

Chapter 28: NICK

I AWAKE TO PAIN, PIERCING MIGRAINE headache pain. A steady stream of ache flashes behind my eyes like a strobe light. My head feels like it's stuck in a vice. I try to move my hands to my head, but I can't. My face is mashed into something wet. I smell wet earth and blood. I roll over and open my eyes; I look up toward grey clouds.

I get that familiar feeling, that dread and confusion I've had so many times over the last decade, that horrible, post–blackout reawakening…a total and terrifying disconnection from reality and self. My mouth is cotton dry. I try to speak, but all I get out is a hoarse cough.

"Hey, look who is up," a voice says.

An unfamiliar voice. I squint and open my eyes enough to make out the figure sitting nearby in a lawn chair. It takes some time to get my vision focused. It is Grey, Jordo's guy. I struggle against what must be rope binding my hands and feet.

"What the fuck are you doing?"

"Enjoying the evening," Grey responds. He smiles and holds up a double–barreled shotgun. He puts a joint in his mouth and lights it.

"Untie me," I demand. "Right now."

"No," he says, exhaling a massive cloud of skunk smoke.

I strain my neck to look around us. It looks to be near dusk. We're alone. I spit dust and grit from my mouth. "Don't be fucking stupid. You can still walk away from this. Untie me, now." It hurts to talk. Every word brings another stab of pain.

Grey responds, "No. Not going to happen. You ain't calling the shots anymore. Get it into your dumb fucking head."

"You stupid fuck. What do you think Tim's going to do when he finds out about this? He'll have you begging for your life, you stupid fuck."

"I doubt it. Tim isn't going to do shit." He gets up out of the chair and comes to me and presses the barrel of his shotgun to my forehead." I just might have you beg for your life right now, tough guy. What do you think about that?"

I squirm to get the barrel off my forehead. He laughs and backs up and sits back down. I look around as best as I can. Tick's Jeep is gone.

"Where's Jordo? Let me talk to him."

"Jordo and Sean took Tick for a little ride into the hills." He points his gun toward the south. "They're out there," he adds.

"What for? What're they doing out there? What're they doing?"

"A burial. Tick's final resting place."

"Bullshit."

"Okay," he says, smiling.

He isn't fucking around. My heart thuds. The throbbing in my head goes up a notch, I groan and roll over, throw up into the sand. My head screams with every convulsion. I roll back over.

"Get me some water at least. Please."

He gets up and grabs a bottle of water from a trailer. He pours it onto my face; I'm able to get a few sips in.

"You know, I asked Jordo to let me take care of you. I really wanted to show you what happens when people put their hands on me, what happens to people that cheap–shot me like you did today. But he wants you alive—for now. But I figure I owe you one for that shot you gave me in the gut, and I wanted you to be awake for it."

I try to roll away from him but he steadies me with his boot and then slams the butt of his shotgun into my stomach, knocking the wind out of me. I gasp for breath.

He laughs. He pulls out a Ziploc bag of powder and a credit card, dips the credit card in the bag, and snorts the take. Then again. He squeezes his nose and tilts back then turns back to back me.

"Big tough guy came down to handle business, didn't you? Big tough guy, huh?"

"You guys are fucked," I say, my voice barely a whisper. "You'll never get away with this. Tim is going to kill all of you. You blew any chance you had at making things right. You're fucked up, man. You fucked up."

Grey turns the barrel on me again, aiming it at my head casually with one hand. He spits the joint out and cracks open a beer.

"Stop talking about Tim. Tim is done. If you had a half a brain, you'd know that his time is up. Jordo's done having that fuck breathing over his shoulder all the time. Fuck it; you still might get the chance to be with us. I doubt it. If it was up to me you'd be in the dirt like Tick, but Jordo said no. Maybe he thinks you'll climb aboard. I don't. You're too much of a fucking errand boy, got your head straight up Tim's ass, don't you?"

"If you guys are dumb enough to try and take him out, fuck, I feel sorry for you, man. You'll get run down by his crew."

He laughs again. "His crew? Ha. Who? Dante, the spook? He ain't shit. And who else, Jake, that old fuck? Ha. Trevor and Saul? With Tim gone they're going to stick by Jordo, no problem. That leaves a few other scattered guys, nothing. You don't know shit."

"You know Tim has friends. You know he's dialed in. They aren't going to let you get away with it." I'm shivering. I don't know if it's from the pain or the fear. Everything is cold right now.

"You overestimate people. All those fucks give a fuck about is money. Why would they battle it out with us when it'll get in the way of making some cash? And with Tim gone we can make some real money, none of this conservative nickel–and–dime shit. You played your cards wrong, hombre. Tough shit."

"You guys are fucking morons. You'll be dead or locked up within a month or two, running around coked up and doing whatever you please, you won't last a fucking month."

"Doubt it," Grey says. "Last longer than you, that's for sure."

I roll over. I'm done talking. I need to think. Jordo didn't kill me, that means he either has plans to, or he thinks that I'll come around and join up with him with a little persuading. I close my eyes and breathe in and out slowly, try to get my damn heart to slow down. The pain in my head eases a bit. I'm afraid, truly afraid. I'm used to fear, shit, like any drunk I've lived my life around it. I'm used to the fear of the unknown, the fear of tomorrow, the fear of what I might have done the night before—but this, this is something new: the fear of the known, the fear of a near and highly probable death. I don't have that life flashing in front of my eyes shit, but I can't help but think about what a dumb fucking idiot I am to have ended up here, ended up like this. Just a few years ago I was looking forward to a career in social work. I made my bed every morning. I prayed. I paid my taxes. I didn't even fucking speed. I fucking babysat for friends outside of AA meetings. I held doors open for strangers. I fucking voted. Nothing like being hogtied and facing the business end of a shotgun barrel to make you see just how ruined you are. Did alcohol really do this to me? Did I manage to drink away the person I was? How do you go from social–work studies to robbing crackheads to beating people senseless with baseball bats in just a few years? How did I manage to trade that part of me away? Perhaps I deserve this. Maybe I *have* gone too far. Maybe there's no return to what I was. I overplayed my hand. I spit on blessings. I saw perfection in the world of sobriety; I saw that people helped change lives, that people had their lives changed, that there are such things as second chances, and third and fourth and as many chances as it takes, for some, and I saw, no, I *felt*, I felt that unbelievable hope in the simple ability to live life on life's terms and be a simple and content human fucking being. I heard it in the words Gary read out of the book. I saw it in that brief time I spent with Rebecca. And I still ended up here. I guess it's my nature to sabotage myself at every opportunity. I'm not so sure about second chances now. Not for me. Not for people like me. I just pray I can get these binds off of my wrists and my feet and find a way to end this before it gets any worse. I don't care if I die trying. I really don't.

CHAPTER 29: HACK

I PARK THE CAB AND WATCH BIRDS eat fast–food scraps from a bag some shithead littered. I get depressed sometimes. I wonder why I do what I do. It's not like I have a choice, but I do wonder what the hell the point of it all is. What's the end game? Will I be here to see the nation in its entirety drift to the lowest common denominator, into a sea of dumb obese mutants too lazy to thrive as they move through life like snails, rolling around in their made–for–fat–asses scooters, brain–dead dumb, clutching onto picture Bibles and unable to point out a single other country on a map, their blood chemical and synthetic, sweating high fructose corn syrup, and in general going through life with a dangerous mix of arrogance and slothfulness? That possibility, that very real possibility, fuck, it's too much. I watch wild animals eat discarded French fries and I wonder why I have to spend my life doing what I do when this world has jumped the shark already.

Chapter 30: NICK

THE JEEP RETURNS. I turn my head and watch Jordo step out of Tick's Jeep. He's covered in dirt. The butt of a pistol hangs out of his waistband. There is a small red stain on his shirt.

"We need to get changed," he tells Sean. "Burn your clothes. Burn everything you're wearing, even your shoes." He turns toward me. I have my eyes shut again, as if this were some bad dream that I could snap out of.

"He up?" Jordo asks Grey.

"Yup."

"You guys go inside for a little bit and relax," Jordo says. "I'm going to talk to my buddy here."

They leave us. I roll over to face Jordo. He sits down next to me.

"So what was that Taser like? I've never been shot with one. You flopped like a fish, man, it was fucking hilarious. I had to put you out with that empty vodka bottle. You got a bit of a knot on your hard head, my friend, it looks like one of those old fucking cartoons where they'd get hit on the head and swell instantly, you know—"

I interrupt him. "Jordo, you gotta think about what you're doing. This isn't the right play."

He laughs. "Oh, Nick, you're amusing. What the fuck do you know about the right play? You're going to tell me about the right play? Before I hooked you up with Tim, you were breaking into cars and robbing nickel–bag street dealers. I was doing work. I've been doing work for years while you were struggling to pay for light beer and fifths of shitty booze. Don't forget that. You might have a degree on your wall at home, but that doesn't mean shit now, does it? I thought you'd excel with me, with my guidance. But shit, Nick, I had no idea you'd take to my uncle like this. You must have real daddy issues."

He laughs.

"It's not about taking to anyone," I tell him. "It's not about loyalty. It's about fucking common sense. Tim runs the show, and he does it well. You, on the other hand, you get left alone for a little bit and you lose all control. You gotta see that, I mean, it's right in front of you, Jordo. You're going to get yourself killed."

Jordo stands up and kicks a little dirt at me. "Fuck, you even sound like him," he says. "Now be honest, would you suck him off if he asked you to? Cuz I think you would."

"What's your plan, Jordo? What're you gonna do?"

"Simple. I'm going to do this job, go back to the city, and tell Uncle Tim that it's time to retire. I'll break him off half of the take as a retirement bonus, but I tell him that he's done. He doesn't like it, tough shit. If he really doesn't like it, well, I deal with it. I deal with him."

"It's that simple, huh?"

He takes a bag of blow out of his pocket and dips two fingers in it, scoops a pile out, and snorts its. He rubs his fingers over his gums.

"Actually it *is* that simple, Nick. And you know why? Because, unlike Tim, and unlike you, I have ambition and I refuse to deny it any longer. And who do you think people are going to side with? Tim, who gets his guys a payday of what, 5–10k a month, 20k at best? Or me, who's going to make that kind of cash seem laughable? Hell, we'll triple our money by taking dope instead of cash for the guns alone, something we should've been doing all along."

He grins a skeletal grin and looks at me with those crazed eyes of a cokehead, wired on little sleep, no food, his entire brain and body numb and drained yet feverish with energy, a near psychosis complimented by great focus. It's a deadly mix.

"I told Grey and I'm telling you. You guys will end up dead or locked up in a month or two. No one plays fast and loose and gets away with it. You know that. That's what makes your uncle who he is. He might not make the huge hits, but he stays above ground and out of the joint. Don't you see that?"

"I see a pussy afraid to take a chance or two. That's all I see. You forget that I'm smarter than he is, and I'm even more confident. That combination will prove itself. Trust me."

"You didn't have to kill Tick."

"Yes I did. I never liked that fucker anyway. See, I can understand why you're like this. You're naïve, new to all this. But Tick, he's been around awhile, and if he hasn't learned by now, he never will. So I had no confusion about what I had to do. None at all. But the real question I have is what am I going to do with you?"

He taps on my ribcage with his shoe. I look up at him.

"Just let me go, Jordo. I'll disappear. I won't call Tim, I won't talk to anyone. I'll leave the state. I'm gone. I promise. I swear."

Jordo takes the pistol out of his waistband and ejects the magazine. He looks at the slot on the side of the mag to see how many rounds he has left. I hold my breath. The world is on pause. If I have ever experienced a true and pure emotion, this, right now, this is it. He puts the piece back in his waistband and looks down at me. I breathe again.

"No, I don't think so," he tells me. "I can't let you go. Not yet at least."

"What, then?"

He takes the coke out and does another bump, then takes two cigs out and lights them, then leans down and puts one in my mouth. I suck deep. Fucking cancer has never tasted so good.

"I think I want you to kill my uncle," he says.

"I don't kill people, you know that. And why would you do that, Jordo? You want to kill your own flesh and blood, Jordo? There's no reason for that, Jordo. I–I don't kill people, man. I can't. There's no way. Please."

"Bullshit. Anyone can kill. It's pretty easy, Nick, especially after you get that first one out of the way. You have such a hard–on for my uncle, and, shit, Nick, you have no idea how many people he's killed. Holy fuck, that man has no problem with it, so why should you? You see, Nick, I don't think you're a lost cause. I think you have the ability to come to your senses and realize that sticking with me is your best bet. I could really use you, Nick. The other guys, Sean and Grey, Trevor and Saul, well, they're decent help, but they don't have the smarts that you do. And, better yet, you can be one tough bastard when needed. So I give you two options. One, I take you out, quick, no pain. I promise. You close your eyes and I put you out. Two, you and me go up to the valley and see my uncle. You kill him, and I hold on to the gun or something that ties you to the scene. That way you ever decide to go against me, I got something on you, something good, something that keeps you in line."

"So what next?"

He goes into his baggie and does another blast of coke.

"Well, if you want to live, I'll untie you and you can come with us to do the job. We keep a close eye on you of course, but I'm going to be honest, I need you right now. Grey and Sean aren't enough for this job. We do this job and we go straight up to the valley and arrange a meet with Tim. You do your thing. It's that simple. But one thing, you make any effort to fuck this thing up from now until then, well," He pulls out a phone out of his pocket. My phone. "Looks like you keep a pretty thorough rolodex on here. You fuck with me and I make sure that that Sarah broad gets done up real good. Shit, I even know where your mom lives now. I can have someone on a flight and to her doorstep anytime I want." He studies my phone some more. "Plus Nicky, these are some pretty hot texts you've been swapping with this Rebecca. She sounds like a nice girl. I'd hate to have to let Grey and Sean loose on her, I mean, I like them, but they get a little scary with the ladies sometimes, know what I mean? I think they might have something really wrong with them, to be honest."

I clench my bound fists. If I didn't have this rope on me I'd beat him unconscious. I would fucking punch him till my knuckles hit brain. I grit my teeth and compose myself.

"I get it. You made your point."

"Good. So you're in? I mean it's really not a tough choice, stick with me and get rich and bust heads or get buried in the desert."

"I'm in," I say. "Fuck it."

It's the only hand to play.

Chapter 31: HACK

I'M ON "THE TRACK" OVER ON Twenty–Seventh Avenue, driving a loop and wondering why I'm wasting my time. That girl in the wheelchair was right. Finding one lost soul in this cesspool of lost souls is like finding a needle in a haystack. I drive by hooker after hooker. After a while they all look the same. They walk clumsily in high heels. They duck into fast food joints when the odd cop car comes around. They do their best to change their expressions from dead to allure when I slow down to get a look at them. I pull into a gas station where I spot an older black guy with the street–worn look, a survivor—the type of guy likely to know the plays around here, who is doing what and where. I pull up next to him, unroll my window, and flash a twenty at him.

"Hey, I need information. You look like you know the area. Got a few minutes?"

"Sorry man, I don't do that, not with the fellas. Not for any amount of money."

"Neither do I. I need a tour guide. Five, ten minutes at most. Twenty bucks. Easy money."

"Forty bucks and you got a deal."

"Twenty–five. I drive a cab, brother, and it's not making me rich."

He shrugs and gets in the cab. He's one of those black guys that ages exceptionally well; maybe it's the heroin. That shit is like the fountain of youth for some people. He has that classic, old–school–junky thing going on, clad in clothes that were hip a decade ago, obviously broke and homeless but still doing his best to look somewhat put together, the kind of guy that lives and breathes these streets and knows all the angles. He pulls out a little blade and leaves it on his lap.

"I ain't trying to rob you, man, I swear," He says. "I have to watch my back, man. Some weird shit going on out here."

"Oh yeah? Like what?"

"People disappear, man, street people, well that ain't uncommon, I mean, you see cats out here day after day, and one day they're just gone; maybe they got locked up or ended up in some other 'hood, but you usually run into them again sooner or later. But sometimes people just disappear, you know? And you think maybe they got straight and moved up the ladder, but shit, we all know that don't happen much. Lately, man, lately people been disappearing. Disappearing and worse. They just found this guy over off Van Buren, this crackhead white boy been around these streets for a damn long time. They found him—shit, they found parts of him, at least. Motherfucker was a mess; word is the way they found him, poor fucker looked like he went through a meat grinder. Someone tore him to pieces, man. We got crackheads out here thinking there are packs of coyotes or wolves or something prowling the streets and feeding off the street folk." He laughs. "It's probably just another fucking Jeffrey Dahmer."

I pull out the picture and show it to him.

"You know her?"

He studies the picture. "Pretty girl. Maybe. Lots of pretty girls out here, but the pretty ones don't last long. Or maybe they just don't stay pretty for long. It's a big city, man, and this ain't the only stretch for girls, you know? It's tough to say. Yeah, she looks familiar. They all do after a while. People ain't that unique, not anymore."

"Who runs the girls around here?"

He peers out the window after I ask the question and then ducks down in his seat.

"You sure you aren't a cop?"

"Yeah. I'm a cop by day and drive a cab by night. Do I look like a cop?"

He laughs. "No, guess not. You look like a motherfucker that spends too much time in his cab. I just had to ask. Why, you sweet on this girl? She that good? What, she rip you off or something? Give you the virus? Why you care about the girls, man? Nobody does."

"I'm doing a favor for a friend. Her little girl is missing. I promised to look around, even if it is a waste of time. So can you tell me who to talk to, who runs the girls around here? These girls might be nothing but shadows now, but they were all someone's little angel at some time, remember that."

"I dig it, man, you want to play the hero or whatever, that's fine, but don't get your hopes up. We're overstocked on disappointment these days. But you want to know the guys running girls around here, that's fine by me. There are always new guys around, young hustlers trying to put a girl or two out to work, but they don't last, man. Young niggas hit a wall real quick, and that wall goes by the name of Andre. He holds it down. Any girl you see around here is most likely his. Or will be."

"Where can I find him?"

"He has a room at that shitty motel three blocks down, around back. He's got a lookout in the parking lot, tall skinny fucker, an Africa dark motherfucker. He don't look like much, but he's one nasty dude. I don't think you wanna bother with it, man. They don't stay on top by doing favors and being nice to people. You talk to him if you want. Anyone who wants to see Andre has to get by him. But like I said, he ain't the friendly type, and you go sniffing around them and their business, well, it's your own ass."

I hand him the twenty–five bucks. He asks me to drop him off in an alley a few blocks away so no one will see him getting out my cab.

"I gotta live out here, man, so don't go around telling anyone nothing about me and this little conversation we had. You do and it's my ass, so keep that on that big conscience of yours."

"You sure you don't want a ride anywhere else? It's on me, man," I tell him.

"Where would I go, man?" He stretches his arms out, presenting the world around him to me. "This is home."

He gets out of the cab and struts off.

I head over to the motel and cruise through the parking lot until I spot the lookout. He's sitting on a bucket, staring out at the cars passing by.

I pull into the open spot next to him. He turns toward me. I unroll the window. The oven blast of the summer heat hits me. He looks at me with big yellow eyes jumping out of his dark face. Sweat's pouring down his face but he doesn't make any effort to wipe it away. He has some of the dullest eyes I've ever seen on a man. I get a read on him quickly, start seeing names and dates and images. There's a lot there. I do my best to block them out. Now's not the time for that.

"I'm not selling," he tells me.

"I'm not buying."

"Well, what the fuck d'you want?"

"I need to talk to Andre."

He looks at me for a moment and then rocks back on his bucket and pulls out a little Saturday night special semi–auto from underneath. He has the gun flat on his palm, displaying it but not pointing it at me.

"Fuck off," he says.

"I just need a minute." I don't budge. This motherfucker is used to seeing fear, but I have none to show. I don't even blink.

"What d'you want?"

"I'm looking for someone, she's missing. She might've been working around here. I just want to see if she's been around."

"Why did you come here, white boy? What makes you think you can come here and ask questions? And what do you know about

Andre? Who told you that name? What're you thinking; you dumb motherfucker, coming up in here like this?

"Not much," I say. "I've been driving this city for years. You learn things when you spend your time doing what I do. I mind my own business and I leave people to theirs, but a friend is missing her daughter, and I said I'd look into it."

"Why should we give a fuck?"

"You shouldn't. I just had to ask."

My read on him gets stronger. That junkie was right; this is one stone cold motherfucker.

I pull out the picture of the girl, hold it up. "This is her."

He leans forward to study it. His eyes widen a little as he looks at it. He leans back and puts the dull face back on. "Don't know her."

"How much do you want?"

"For what?"

"Information. I saw the way you looked at the picture. I think you maybe recognize her. I don't want to bother you. I just want to know if she's been around lately. I'll make it worth your while. So how much?"

"Hold on a moment." He gets up off his bucket and tucks his piece in his pocket, then walks to make a phone call. He comes back two minutes later.

"Can't help you," He says. "I don't know the girl, and even if I did I wouldn't tell you a goddamn thing. Now get out of here, white boy, or I'll whup your ass. And don't come back. I ever see you around here again I'll slit your fucking throat."

"Hey, I'm sorry, man; here, let me give you some money for your troubles."

I dig in my pockets for some cash, carefully cracking my door open as I do so. He doesn't notice. I hold up the money inside the cab so he has to get close and lean in to grab it. The sight of the green hypnotizes him; he gets up off the bucket and leans in to grab the cash. I wait for his arm to enter the car and I jam my shoulder as hard as I can into the door. The door flies open, slamming into him and knocking him off of his feet. He falls back; his head hits the bucket on his way down. I get right on him as he attempts to get up, I get my pistol out of my waistband and start pistol whipping him, slamming the metal into his face. The junkie was right. This is a tough son of a bitch. He struggles against me even as I slam the heavy .45 into his face over and over. He almost gets to his feet but I get one good shot to the temple that has him on queer street. One final shot to the jaw with my boot and he's out cold. I look up and meet the stunned gaze of a passenger in a passing vehicle. They speed off.

I get this fuck into the backseat and then find some duct tape in the trunk. I tape his hands and legs and get his mouth, too. He isn't going anywhere. I get in the cab and peel off. No problem.

Chapter 32: NICK

I WALK INTO THE TRAILER WITH Jordo behind me. Grey's mouth drops when he sees me. He points his shotgun in my direction.

"What the fuck, Jordo? You untied him?"

"Yes. We had a talk. He came around. Now lower that gun. You know you can't handle that thing worth a damn."

"This is bullshit, Jordo. That fuck is going to—"

Jordo grabs a beer off the table and throws it right over Grey's head in one sudden, furious flash. The bottle explodes and sends foam and glass shards flying. Grey sits there, stunned. Jordo shouts at him.

"If you fucking question me again I'll shove that shotgun up your ass and pull the trigger. I call the shots. Don't forget that."

Jordo sits down at the table. "That was a waste of a perfectly good beer. You see what you did, Grey? You made me waste a perfectly good beer. That isn't right." Jordo takes a joint out of Sean's hand, who is zombie stoned. Jordo takes a few puffs and continues: "As I said, Nick has come around. I saw it in his eyes. He's a changed man. He has come to Jesus. And he knows what's at stake if he doesn't play this right. Isn't that right, Nick?"

I nod and light a cig. I find a jug of water in the fridge and chug. My headache is getting better but it still hurts like a motherfucker.

Jordo continues: "Of course, Grey, if you really have a problem with Nick we can always find a way to deal with it. You guys can fight it out, man–to–man, one–on–one, outside. No guns, just scrapping. Loser leaves town. How about that?"

"Fine by me," I say.

Grey just sneers in response. Sean, his nose powdered white from coke, cackles and laughs like a retard.

"Thought so," Jordo says. "Now let's talk about this Packridge thing."

Jordo lays it out.

"Okay, so this fat fuck Packridge lives on a cul–de–sac in one of those shit developments full of white trash McMansions. Good thing is that it's pretty damn empty, given that they started building it right before the economy tanked. Packridge only has one or two neighbors in his little cul–de–sac; the rest of the houses are empty. His house backs to an empty lot a little bigger than a football field, with a block of unfinished houses beyond that. We park by the unfinished houses and get to his house across the field. We don't know the house; it's a two–story build and he lives alone, so the bedroom is likely upstairs. Sean prowled it a few nights ago and doesn't think he has an alarm system or a dog. We get into the house through the back door; it's a cheap slider and will be easy to pop with a crowbar. So we get in nice and quiet, catch fatso asleep, get the jump on him, and work our magic to get him to give up the cash. It's that easy."

It sounds like a simple plan, but the way these guys are drinking and smoking weed and blowing coke, I have serious reservations they can manage this. I also have no doubt these fucks are going to kill Packridge in the process.

"What about the guns?" Sean asks. "Are we still doing the drop?"

"Yes. We go straight from the Packridge job to Three Points to meet up. We have more than enough time to get to Three Points and set up, even if we have to work on Packridge a while to get him to talk."

"You selling the AKs to those same guys?" I ask.

"Yeah. At a pretty nice price too. They were more than happy when I finally accepted their offer of paying in dope. This is going to be a very enriching evening, gentlemen. You think you two can play nice?"

Jordo looks at Grey and me. We both nod.

"Hey, Jordo, what about the bikers," I ask.

He looks at me and blinks. "What about them?"

"They think we're giving them the guns to make up for you guys beating on their guy the other night. They're gonna be calling sometime tonight to set it up. We don't answer, they know about this spot, man, and they're going to come out here."

Jordo snorts. "Fuck them. We do the Packridge job and we head to Three Points right after. They can come out here all they want. Won't be anything here. If they want to come up to the valley and make a fuss about it, so be it. It won't turn out well for them."

Jordo's coke–fueled insanity is getting worse by the moment. He thinks nothing of going at it with Tim and the remainder of his crew and the bikers at the same time? No way that turns out well.

We sit at this fucking table for two miserable hours. They drink and snort and pass joints. Sean stares off into space. Grey mean–mugs me. I chain–smoke and pop ibuprofen. I hold a bag of ice over the knot on my head. Jordo holds court and talks nonstop, sharing long rambling war stories about girls and robbery. One a.m. hits and we get geared up. Jordo pulls out that crate of SMGs, ski masks, and body armor from a hidden hatch under the trailer. We pack up whatever is left in the trailer into the back of my Jeep. I guess I'm driving. These guys are so fucked up I have to remind them about Jordo's car, how he probably doesn't want to leave it here in case the bikers stop by. Grey hops in the BMW and I follow him to a nearby grocery store. He parks the car and gets into the Jeep. And we're off.

Chapter 33: HACK

"DID YOU KNOW THAT THE U.S. HAS one of the highest rates of fire–related deaths in the industrialized world?"

I take the torch and bring it close to his shorts, close enough that it singes the stray hanging threads.

"Oddly enough, black men, such as you, have a much higher risk of dying by fire than any other group."

I bring the torch up. Flames tickle his face. He screams. No one will hear him. I took the cab on some very bumpy roads to get here, way out here in a part of the west valley that few travel to, particularly at night. I pull the torch away from his face and wave it above my head; the torch makes that crackling *whoosh* sound. I point to the nearest light, a red blip from a radio tower far, far away. The torch gives a small circle of light carved out in this immense land, a faint yellow glow like a lit jack–o'–lantern.

"No one is going to hear you. Scream all you want. But tell me something, have you ever smelt burning flesh? Strange question, I know, but you're a killer, right? And how many people have you killed? I think….um….four? No, its five, isn't it? Two drive–bys, one stabbing, one shooting—up close and personal—and there was that time in prison that you and some boys gang stomped that guy to death. No fire though, huh? You never burned a man to death. You lack imagination."

"Fuck you." He spits at me and misses; the four stakes I have his limbs hog–tied to don't exactly help him with his coordination.

"Burning flesh is really a one–of–a–kind smell. You see, in 'Nam we dropped a shit ton of napalm, and that shit burns right through the muscles. It's really incredible stuff, makes plain old fire look so pussy. It's one thing to see someone burning to death, that's something you may forget or blur out, the sight of it, but the *smell* of it, that never leaves you. The memory might fade, but the scent never leaves. It's hard to explain—it's kind of like cheap beef burning on the stove, but with this odd sweet hint—somewhat rubbery. It gets in your nostrils and throat and just stays there. I got used to it at some point, hell, I even got to like it somewhat, that smell of burning flesh. Well shit, why'm trying to explain it to you when I can just show you?"

I jam the business end of the torch into his bicep and push. He screams that desperate scream.

He tries to pull away but I have him bound too tight.

I make a point of smelling the air, holding my head high like a chef admiring his work. "There it is. Now you know it."

He pants and then howls again.

"It hurts, huh? Yeah, the funny thing about burns is that the worse they are the less they hurt, at least initially. Can you believe that? If I'd pressed a little longer and harder, that burn wouldn't even hurt right now; you see, once the nerves get burned out, that part of you no longer feels pain. I mean, you can still die from them, but it's not going to hurt as much as a more superficial burn does. But really, Slim, as fun as it is teaching you about the world of fire, I would prefer to get back to the city. I can talk about and play with fire all night. But something tells me you might not enjoy that as much as me. So for your own sake, please tell me what I need to know. The girl in the picture—tell me everything you know about her."

"Fuck you. I ain't telling you shit. You just gonna kill me either way, so I ain't telling you shit. So suck my dick." He struggles against the ropes. All it does is chafe his wrists and ankles raw.

"You're not used to being dominated, huh? Real mean motherfucker like you, you don't know the feeling of helplessness all that well. Strange, isn't it?"

"Fuck you. Just kill me and get it over with," he says.

"Kill you? Believe it or not, I don't think I've ever killed anyone. I've been around it plenty, sure, but I don't think I've ever actually killed someone. Well, of course I did in the war; that goes without saying. That doesn't count, in my opinion, and I've never killed since, not in all these years. And I'm not about to start tonight."

"So what, after you torture me out here you just gonna let me go? You gonna just drive me back to the city in your cab? Bullshit."

"Like it or not, I'm not killing you tonight. I'll get you to break, and tell me what you know, which is probably not that much, but I *will* get you to talk. Everyone has a breaking point. I mean, I have a fair amount of tools to use in the trunk. You'd be amazed at all torturing you can do with your everyday emergency car kit. But, I swear to you, I will *not* kill you. You talk and I let you walk. No rides. You walk out of here. You tell me what you know, no bullshit—I'll know if you're bullshitting, trust me—and I let you go. You walk off into the night. I mean, we are pretty far out, but if you walk long enough in any one direction here you're bound to run into someone, or something. Eventually."

"I don't believe you. You full of shit."

"Of course, if you don't want talk, I could just leave you out here like this, tied up to these four stakes. No guarantees you survive that. You'd be seriously dehydrated by early afternoon tomorrow. It's supposed to top a hundred and twelve tomorrow, and you, tied up like that, I'd give you a day, maybe two, until you die of heat stroke or dehydration. It'll be a long and torturous process. Maybe a coyote or something nibbles on you along the way. Man…bad way to go. So look, you can choose to not tell me anything, and go like that, or you tell me what you know, gamble that I'm a man of my word, and then you walk off into the night with no more than a little burn on your arm and a few bumps and bruises on your face. You dig?"

He doesn't respond. I give him a minute and then I hold up the torch. "Fine, I always enjoy a little demonstration and lecture about the amazing abilities of fire. Have you ever seen someone with their eyelids burned off?"

I get up close to say "hi." I bring the flame closer and closer.

"Okay, okay, okay! You crazy fuck! You want to know about her, the girl, Melody, she got strung out and owed some dealers a few hundred bucks, so they came to Andre with her, she was all fucked up and Andre bought her from these guys for two hundred dollars. She's real fucked up, right, but when Andre got her cleaned up a little he saw that she was a good–looking girl and he took a liking to her and kept her around. I told him he oughta put her out and make some money, what, with a sweet look like that, but he liked having her there to order around and shit except he got stupid and careless and one day he wakes up and she's gone. And she somehow found his stash too; bitch cleaned him out, a few grand in cash, a watch, a chain, and some rings. She cleaned him out. We spent the next three days and nights looking for her, every fucking junkie spot, every crack house, every block we could think of, but we never found her. We figured she skipped town. But we let everyone know if that bitch comes around, we'd pay top dollar for her. So that's what I know. Just another dumb dopehead bitch. Worthless like the rest. You go and tell your friend that, too, her daughter's a no–good worthless street bitch. Probably smoked through all that money she stole already and is back to sucking dick for rock."

I pull out my pocket knife.

"What the fuck you doing? You said you'd let me go if I told you."

I cut the first rope. Before I cut the third I pull out my pistol. He leans forward and tries to untie the last rope on his ankle. It's a difficult knot. This shithead won't figure it out.

"I know part of you thinks that when I cut this last rope you can get a jump on me and take me out. But that isn't going to happen. You got it? You take one step toward me and I take your knees out. And trust me; I got pretty damn good with a .45 in 'Nam. You got it?"

"Whatever, man, just lemme go. I ain't trying shit."

"When I cut, you turn around and you run. You turn back around and try to come at me and I'll shoot out your knees and let the vultures pick you apart."

I cut the last rope. He hops up and looks at me, at the gun I have aimed his way.

"Which way do I go?"

"Doesn't matter," I say. "It's all the same for you."

He turns around and runs off, disappears into the dark. I throw the torch way up in the air and watch it fall in slow motion, each spark and ember and flame fall so perfectly. Then I get back into the cab and head back to town.

Chapter 34: NICK

I DRIVE CAREFULLY. We get pulled over with a car full of illegal full–auto weapons, bullet proof vests, ski masks, and whatever amount of dope these guys have in their pockets, fuck, that's a life sentence. Jordo directs me to the development. The storm is gone and has left the air thick and swampy. A bright half–moon towers above. No stars. We cross from the city into suburban Tucson, over a hill and into a wide expanse of development that looks like a massive glowing fungus invading the desert.

We turn into a ghost town of a development with fresh asphalt roads, open lots, and houses in various stages of completion. Jordo starts humming and then pounds me on the shoulder. "This is what it's about, man." He smiles and takes out some coke. "One more blast before the job, boys. Nick, you sure you don't want a little boost?"

I shake my head. He directs me to an almost–finished garage. We pull in and get out.

"Perfect, huh," Jordo asks me.

We double –check our weapons and put the ski masks on. Jordo, crowbar in hand, leads us onto the open field. "Watch your step, not like you can see shit, but this area is crawling with rattlers."

We cross the football–field–sized lot of kicked–up sand and rock and reach a back porch.

"This is it," Jordo says. "Remember, no shooting unless he shoots first."

We step onto the porch. I peer into a window. The house is pitch black. The neighborhood looks abandoned, lonely even; from here it looks like we're alone for miles. Jordo uses the light from his cell phone to study the door. Big beads of sweat pour down my brow; the stink of Jordo and the other guys, that nasty, chemical–coke sweat fills the air.

"It's cheap," Jordo says. "Figures. I swear they build these fucking houses with tin foil these days. Easy."

He pries the handle off the sliding door and pokes his finger through the hole to unlatch the lock. The door slides open and we step into the total silence of the house. I wait to hear an alarm. Nothing. My heart pounds against my vest.

"Grey, come upstairs with me. You two keep an eye out down here," Jordo whispers, pointing at Sean and me.

They head upstairs. I motion for Sean to watch the front while I look out the back. It's quiet for about thirty seconds, until I hear a gruff voice shout "What the fuck?" and then the sound of impact and a loud but brief scream. Something falls and breaks in the commotion.

"Nick, get up here!" Jordo yells.

I run upstairs, cursing Jordo for using my name, and follow the noise to a bedroom down the hall. Grey and Jordo are struggling with this guy; Grey is trying to get him in a headlock while Jordo is wailing on his legs with the crowbar. This Packridge is bigger than I expected. He's fat but thick, too much for the party–weakened Jordo and Grey. He shrugs Grey off and gets ahold of the crowbar and rips it out of Jordo's hands. Grey starts to bring up his gun, I swat it down and shoot a wrestling double–leg takedown on Packridge, getting his legs together and picking him up slightly before dumping him back down on the ground. He hits with a hard thud and I quickly get my knee on his stomach and pin his arms. I get my weight balanced on top of him and he's stuck. He starts to shout, so Jordo grabs a pillow and buries his face with it.

"Careful, dude, you're going to suffocate him," I say.

Jordo doesn't listen to me. His eyes are wide and crazed. He trembles as he pushes down with the pillow. Grey picks up the crowbar and slams it into Packridge's gut.

"Seriously, cut that shit out! We need this guy to talk. Stop it!"

Jordo looks at me and then releases his hold on the pillow. Packridge gasps for air and tries to scramble but I have him pinned.

Jordo puts his hand over Packridge's mouth and puts a gun to his forehead. "Listen, fucker, we aren't here to kill you, but if you shout or make noise I'm going to rip your fucking throat out. Got it?"

Packridge nods. Jordo keeps his hand on his mouth. "Grey, go downstairs and find some fucking tape or rope."

Jordo, the stupid fuck, is so high he actually used Grey's name when he spoke to him. Not good; now Packridge can identify two of us. I tap Jordo on the shoulder and whisper in his ear and remind him not to do that.

Grey heads downstairs. Jordo pulls a knife out of his pocket and flips it open. He puts it to Packridge's throat and releases his hand off of his mouth. I feel warmth on my leg. Packridge pissed himself. The air conditioning kicks on and hums above us.

"Okay, listen," Jordo tells him. "You can make this very easy on yourself. You tell us where your money is and we're gone. You don't, and I have my big buddy here beat it out of you. In case you haven't noticed, there aren't a lot of people around your neighborhood, so we can take our time. So where is the fucking money?"

"I, I don't know what—"

Grey comes back upstairs with the duct tape. We bind his feet and hands.

"One more chance," Jordo says. He pushes the knife into his neck, just short of breaking the skin.

Packridge breaks: "Okay, okay, downstairs, there's a false wall in the closet with the water heater."

Jordo sends Grey to go look for it.

"Don't kill me, please," Packridge begs.

"You give us the money and we won't."

Grey runs up the stairs and into the room. "We're good. Real good."

"Okay, that's it. Easy," Jordo says. "Both of you go downstairs. I have one more item of business with our friend here, one more piece of information I need."

I don't move. Something about this isn't right. Jordo looks back at me, knife in hand, big bulging eyes peering out of the ski mask." Go downstairs."

I walk downstairs listening to the sound of duct tape being ripped off of the roll as I do. Sean and Grey are waiting by the back door, a big duffel bag at their feet. Grey taps the bag with his foot.

"Our money," Grey says to me. "And trust me; I'm going to see to it that you don't get a fucking penny."

I don't respond. I peer out the back window. I look for lights, people, anything. We're all alone. I get more and more nervous with every moment we wait. Jordo finally comes downstairs. "Sean and Nick, go outside. Grey, help me for a minute."

We go outside and step off of the porch onto the field. I look up at the sky. My vision is blurry from the heat and adrenaline. I need to get this vest off; my body is overheating from the fear and the humidity. Every inch of me is soaked in sweat.

Jordo and Grey walk out of the house and off the porch.

"Let's go."

I turn back and look at the house. A faint orange glow appears in the kitchen window. *What the fuck is that?*

Jordo sets a brisk pace and we cross the field and get into the garage. We peel off the ski masks and vests and put them and the guns in the back of the car.

"I'm driving, I know the way," says Jordo.

I hand him the keys. Halfway out of the garage I hear what I think is the sound of thunder. We pull out of the driveway and I hear another roar, like a gigantic growl, and I look across the field to see a huge fiery blob of orange. Tall columns of reddish flame rise up into the sky from Packridge's house. Then another rumble. The house is engulfed in flames.

Jordo drives out of the neighborhood nonchalantly.

I look at him and he grins.

"What the fuck was that?"

"Fire," he answers.

"No shit, but what did you do that for?"

"Does it matter?"

I shake my head.

"You know Nick, it was smart to let me know I fucked up and said two of our names. I was going to just leave him be, but I couldn't do that after I fucked up like that. See guys, this big dope is worth having around. You see how easily he pinned that fat fucker? Me and Grey were having quite the struggle and then big Nick comes in and pulls some WWF shit. Then he catches me using names. Smart fucker. So yeah, Nicky, me and Grey cut a little leak in the gas line and started the burners in the kitchen. It's not like we had any choice. It was my fuck–up that he learned two of our names. Do you really give a shit, Nick? But fuck, I didn't know the house would blow up like that! I thought it would be a nice little fire to burn our buddy to a crisp. Now they're going to have to identify him through his dental remains. Ha!"

They laugh. The coke comes out and they are at it again. We get on the highway and blend in with the rest of traffic and head toward Three Points.

Chapter 35: HACK

I STOP AT A DINER TO DRINK SHITTY coffee and think. I can't get that picture of Melody out of my head; it blurs everything and I can't get a decent read on anyone. Am I wasting my time, trying to find a fucking ghost? After all that work I did on Slim and all the driving and watching the streets, I'm still at square one. Melody is most likely alive, but she has some bad people looking for her, and if they find her she won't be alive for long. She most likely smoked through or shot up all that cash she stole, fast, too; you give a dope fiend a few grand and it's gone in record time. I imagine her strung out somewhere in the city, oblivious to anything but the next hit. I don't know if there's much I can do to help her but I can't help but try…even if I don't want to. *Where did this fucking care come from? Why now?* It doesn't make any fucking sense.

I want to go find this Andre motherfucker and put a bullet between his eyes and have the whole thing done with; at least that way the heat would be off Melody and she might be easier to find. I can't do that. It doesn't work that way. I can't kill. But if I can get Andre in my cab somehow, then, then I get the read and he'll be taken care of. No way do I not see something in him, something dark and horrid, a picture of the past that'll lead to his inevitable brutal end.

I guess I have one card to play. I don't want to, but I can't spend much more time with this girl and her poor mother on my mind. I just can't. I can't feel responsible for this for much longer. So I'll play the card.

I dial up the Phoenix Police and ask for Lt. Granges. He's there, of course. He's always there. He takes my call.

"Holy shit! You, calling me? I'm amazed. Must be something very interesting going on, huh?"

It takes me a long moment to get the words. "I need your help. Can you meet me somewhere?"

"Sure, got a place in mind?"

"I'm at the diner on Camelback and Seventh. That okay?"

"I'm on my way." He hangs up.

I go outside to smoke. Granges. Fucking Granges. As much as I want to see him, as much as I truly crave his friendship, I fucking adore him and the bond we have that stretches back so many years, as much as I covet him as a person, who he is—being around him is terrible. People like us, who we are and what we have, what we do, the vision, this thing inside—we aren't meant to be around one another, even for a short time. It brings something to the surface, a filthy stew of suppressed emotions and memories, bubbling and churning to a fevered pitch that, left unchecked, is nothing short of agony.

I go back in and order some food. This meeting will make me weak. Sick even.

I'm halfway through my French toast when he arrives. He steps into the shitty diner, glowing, wearing a sharp–looking suit with his shield on his belt. Despite the grey hair, the subtle wrinkles, and other signs of aging, he still has that aura of confidence he had the day I met him in Vietnam. He commands attention; the fellow patrons and employees of the restaurant look up at him as he walks by, they take notice of his Paul Newman looks and the way he navigates a room like it's full of dear friends. He is the black to my white; I have always been the one short on personality and long on thought; he oozes personality in a manner that has proven over the years to be just as much a detriment as my lacking.

He walks up to my table and looks down at me. He smiles.

"I'd hug you or shake your hand, but, well, you know," he says. His voice hasn't changed a bit since we were terrified kids clutching rifles and a simple desire for survival.

I nod and smile. Being around one another stirs up a lot; touching one another is like putting your hand in a fire and leaving it there.

"I'd also say you look great, but you know me, I'm not a very good liar," he says, sitting down.

I laugh. "I know. I wish I felt as good as I look, I'll tell you that much."

"Ohio, you just have to bear the weight of the world on your shoulders, don't you?"

I shake my head. "I can barely handle this city."

"I understand," he says. "Believe me. And honestly, my friend, I don't know if we're making any difference at all." With that he lets his guard down and that million–dollar smile of his falls to pieces.

We do the same thing. We have the same gift. We just go about it in different ways.

He orders coffee.

"So what is it? I call you all the time and you never get back to me, I get it, I know the drill. Now I don't care if the only time you contact me is when you need something, because it's obviously something very important. But...fuck Ohio, sometimes I worry, you know?"

A mild electrical zapping feeling starts around my temple. Here it comes. I take a deep breath and a drink of water. I'm getting dizzy and the smell of this diner, the ancient soiled carpet, the shit food, the hint of aerosol cleaner fighting against the remnants of decades of cig smoke–I'm left with a growing disgust, not for anything in particular — just a mounting disgust for the way things happen to be. We have to get this over before the headache and nausea start. I blurt it out:

"I need this. It's important. I need you to pin a case on a scumbag. I haven't read him but I know he's dark. Real dark. His name is Andre. I don't have a last name. He's a street pimp, runs girls over on the track on Twenty–seventh Ave."

He doesn't respond. His coffee arrives and he pushes it aside. "Funny. MCSO just found a guy known to hang around that area, Echo was his street name; he worked that track too, anyway, poor Echo, some hikers found a big mess of bone and gore out in the middle of nowhere. The Sheriff's guys would never have identified him had not his ID still somehow been in one piece. And he was just like all the rest, all the other mutilated messes we find across the valley; he'd been ripped apart, as if he exploded from within. You know anything about that?"

I lean across the table. "Why do you always ask questions that you already know the answer to?"

He shrugs. "I get nervous. I worry that I wake up one day and these things start happening more and more until they are damn near routine. And it scares me. I know there's nothing I *can* do about it, I know there's nothing I *should* do about it, and I know I shouldn't *want* to do anything about it...but it still fucking terrifies me. " He pauses to sip his coffee, then peers out the window and back at me. "I'm not scared for the dead. I'm not scared for this city or the normal folks. I'm scared for you Ohio, I'm scared because I know that you walked these scumbags to their end, and yes, a well–deserved end it is, but it terrifies me to know that you spend your whole life teetering on that odd little line between reality and...fuck it, what's the point. I'm not trying to lecture you. I don't judge you. I never have. How could I? It's all out of our hands. But fuck, Ohio, you have it the worst, and it terrifies me. I care. I fucking care. That's all I'm trying to say. I wish things were different. I wish you didn't have to be...you."

I push my food out of the way. It looks and smells revolting all of a sudden. I digest his words...fucking Granges, always the savior. I respond:

"Like you said, I, just like you, have no control over it whatsoever. So what do you want me to say? I wish I could read like you do, I wish I could use it to collar scumbags and pin cases on them, have all the accolades of being an amazing cop with a sixth sense for figuring out criminals, well on his way up the ladder. Shit, you'd probably be knocking on the chief's door if you didn't insist on staying on the hands–on side of the police force, huh?"

"My talents are no good behind a desk. You know that."

"I do. Just like you, I can't help what I do. And trust me, any time it leads to one of those horrid finds, the ruined mass of what was a body, don't ever forget that they deserved what they got. Fuck it, they deserve worse. We're not allowed the luxury of sympathy. You know that. Don't try to bullshit yourself."

He stares out the window.

"You ever talk to Geddy?" he asks me.

"No."

"Why not?"

"I have no need to."

"I guess you don't talk to anyone, do you?"

"Just the people in my cab. That's about it. I don't really have the liberty to be social. You know that."

"I'm sorry."

"Don't be. It's the way it is. I'm at peace with it."

"So why now? It's been almost two years. You need a favor and it's this? Getting some street garbage locked up? Why now? Why this pimp?"

"I have my reasons. It's very important. Not just for me, but for a troubled young lady out there somewhere. Speaking of which," I pull out the picture of Melody and hand it to him. I don't need it anymore. It's burned into my mind. "I need you to lean on whoever is in charge of looking for that girl, get them to put some actual work into it. Her name is Melody."

He takes the picture but doesn't look at it. "Didn't you just say we aren't allowed the luxury of sympathy, or something along those lines? So what is this? Are you taking on missing person cases now too?"

"It's not about sympathy. It's something that needs to be done," I tell him. My words are flat and without emotion.

He looks at the picture. His eyes squint then he closes them, puts the photo down, and rubs his temples. "I think I understand," he says. "Something about this picture, this girl; fuck, I don't know. I don't know the details, but I understand somehow."

"I don't," I say. "I don't understand at all. I just know that I have to find this girl. I don't know why. Maybe it's not my role to know. But I need this Andre fuck out of the picture. He's looking for her too, and if he finds her she's dead. I have to see this through. I have to. And as you know, I don't do well with commitments or expectations. I never have. That part of me didn't come home."

"You should call Geddy," Granges says. "He'd love to hear from you, just to hear your voice."

"How is he?" I ask. I ask because I care. I really do.

He smiles. "He's Geddy. Doing what we are, of course, just in a different way. He's like us, Ohio, out there suffering with the power of Gods. "

I start to salivate. I swallow. My stomach churns with acid. The first hints of a horrible headache navigate the top of my skull. I look at Granges. He's pale. His blue eyes have gone red and bleary since he arrived. He's feeling it too.

"I guess that's my cue to leave," he says.

"His name is Andre. He runs his show out of a room at that Budget Motel on Twenty—seventh Ave. He needs to be dealt with."

"He will be. I promise you. I'll have him picked up tonight. And after I get one look at him—well, you know."

I nod. He stands up and smiles that movie star smile of his.

"I always think about it," Granges says. "Everyone talks about leaving a piece of themselves in a war, but you, me, Geddy—we came home with more. How many people can say that?"

I shrug. "I don't think about it. It's doesn't matter."

"Well you know what Johnny Cash said?"

"Huh?"

He strums an air guitar and does his best Johnny Cash: "You're a walkin' talkin' miracle from Vietnam." He smiles again. "You are a goddamned titan, Ohio. A true child of God. And don't you ever forget that."

I watch him walk away, this caricature of a man, fucking potent and false, equally flawed and powerful; He is the best I've known. He steps out into the Phoenix night. I flee from the booth and barely make it to the bathroom. I throw up violently until the screaming pain in my head goes away. I lie on the dirty floor and pant. I won't feel right for days, maybe weeks. I won't sleep well, and my reads might be a bit off. But it was worth it, just to see Granges, even for minutes, just to be with my fucking brother. It was worth it. I bury my face into the cold dirty tile and I cry with an emotion that I haven't felt for years, many, many, years.

CHAPTER 36: NICK

THREE POINTS. We stop on the way to get smokes. The guys got a few cases of beer and two bottles of whiskey. Whiskey fumes poison the air. I get dizzy from the scent, nauseous even. The strange thing is that I don't crave it. I don't crave the booze at all. This isn't me. A month ago, even a hint of booze in the air would have me screaming for a drink. Somehow today I'm spared the obsession of alcohol. I can't stop with the cigs and the energy drinks though, shit, it's one after another and all they're doing is making me more attentive to how fucking nervous I am.

We pull off the road and onto that rugged trail. Jordo fills me in on the guns. They're stashed in that wash where we met up last time. Trevor and Saul are waiting for us. They might be Tim's guys but their true loyalty is cash. They were easily won over by Jordo's offer of making some "real cash." Tim doesn't know about this, this little coup. My loyalty lies with him, and no filthy pile of cash could change that. Tim is cold and calculating, perhaps cruel, but there is also this incredible warmth about him. The fact that he's a crook and killer doesn't take away from that; he shows that hint of extraordinary; good or bad doesn't matter, Tim is a man made of an entirely new mold.

You don't turn your back on someone like that, someone with such magnetism, primal magnetism, and fuck, maybe this is the way cult members feel when they get conned by their messiah, but as much as I don't trust myself, I will never be able to deny my instincts, not after all the tests they've gone through. I don't think I've ever known anyone as fucking real as Tim. He reminds me of that drunk I met that night years back in detox, that strange, faceless man who was so sure about his place in the world and the things he knew about it. Tim is the same way. He's a killer, a criminal, maybe even evil, but he is as authentic and comfortable in his skin as anyone. There's a saying in AA that you pick your sponsor or sober friends by finding someone who "you want what they have." Don't ask me to explain it, I'll just ramble on some more, but I want what Tim has. I want to feel comfortable in my own fucking skin.

Jordo turns up the radio, breaking me out of my reflective state. A scratchy signal of a ZZ Top song blasts through the speakers. Jordo drives with one hand and pulls from the bottle of whiskey with the other. He watches the road with that laser–like coke focus, anticipating and handling every slight bump and rut of the rough road. I look at Jordo and all I see is chaos, a person loyal only to his desires and indulgences. He only cares about himself, that much is clear. The more time I spend with him, the more I realize he is little more than a skilled actor, a person that might not be able to feel and express emotions like a normal being but is a goddamned expert at mimicking them. *Who is Jordo?* I ask myself, and the answer will always be that Jordo is whoever he wants to be that day, a shadowy being made as much of deception and insatiable hunger as he is flesh and bone. I don't think Jordo is comfortable in his skin. I don't think he ever was or ever will be. When your inherent creed is more, more, more you are never going to be okay with the reality of the meager things that make us all human and whole. Maybe I shouldn't bother thinking about this shit. If life is truly understood via trial and error, I have been a little too heavy on the error side…what the fuck do I really know?

The Jeep kicks up sand as we follow the trail over the hills and down into the wash. Visibility is low, just a few feet ahead of us, beyond that is an eerie blur of the occasional cactus or brush that float past like ghosts in the dusty wake the Jeep creates. We crawl over the rock garden. The bed of the Jeep groans and clanks as it makes contact with the rocks. We pull up to that old shack and watering hole and park. We step out into the bone–dry heat. We cut the lights and a flashlight comes on; Saul sits alone on top of a crate with an AK in his hands.

"You're late," He says. "Trevor took the ATV up to the lookout spot already."

"Good. Very good," says Jordo. He takes his baggy of coke out and tosses it to Saul. "We have twenty minutes until our friends arrive. Let's get going."

I help Sean unload the crate with the guns and vests. Jordo pulls on the bottle of whiskey and starts describing the night's events to Saul. Jordo gets really into the story, his speech comes out staccato fast as he waves his hands in the air. He dramatizes the explosion of Packridge's house by shooting his hands up, which sends my car keys out of his hands and onto the ground near me. He doesn't notice.

"We should get going," I remind him, interrupting his story. We gear up.

Grey takes the other ATV. Sean gets in Saul's truck with the crate of AKs in its bed. They take off, crawling up out of the wash toward the meet–up. That leaves me and Jordo. He runs his hands through his pockets, looking for the keys.

"Looking for these?"

I swing them back and forth. He holds his hand out for them and I take the opportunity to unload a heavy overhand right square on his jaw, putting all of my two hundred and thirty pounds into it. He falls back stiff as a board, unconscious before he hits the ground. I shake the ache from my hand and turn to watch Saul's truck go up the hill, anxiously waiting to see if he happened to see what I just did.

Jordo is out cold. I go to my Jeep and look for something to tie him up with—rope, tape, anything. I'm digging behind the back seats and I hear Saul's voice call out from the walkie talkie lying next to Jordo. It wakes Jordo up. He starts to punch–drunk mumble into it before I get to him and kick the walkie out of his hands. I look up the hill. Lights. Saul has turned his truck around and is coming back...fuck. I panic for a moment; this was the perfect opportunity to gift wrap Jordo for Tim. I cock a round into the SMG and point the barrel down toward Jordo. I tell my finger to squeeze the trigger, to give it that bare exertion required to blow his fucking brains out all over the ground. I grimace and wait for the squeeze and the flash of full auto fire...but I just can't do it. Jordo looks up at me, semi–conscious, like a child woken up in the middle of the night. I lean over and give him another straight right to the jaw that puts him back to sleep. Saul is halfway down the hill by now. Fight or flight kicks in; I jump into my Jeep and gun it, the bed scrapes against the rock garden and I hear a *thud*. I go as fast as I can without risking blowing out my axles. I look in my rearview. Saul has stopped and found Jordo by now. My Jeep slams into the rocks beneath me, loud enough to make me duck my head, not knowing if it's gunfire or not.

My heart pounds as the engine whines with the steep incline of the road coming out of the wash valley. I hit the top and push the gas up to thirty—dangerously fast in this terrain. I hit a rocky curve and almost flip. I correct the wheel just in time. I fly over the rough terrain, sneaking nervous glances in the rearview and waiting to see lights behind me. I follow the road out of the desert and onto the highway. I'm alone. For some reason they let me go. Why? Why the fuck would they do that? I have to call Tim and warn him. Jordo has my phone still, with all of the names and addresses. And I have the money from the Packridge job still in the back of the Jeep. My heart hasn't beat this fast since the first and last time I tried meth, when I did too much too fast and spent a nervous twenty–four hours with a racecar paced heart I was certain would explode at any moment. I hit the highway and cringe at the sight of every pacing car, for some reason certain that everyone in the world was privy to the events of the day and the fact that my life has quickly devolved into a fragmented mess of the worst possible emotions available: dread and horror, added to a tightrope anxiety and the utter bewilderment of my ability to put myself right in the center of a major fault line that is now tearing apart whatever semblance of a life I have managed to piece together in my twenty–seven years.

Relax, Nick, life is not only unfair but indifferent as well. Lucky for you, even if the world was privy to your situation, the vast majority could give a flying fuck about it. So push the gas to three miles above the speed limit and settle back into the safety of being one stupid fuck in a sewer clogged with them.

I stop at a rest stop twenty miles out. It is deserted, luckily, as I am so frantic that I get out of the Jeep without realizing I still have the vest and the SMG strapped around my chest. I still have that piece of paper in my pocket with Tim's burner on it. I call him three times in rapid succession until he finally answers.

"Jesus, I'm fucking sleeping. What the fuck is going on?

I let it out, all of it. I unload the situation in one giant string–on sentence, pure word vomit. I tell him about Jordo killing Tick, about the guns, the coke, the Packridge job, the gun deal in the desert, about Jordo's plan to force Tim into early retirement. How he wanted me to kill him. How I knocked Jordo out and just barely escaped. How I'm here now, alone at this rest stop and shaking like I have the DT's, and…I just need to know what to do.

I'm out of breath. I wait for some fucking words that will make me feel better. Tim, as calculating as he is, thinks about it a bit before answering, some thirty odds seconds of dead–air agony.

"Okay, Nick," he says calmly. "I can't say I'm surprised. This is my fuck–up. I saw what Jordo was—what he is—I saw it a long time ago, and I was stupid. I ignored it because he's family, even though I knew it was wrong and that I was ignoring the blatant truth and I alone am to—"Tim starts to ramble, showing a rare divergence from his usual rigid and controlled self. He catches it and stops to gather himself. He continues: "This is my responsibility. Listen, Nick. You don't need to be caught in this shit. You're better than this. You take that money and you leave. Ditch the guns and vest, just get on the highway and disappear. Ditch the car when you can—"

"No. That's not how I'm playing this. I got in this mess, I made the decisions, and I led myself here. I'm gonna do what I have to do to straighten this thing out. I won't be able to live with myself if I don't see this thing through. I'm not going to run away and let these fucks off like that. You want, we do this together, but if not, I'm doing it alone. I'm taking them all out."

Silence. Then, "Okay. Let's do it then."

"So what's next?"

"I'm going to make some calls. Head back to the valley and meet me at the yard." He hangs up.

Chapter 37: Granges

LT. GRANGES LOOKS UP AT THE door as the officer brings in a handcuffed Andre and sits him down at Granges desk. The officer leaves. Granges stares at Andre and Andre stares back in a brief competition of who can look the most aggressive. Granges wins.

"You mind telling me what I got picked up for?" Andre asks.

"Marijuana. You had a joint behind your ear, in plain sight, when you opened the door to your motel room."

"No, why the fuck did the pigs knock on my door in the first place? I didn't do shit."

"Because I told them to," Granges said.

"Why?"

Granges gets up and turns off the lights in the room. The room goes dark. Andre says, "What the fuck?" and starts to stand up but Granges shoves him back down in his seat with one hand.

"Sit. You try to get up again and I hit you with an assault on an officer charge. Guaranteed time."

"What the fuck? Why the fuck you turn the lights out, man?"

"I see better in the dark."

"What the fuck sense does that make?"

Granges doesn't respond. He closes his eyes for a moment and then opens them. The room, as he sees it, is now an intense blur of white and grey, not unlike a photo negative or a streak of lightning.

"Turn the lights back on, man," Andre says.

Granges doesn't respond. The light in the room gets brighter, more vivid. A hue of streetlamp–yellow mixes with the brilliant whites and grays. Andre, of course, sees only darkness.

"Lawyer. I want a lawyer. I want a fucking lawyer. Get me out of this fucking room."

"No."

"You have to get me a lawyer. You know that shit."

"I don't have to do anything," says Granges.

Granges watches the yellow and whites and greys bleed into one another, swirling and mixing until it becomes a single ball of furious light, blinding, spinning around. Screaming. Granges closes his eyes again and the ball of light moves toward him and explodes upon contact with his forehead. The movie starts. He watches it. He sees it all, very clearly now. He opens his eyes and the room is dark again. He walks over and turns the lights on.

Andre looks up at Granges with the eyes of fresh road kill. Granges tell him how it is. "You're going into the other room with the detectives, and you'll tell them about that little Mexican girl you beat to death last year. You tell them where you put her, in that dumpster on Thirty–sixth and Camelback. You're going to tell them how you still have those jeans hanging in your room at your mother's house, the jeans with that blood still on them. You tell them every little detail about what happened that night. You tell it all, and once you're done you will never deny or dispute any of it. You got that?"

Andre's eyes fill with tears as he nods vigorously. He will never be the same.

Chapter 38: HACK

ANY FUCKING NOBODY CAN LOOK in the mirror and try to judge themselves. Ask someone who has seen their reflection in a knife, a knife held to their wrist, the blade ready to go with the tracks instead of against them, meaning that this is to be a real–deal attempt and none of that cry–for–help bullshit, and someone like that, someone ready not just to cut open their veins but to drag, drag a blade beneath the skin and carve out their life, and in that moment you see your fucking brilliance and your idiocy, your dumb pride and crude humiliation, your sparkling talents and your natural dullness, your petty ego telling you that you have the right to end your life, as if *you* are worthy of such grand notions, let alone actions. Pathetic.

I drive my cab in the suburbs. I drive through mazes of identical houses and towering brand–new–and–rotten mega–churches, churches that from a distance might be confused for a shopping mall. I drive past chain restaurants and box stores and it's so predictable and bland and lazy, but I know that in these streets, behind cheap doors—cheap doors made to look expensive—great horrors thrive on shame and spit–vile secrets, and there is something delicious about a darkness wrapped in fluff and comforts and desperate veils of normalcy, so the truth is that there is nothing false, nothing fake, nothing weak about the people living in these sprawling communities of cookie–cutter houses, communities with disgusting names like Valley Spring Estates and Sun Eagle Meadow. There are horrid secrets anywhere, it doesn't matter if it's the worst goddamn piss–stained ghetto or the vertigo lines of McMansions sprawling out toward wild lands in haste...none of it matters when you sit down in my backseat. Welcome to the great fucking equalizer.

A couple months ago I picked up an old man on the far edge of Gilbert and Mesa after his car died along a stretch of old farmland. He was old school and didn't have a cell phone. His car died and he set out for help on that early evening. I happened upon him, this caricature of an old man, the sweet old timer in his dated clothes and with his slow gait, struggling slightly with the heat as the sun set behind him. I pulled on the street and I saw the old man; what I saw, that image of the old man, well it was like fucking Norman Rockwell, with the sun setting in the past and this gentle old soul walking next to an open field of sprouts, and he got into my cab and it took one moment, the old man got in the cab and offered his thanks and he smiled, and in an instant that whole oasis boiled over Rockwell into one cancerous tar spew; you should have seen what I saw, the things this man had done...holy fuck. It's all in plain sight.

Chapter 39: NICK

I PULL UP TO THE STORAGE LOT. It looks empty. I wait. The gate opens after about three minutes. I pull in and park, look around but don't see anyone. A figure emerges from the dark. It's Dante. His huge gold cross shimmers in the dark. He has a sawed–off shotgun by his side. I get out of the Jeep with the SMG slung over my arm.

"Sorry for the wait. I had to make sure it was you," he says.

"Well it is." I say. "Where's Tim?"

"On his way."

We sit down by the tool shed.

"Why are you here?" He asks me.

"What do you mean?"

"I mean *why are you here?* Why did you risk your life and run out on Jordo and his guys like that? What for? What's in it for you?"

"I don't want any part of that. Of them. It's not who I am."

Dante chuckles. "Then who are you?"

"I don't know," I say. I really don't. "Not that. Not them. What the fuck are you getting at, man?"

A car passes by, slowly. Dante gets up and peers out through the fence. He holds a hand up to me and I grab my SMG tightly. The car disappears down the street and we relax. Dante walks back but doesn't sit down; he stands in front of me and looks down at me, starts lecturing:

"You need to think about why you're here right now, in this shit, right in the center, about to step headfirst into a big fucking mess that might cost you your life. You need to ask yourself why, why are you willing to see this thing through," he tells me.

"Do I?"

"Yes."

I get up off my chair and stand in front of him, now looking down at him. If this weird fuck thinks he can intimidate me or lecture me he's got another think coming.

"Well let me ask you, then," I say. "Why the fuck are *you* here, huh? What's in it for you?"

"Because I believe," Dante answers.

"You believe? What the fuck does *that* mean. In what?"

"Tim."

I laugh. "You are out of your fucking mind. You believe in Tim? What the fuck does that mean?"

He stares up at me, gives it a moment. "Sooner or later, if you make it, you'll understand."

I wave him off. He keeps talking: "There was this night, like eight, nine months ago, you weren't around yet, and I wake up to a knocking on the door, middle of the night, and I answer it all sleepy and shit and its Tim, he's there at my door at three am. I was gonna ask what was wrong, him coming unannounced so late and all, but I swear, Nick, I never saw a man look as calm and cool as Tim did that night. And that's why I got dressed and went with him without speaking as much as a word about where we were going or what we were going to do."

"I'm not in the mood for story time, dude," I tell Dante.

He goes on anyway: "So we get in the car. You see, before this night, I was like you, working for Tim on the crew, swinging a hammer and hauling rocks and shit, and sometimes after work we'd go do some work, you know, shaking down a small–time bookie or maybe rob a dope house or two; nothing too heavy. So this night Tim gets me and we ride in silence, right, out by Glendale, the 'burbs, and we pull up to this house, a house like any other you see, and Tim, he parks right in front, he didn't tell me a thing about what was what, I follow him and walk to the carport, everything is all dark and shit, and he goes under the welcome mat and gets this key so I figure that he knows whoever this house belongs to, and he motions for me to stay quiet and we walk into this house, into the kitchen—it had that dusty old white–person smell, right, and we creep to a back bedroom where this guy is snoring and before I know what's what Tim pulls this sleeping fucker out of his bed, this middle–aged balding motherfucker, Tim pulls him out and it's dark in the room and I don't know what the fuck is going on and I hear this *Clank! Clank!* sound and Tim is putting a real beating on this fuck. I don't know what to do so I just sit there and watch Tim swing away, *clank, clank,* and this poor fuck is getting his ass whupped solid in his tighty-whities, an ass–whupping so solid that he doesn't even get the chance to yell or cry or whimper or any of that shit, and it's over fast and Tim turns and looks at me and it was like the moon hit the perfect light through that bedroom window and I see Tim. He had blood all over him; it's all over his white tee shirt and his hand is all red and he's gripping brass knuckles, that was the *clank clank* sound, Tim just smashed out this fucker's teeth, and Tim's looking at me, right, in that perfect light, and he still has that calm, fucking *serene* look on his face, his face splattered with blood. This guy Tim just beat the shit out of, he's coughing and wheezing on the ground, and I don't know what to say, and Tim motions for me to follow him and we go down the hall and into this room with all these computers and shit, like eight of them, and Tim asks me if I wanted to know why we're here, and all I said was the truth, that whatever this guy had done had to have been pretty bad for Tim to fuck that dude up like that, and Tim tells me that if I saw what was on those computers I would do the same, if not worse, and he asks me if I trusted him, and shit, Nick, I said yes because I've never seen a more honest look than his, that night, and we walk out of the house then, leave the dude half dead from the beating, and I hear on the news a week or two later about how the neighbors smelled this smell, and they call the cops and the cops go into this house and find a dead man, dead from suicide, gunshot to the head, he was all decomposed in shit, and in that house, down the hallway, they find this man had all these computers, and he was running his little business there, selling this child porn all over the world, and I asked Tim about it, what it felt like to beat that man so bad, did it feel good to beat that piece of shit, that fucking chomo, and Tim tells me that the man was more evil than I knew, that the man wasn't a chomo at all; he just distributed the shit for the cash, and he told me that no one chooses to be a chomo, didn't make it right and didn't mean they don't deserve to pay for it, severely, but the kind of man that sold that shit, just to make a buck, well he had to learn a lesson. You can only bear to learn so much about yourself, Tim says, and then he told me to never bring it up again. So what I'm asking you, Nick, as we stand here—you, *you* stand here—ready to face what may be coming, even though you had the chance to flee, to drive away from this mess with a big bag of money and no worries, what I am asking you, Nick, is *why are you here?*"

I take a step back from Dante. I hear the crickets I heard growing up in New Jersey summers. But there are no crickets here, not in this part of town.

Tim's truck arrives. Dante opens the gate and Tim pulls in. Tim gets out of the car, tucking his Colt 1911 into his waistband. He looks around the lot with the same steady demeanor he always has, as if this were any other day, and his coked-out nephew and his crew of thugs weren't out to kill him.

"You guys getting along all right?" he asks us.

"This fucking guy is out of his mind," I say, pointing at Dante.

They both laugh.

"So what now?"

"We wait," Tim says.

"Wait for what?" I ask him.

"Granges."

Chapter 40: HACK

I HAVE IT UNDER CONTROL. Yes, I want to do it. I want to do it all the time, with no restrictions and no concern. But I don't. When I get the jones to burn something, and it is just that, a jones, an urge, an absolute need—I restrain myself. I start fires in unoccupied structures and unoccupied areas only. That's the rule I have to follow. While I don't feel the need to put people at risk with my fires, I do sometimes tingle at the thought of creating a truly monstrous fire, to watch it go from a single match to a block–long fiery beast that consumes and collapses upon itself and grows, grows, grows...

But I don't do that. Somewhere along the way I was gifted the curse of self–control.

I drive to an abandoned scrap lot on the edge of South Phoenix, toward the tail end of the industrial area where meager desert tries to make its comeback. The lot is ancient and anonymous. Its rusted fence is all but gone; scavengers have pillaged whatever could be carried away. All that's left of the lot is trash: bundles of yellow weathered newspapers, broken glass, mutilated tires, and old twisted heaps of metal not good for anything and too heavy to move. I pour lighter fluid into two bottles of vodka I found in a dumpster—holy fuck, for one bright moment that odor of vodka sent chills down my spine. I jam a rag in each, each rag delicately soaked with lighter fluid. I pick up the first bottle, light the rag with a Bic, let it catch a little air. The flame pops up and I heave the bottle in the air. I try to aim for something that will burn. The bottle crashes and explodes with a popping noise. A ball of orange flame appears for a second but disappears. Small spots of fire burn themselves out within seconds. So disappointing. I do a little better with the second cocktail; it hits the bundle of paper I aim for. The paper goes up fast, and I get the lovely queasy lust in my stomach and below. It's a modest burn. It won't go on for long. It won't grow. It reaches its peak, a simple three– or four–foot blaze. It's all downhill from there. I leave. I'm disgusted with myself; this base and neurotic desire is the only real thrill I seek from life. I have the ability to see people, to see the vilest things they hide within, yet I feel nothing but apathy for that extraordinary gift, at the truth that *I* am the catalyst that can send awful people to an awful end. I have this ability—who knows how many people have it? Only two others that I know of, but I'm sure there are more, perhaps many more. Whatever it is, it is nothing short of a miracle, otherworldly, demonic or divine, I don't know and don't care. I have it and it does nothing for me. All I really want is to see things burn, and for whatever reason I can't allow myself that. It's like thinking about fucking all day and then finally getting to it and you come in ten seconds, left with nothing but shame shadowed all over you and your bare animal skin.

The urge for fire grew greater after I quit drinking. I suppose I simply traded one compulsion for another. The difference is that unlike my drinking, I can control my firebug. I guess this Melody distraction is a blessing in disguise—it's tough to fixate on fire when somehow the fate of another—decent—human being is placed squarely on my shoulders, and when I close my eyes all I see is that picture of a smiling Melody; I see that or see her mother's tear–stained face. Her mother, fuck, I don't even know her name, what does it matter, all she wants in the world is to know her daughter is alive, maybe even be blessed enough to see her again. It's such a simple want, and for whatever reason I share it with her now. At the strangest and darkest times in my life, when everything has seemed to be innate chaos, nonsensical, not even coherent enough to be worthless—I never expected the next development, the next tick, the next hint—how a series of random events, people, places, and things somehow all come together to make sense. Resolution. I've never gotten used to it. To this day I'm still surprised when the fog clears and the events of days and weeks, months, and even years somehow warp together and form one clear and irrefutable conclusion. And it is a fleeting moment, that moment of clarity, just enough time to take maybe one breath, to have one thought, and then I find myself diving right into the next bizarre and unpredictable period of time, of events, of people, and days spent sleeping and nights spent on autopilot in my cab, and I drive the streets of Phoenix over and over, always wondering if the next person to get in is the next piece of the puzzle.

CHAPTER 41: NICK

"GRANGES? WHAT'S THAT?" I ask. I stand right next to Tim and Dante. We stand close, yet I feel so peripheral around them. There is this nervous energy between them, around them. The feeling it gives me is that I'm on the outside looking in, that there are big glaring secrets being held just out of my reach. *Please let me in on your little inside joke, please, pretty fucking please.*

"Not what. Who." Tim says. "Granges is a friend, a friend that's helping us sort this thing out."

Tim is so calm, almost too calm, as if the prospect of dealing with his insane nephew and his drugged–out crew of thugs is not particularly pressing, ordinary even. He shows no panic, no worry, and no anger even—just his massive air of pure fucking confidence. Who can be this relaxed in the face of these kinds of problems? Not me. I smoke one butt after another. I pour sweat. My head tingles with the dread of a bad mushroom trip, but this paranoia is real and it has my head on a swivel, looking around, expecting something to go wrong at any moment…my God, this fucking tension.

My heart skips a beat when a car pulls up to the gate; my finger travels to the trigger of the SMG. Tim holds a hand up.

"Relax," he says to me. "It's him. Open the gate, Dante."

"Let me check first, It's dark out here, could be anyone," Dante says.

"No, it's him. I know it is. Open the gate," Tim says.

Dante walks over and unlocks the padlock and swings the gate open. A silver–gray Lincoln pulls in. It looks like a cop car. The driver turns off his lights. Dante relocks the gate. The driver gets out and walks toward us. It's damn near pitch black out here but he knows his way I guess.

"Hello Granges," Tim says.

"Geddy. You and Ohio in one week. The world must be ending soon."

Tim shifts suddenly after this Granges guy says that, shows a rare startle. His words come out fast: "You talked to Ohio? Did you see him? How is he?"

"The same. Maybe worse. Shit, maybe he's better. I don't know. I told him he should call you."

"He won't."

"I know."

Granges walks up to Tim to shake hands; they both hesitate at the last minute and keep their hands to themselves.

This Granges guy walks to me. He stands right in front of me, uncomfortably close, just a few inches inside the normal distance people tend to keep from one another. I can't make out much of his face in the dark. His eyes are closed. The creepy feeling of being watched comes over me. Nobody speaks. Granges finally opens his eyes and looks straight at me.

"Geddy, you going to introduce me to your friend here?"

"Nick. That's Nick."

He puts out his hand and I shake. As I pull my hand away I notice the badge clipped onto his belt. This guy is a fucking cop?

Granges nods and says hello to Dante.

"It's good to see you, Granges," Tim says.

"You too, Geddy," Granges replies. *Why is he calling Tim "Geddy?"*

"I guess we should hurry it up, well, before, you know—"

"Yeah. We don't have much time. Not at all," Granges says.

"So what do you know?" Tim asks.

"After I got off the phone with you I called my buddy with the border patrol, told him I had a tip from a CI that a big gun or drug buy was going on in the desert past Three Points over by Hallow's Wash. They had a unit not far off and they picked up their trail. A spotter got them and a crew of local cops and border patrol got to them on their way out back to the 86, set up a road block and had em' pinned down. Your boys tried to go back on the trail, back into the desert, but they ran into another unit and had a little shootout. The border guys took two of them out. One border agent caught one in the neck and is critical. Two of your guys got away on foot. Based on the descriptions you gave me, it's likely your nephew was one of them. They found one of them about a mile away, shot in the head. I guess he was slowing your nephew down; there's no way he got that headshot before he made a run for it. So, Geddy, your nephew is somewhere out in that big spot of land. They'll find him eventually. He isn't going to last more than a day or two out there unless he has a horseshoe up his ass. Not this time of year. You know that land. Unless he lucks out and picks the right direction, he's pretty much fucked. He better pray the border guys find him in a day or so or he'll die out there."

"You said there were two guys dead at the scene, and two made a run for it, right?" I ask.

"That's right," says Granges.

"There were five guys out there: Jordo, Trevor, Saul, Grey, and Sean," I explain.

"They only counted four: three dead of gunshot wounds, and your nephew, out for a walkabout in that miserable fucking desert. Don't know about anyone else. Let me check."

Granges goes back into his car to make a call.

I turn to Tim. Something about this story about the Border Patrol getting the jump on Jordo and his crew doesn't sit right with me. "We need to make sure Jordo and whoever else gets taken out, they get caught they might sing, I—"

"Relax Nick. That happens and Granges will take care of it."

"Why would he do that?"

"Because he has to."

"But why?"

"He just does," Tim says.

Granges comes back from his car. "Yeah, they only saw four. The fifth guy wasn't with them. I'll have them check that wash and the surrounding area."

Tim starts to rub his forehead. He is pouring sweat and now wears a rare grimace of discomfort. I guess this is all finally starting to get to him, cracking that stoic exterior of his.

"Headache?" asks Granges.

"Yeah," Tim says. "It's bad. I don't remember it being this bad, this fast. I guess we're getting old, huh?"

"I feel it, too. Won't be more than a couple of minutes and we'll both be puking. Shit, you should have seen Ohio; I never saw someone get so sick so fast. He practically turned green."

"So what next?" Tim asks.

"Sit tight. I got it set up that your nephew is wanted for questioning on a drug rap up here, big case. So if they get him I'll get a sit–down with him for sure. That's a big if though. He isn't going to last long out in the middle of nowhere like that. As for the other guy that's unaccounted for, I'll see what I can do. Just watch your back for now. This'll all be over soon. Everything's going to be okay."

"Thanks, Granges."

"No problem. I suppose this is all part of some bigger plan. It always is."

He looks at me as he says that.

"Good to see you, my brother," Tim says.

Granges winks and gets back into his car. Dante opens the gate and Granges leaves. Tim falls to his knees and pukes violently, over and over. His entire body spasms and convulses as he pukes himself dry, hacking and wheezing. Dante motions for me to give him a hand and we carry Tim into the backseat of my Jeep. I crank the AC full blast. Tim tries to wave us off, but Dante finds a clean rag in the shed and wets it, brings it to Tim's brow. Tim sighs and soon falls asleep.

"I'll take him home," I say. "He's in no condition to drive."

"Okay," says Dante.

"Or should I take him someplace else? Maybe hide out for a bit; I know a spot up in Payson where we can lay low."

Dante shakes his head. "No, you don't need to worry. Everything is going to be okay."

"Really? And how do you know this? I'm not okay with jack shit until I know for a fact that Jordo and whoever else is still out there are dead or in cuffs."

"You don't have to worry Nick," Dante says. "Granges said everything was going to be OK."

I laugh. "Oh, well if Granges said everything is going to be okay, then no worries. Granges said everything is okay. Fuck, man, what is with you? The guy's a fucking cop, not a miracle worker. Or wait, maybe he's psychic? Is that it? Get the fuck out of here."

I get in my car and slam the door shut. I flip Dante off as he opens the gate for me. Fuck that crazy bastard.

I pull out onto the street and stop. I realize I have no idea where Tim lives. I lean back and nudge him to ask. He doesn't respond. I grip his arm hard and shake it. No response. I slide my fingers down his arm. His skin is cold and clammy. His breaths are weak, wheezy efforts. I check his pulse. It's faint. Something is very wrong here. I dial 9–1–1 and ask for an ambulance.

Don't die on me, Tim.

Chapter 42: Hack

I DON'T UNDERSTAND ANYTHING.

Chapter 43: NICK

"YOUR BOSS HAD A STROKE. A serious stroke," the doctor tells me. "It was a smart move to call the ambulance when you did. You might have saved his life."

I lean over the chart the doc is holding. I look at it as if I could actually understand a fucking thing written on it. I look back at the doctor. "*Might* have saved his life? What do you mean? Is he going to make it?"

The doc shrugs. "It's touch–and–go from here. We just have to wait it out and see how bad the damage is. Strokes can be like earthquakes. Sometimes there are mini strokes afterward, like aftershocks from an earthquake. We have to watch him closely for the next twenty–four hours. Can you notify his family? They should really be here."

I get Tim's cell phone from a nurse and find the number to his wife. It's almost six a.m. I wake her up with the horrible news. She is frantic. I get her calm enough to let her know where we are and that his situation is touch–and–go. I leave the waiting area and go outside to have a cig and think things over. I scroll through the rest of the numbers in Tim's phone, stop at Granges. Something tells me I should call him too.

The phone rings five times before Granges picks up.

"Christ, Geddy, I just got to sleep. What's up?"

"This is Nick. We just met at the yard. Tim had a stroke of some sort after you left. I don't know if he's going to—well, I just figured you should know. I don't know your relationship, but you seem close. The doc says its touch–and–go. I don't know. Fuck, it didn't look good when they put him in the ambulance."

Granges tells me he can't come to the hospital, he can't even come close; I guess he can't be seen near Tim. He makes me promise that I'll keep him up to date. Before he hangs up he lets me know that he'll keep me in the loop about the Jordo situation. He tells me to get rid of anything that could connect me to Jordo and his crew.

I go back to the waiting room in the ICU and sit amongst the hustling nurses and panicked family members. I fall asleep sitting up.

I awake to a hand on my shoulder.

"Nick?"

I open my eyes to a beautiful older woman. She has gorgeous thick reddish–blond hair and a mother's smile. I blink.

"I'm Meredith," she says. "Tim's wife."

I stand up to shake her hand. She hugs me instead. She smells like lilac. I stay in her arms until she releases me.

"Thank God you called the ambulance," she says, gripping the back of my neck. "The doctor said you might have saved his life."

She releases her grip on me. She is so gentle looking, almost hippy–like. I can't believe this woman is married to a hard–ass like Tim.

"Our daughters are on their way."

"I'm sorry Meredith. He's a tough guy, I'm sure he'll make it through this."

"Oh, don't buy that hard–ass routine he puts on. Trust me, you get him away from his work and he's a big teddy bear."

She smiles and then holds her hands to her face as she tears up. "I've been trying to get him to quit smoking for years, I know he gets so stressed about what he has to do, and…"

She goes on talking, but I'm stuck on "what he has to do." What does that mean? I don't know if it's from sheer exhaustion or what, but, again, I swear everyone around me has been talking in code all night.

Dante arrives. He and Meredith embrace. "Let's go into the chapel and pray," Dante says.

"Nick, will you come with us?" Meredith asks.

I look at her, notice the cross on her neck. Another holy–roller I guess. "Of course," I say. Now is not the time to tell them I have no idea what to pray to.

I follow them down the hall into the small generic hospital sanctuary. It has a few benches and a big plastic–looking cross. I follow their lead and kneel on the bench in front of the pew. I bow my head to my hands. The room goes silent.

Meredith prays: "Dear Father, please watch over Your faithful servant in his time of need. We pray not for our wants, but for the desire to be at one with whatever Your will may be. We ask for nothing but strength in the face of doubt, for peace in the face of pain, for understanding in the face of fear. Please watch over us as we seek to do Your will. Please guide us and direct us. We pray for the tormented souls, that their release may be swift and without hesitation. "Thank you our Father, Thy will be done. Amen."

"Amen," I say.

Meredith smiles as we get up. She puts a hand on my shoulder. "You're a good guy, Nick. Tim really likes you. He talks about you all the time." She stops and puts a hand on the side of my face. "I'm sure you question yourself, Nick. We all do. I'm sure you question the things you've done, the things you continue to do. But nothing happens without a reason. Ever."

She kisses me on the cheek and leaves the room. I start to follow her but Dante puts a hand on my arm. "You look tired, man. You should go home and get some sleep. I'll stay here for a while."

"Okay, Dante. Sorry I snapped on you earlier. It's just been a long fucking day." We stare at one another for a moment. "Nothing makes sense," I say.

"Don't worry about it. Everything will make sense soon."

He pats me on the back. I leave the hospital. Exhaustion sets in. I drive the ten miles home. I chain–smoke and squeeze my fingernails into my arm to stay awake. I get into my apartment and fall asleep on my bed with my clothes on, the SMG, vest, and big bag of money lying next to me.

CHAPTER 44: HACK

I'M SITTING ON THE HOOD OF MY cab outside a 7–Eleven, smoking and watching the last bits of pink daylight glow over the top of South Mountain. Something is wrong. I feel… it's the feeling you get when you realize you left the house without your wallet or your cell phone. But I have everything on me that I need: cigs, lighter, phone, wallet, and gun. There is unease. I watch a mother pull a dirty toddler into the store and then come out with her daughter in one arm and two tall cans of beer in the other. A demented bum, reeking of seven shades of awful, walks by me, mumbling. He checks the payphone change–return slot. He frowns a pathetic sad–puppy face when nothing comes out. I dig into my pocket and hand him a dollar. He tries to say thank you but his mouth is all rot. He can't speak. I nod and he moves on. A car pulls up next to me, a car full of younger guys blaring bass–heavy rap music. The rich scent of marijuana fills the air. A young guy, no more than seventeen or eighteen, gets out of the passenger seat and readjusts his tank top to cover the pistol he has tucked into his pants. He walks inside and buys a rack of beer. I watch the guys in the backseat fill little packets of what looks to be crack. They peel out of the parking lot without a care in the world. A truck pulls up and a worn–looking couple, white trash is the proper term, get out. They argue and hurl insults at one another as they scrounge through their pockets and the seats of the car for change. They find enough to buy a pint of cheap vodka.

I watch it all and I wonder what the fucking point is. I start almost every day telling myself that I'm going to work the nice parts of town, Scottsdale or the suburbs, drive in clean and compartmentalized areas that don't scream of desperation and weakness…maybe a little greed, but that's about it. I fucking hate to admit it but I just don't fit in anywhere but here. I guess it's not up to me anyway.

I get back in the cab and drink coffee, wait for a call to come in. It's a little early yet, I suppose. Give it a few hours and the streets come alive. My cell phone rings.

"Yeah."

"Ohio."

Fuck, its Granges. "Hey buddy," I say.

"Listen, I have to tell you something—"

I interrupt him. "You got any news about that Andre fuck I asked you about?"

"Yeah. I took care of him. No problem. But that's not what I am calling about—"

"What about Melody?" I interrupt him again. "Did you light a fire under the asses of the guys in charge of her case?"

"Yes. But listen, that isn't important right now, that's not why I called. Geddy's in the hospital. He had a stroke, and it was right after we saw each other. I don't know if he's going to make it. It's pretty bad."

I turn the cab off.

"Ohio? You still there?"

"Yeah. I just, I don't know what to say."

"I know. Look, something's going on. I feel it. I don't know if Tim having a stroke has something to do with it, but it's like, it's like—it's like I'm walking and the ground is moving under me in all different directions, yet I'm still walking straight and I have this feeling like everybody is fucked... and I'm the only one who knows about it...does that make any sense? "

"Yes, it does. A lot of sense, actually."

"I'm scared. I really am. Geddy might not make it. I don't know what happens when one of us dies."

I don't respond. An old, almost forgotten pain in my stomach resurfaces—that burning and tickling hollowness of a drunk's ulcer I suffered from years ago. Stomach acid crawls up my throat.

Granges goes on: "What if it all comes apart? What happens to us, Ohio? What happens when a wheel falls off?"

"I guess we won't know until it happens."

"So cold as always, Ohio. So cold. You know, I've never bought into this cynical front you put on. You know that, buddy? This fucking cold, nihilist, I–don't–give–a–fuck thing you have going on–I've never bought it for a second."

"Neither have I," I say.

A car screeches at a nearby intersection, nearly hitting oncoming traffic. Disaster is averted.

"I'm sorry," Granges says. "I don't mean to take it out on you. I'm sorry."

"Don't be. I'm not. I wouldn't change a thing if I could. I wouldn't change a fucking thing. Don't be afraid, Granges. We've come this far, right?"

"Yeah."

"A walking talking miracle from Vietnam, right?"

"You got it."

"Geddy's going to be just fine, Granges. One way or another, he's going to be just fine."

I hang up and get back inside the cab. A call comes in.

CHAPTER 45: NICK

I WAKE UP AND CHECK THE CLOCK. I slept a solid fourteen hours. I open the bag of money and run my hands through it. I always figured the sight and the feel of this much cash would be pure fucking exhilaration. I grew up watching movies where the hero or the villain got the big cash score and it always seemed like that neat pile of paper was the missing link to true happiness. But I'm disgusted. This isn't a fucking movie, where the money is always brand new and packaged in neat little bundles and fresh off the press. This money is real. It's dirty and stained and wrinkled, bound together with rubber bands in huge clumsy clumps. I know where this money came from. It is not anonymous. This cash bought a supposedly safe passage for who knows how many people; people looking to cross that invisible line in that desert and on to a better life. Each filthy bill in this bag was at one time as precious as anything to someone. It was a piece of their new life. Jordo told me about the bodies in the desert, the border crossers that got lost or abandoned and left to die on that brutal fucking scorched earth. I can't help but think about how many people used this money to buy an unmarked grave out in the middle of nowhere.

I guess with every booze–free day underneath my wings I regain a little piece of that bleeding heart I had once upon a time. Part of me doesn't want this money at all, even if it might be my ticket past my own invisible line toward a better life.

I stash the bag in that vent above my bed, where I find a Smith and Wesson .357 six–shooter I had forgotten about. I'm going to ditch the SMG and the vest and whatever else might tie me to Jordo and his crew, so the .357 will come in handy. I still need a piece. I have the Colt M4 in my Jeep but I need something to carry. Until I know for sure that Jordo and whoever else survived are either dead or in lockup, I need a gun. Fuck, for all that I've been through, I'll probably need one close to me for a long, long time. I'm okay with that.

I leave the apartment and go to a coin–operated car wash. I wash the car. I scrub and scrape at the tires to get the trail grit out. I spend ten minutes vacuuming the carpets. I toss out whatever trash is left. I leave the car wash and pull into a random alley to ditch the vest in a dumpster. Next I break down the SMG into parts and stop off at the canal to throw them in. I grab a new burner at a corner store. I then swing by Rebecca's to leave a note on her door: *hey beautiful, lost my phone in Tucson, sorry. Call me, pleassseeeee…* I leave my new phone number. I sign the note with a heart and a clumsy smiley face.

I pull out of her apartment complex and I shudder when I think about Jordo's threats. He said he would come after all those people in my phone if I ever crossed him. I don't doubt that he would. He has it in him to do pretty much anything. This whole thing is about done, I suppose; my foray from petty crime into assault, robbery, drugs, guns, and accessory to murder… I jumped right into the fucking deep end. I have the chance to get out before it consumes me and gets routine. I don't want to wake up every morning to yet another day in the ragged, diamond–bright landscape of violence and greed. *You hang out in the barbershop long enough and you're going to get your hair cut*—a Cajun guy I lived in a halfway–house with told me that, the same guy that confessed to me that he had killed a guy and dumped the body into a Louisiana swamp. *You hang out in the barbershop long enough and you're going to get your hair cut.*

I head over to the coffee shop to meet with Gary. I sit and drink two Americanos back–to–back. I chain–smoke and get that pure sun–enhanced tweak of caffeine and nicotine.

Gary sits down. "Didn't hear from you for a few days there," he says. "Thought we might have lost you to Jim Beam again."

"You'll never lose me to Jim Beam. Johnny Walker maybe, but never Jim Beam."

He laughs. "It's strange, Nick, you look worn out but you seem good. What gives?"

"I don't know. I guess I'm getting to the point where I can't even remember the last day I really craved a drink. So that's pretty fucking exciting. A little scary too, I mean, it's a strange thing to have something that was such a big part of me kind of slip away. I'm not expecting it to be permanent or whatever, but for now, the obsession is gone."

"Well, sounds like you're doing something right."

"I don't feel like that at all. I feel like I'm doing all the wrong things just to get to the right place."

"It works that way too. You fuck up enough and the last place on the block is—"

"Jails, institutions, and death," I say, repeating the well–worn AA phrase.

"Pretty much. So what about the second step?"

"I got it."

"You do?"

"Yeah. I don't know. I was in a strange spot the other day. I got to thinking about how I spent this night in detox before I got sober the first time. I don't think I've ever been as afraid as I was that night, waking up in a strange room, not knowing where I was or what I did to get there—assuming the worst, of course. I'd never felt that kind of terror before. It was like I was in some limbo of sorts, not knowing what had happened, but not necessarily wanting to know either, on the chance that whatever it was might be something I couldn't live with.

Well there was only one other guy in that detox, this old–timer drunk I guess—I never saw his face. He sounded old. Maybe not so much in his voice, but the way that he talked was just... weathered? He talked me down from that fear, and he told me about the fear, he told me that If I kept it up long enough, the drinking, that the fear wouldn't go away, not entirely, but a day would come when something worse came than fear, and that was indifference, indifference about who you are and what you are and what you may or may not have done. I think about that, Gary, I think about that indifference, and how close I've come to accepting it. But I never crossed the line. I came close, Gary, but I truly believe that there is still room for second chances for me. And—"

I take a long sip of espresso and a drag of my cig as I gather my thoughts. A low–flying jet passes overhead. I wait for its rumble to die down. "And if I can believe in that, believe that my life can still change directions in any crazy way, whether I want it or not, well, I guess I have no choice but to believe in something greater than myself. Do you know what I mean?"

"I guess so," Gary says. He grins. "To be honest I really have no fucking clue what you're talking about, but if it makes sense in that head of yours, well, that's all that matters. The book says "of your own understanding" for a reason. So if it makes sense to you, and you aren't bullshitting yourself—that's it."

"It does. It really does."

"Good stuff."

He starts talking about the third step and God and I start thinking about that prayer Meredith said while we were in the chapel, about how her voice was so sure and steady; with her husband dangling between life and death she said that prayer, and she meant it, too. Anyone can rattle off a prayer. I've heard a lot of prayers in my life, but I don't recall hearing many that sounded like much more than a formality. But Meredith's prayer—her prayer was real. She meant it. She believed. I'm not saying that I'm any closer to the God kick or anything like that, far from it, but if she can have that stout of a conviction, that must mean something. Right? Right?

Chapter 46: HACK

A SOBBING MIDDLE–AGED WOMAN flees from my cab and runs away into the underwhelming streets of downtown Phoenix. An hour earlier she was drinking and laughing with friends. Now she runs. Ordinarily I would feel some joy knowing that a piece of shit like her was running straight to her end, all hysterics and all alone, but tonight I can't get over the fact that even all–powerful me can't do much of anything when left to my own capabilities. Melody, you're out there somewhere, right? I close my eyes and see that smiling picture of you, but it warps into an image of you sprawled out on the floor in a filthy crackhouse; the image is of my own making, just like the naïve vision I had of you, it's such a delightful cliché, this image of you on a bus or an airplane staring out the window in wonder, as if all that you need to conquer your trashed life is a good solid change in geography. Can you please just find a way to drag yourself back to your mother's house, to see her and cure her of her sickness? While you're at it, can you please explain why I give a fuck about you, you a complete stranger, when the second–best man I've known is barely clinging to life in a hospital just a few miles away? I don't know the first thing about you, only your mother's claims that you're a good soul led astray, but what happens,

Melody, what happens if I do find you? What happens if you get in my cab and I take one look at you and something horrible pops up? What happens if you happen to turn out to be just like the hundreds of others who died well–deserved deaths mere minutes after they left me? How would I return to your mother if I find you and you turn out to be one of them, Melody? Am I supposed to tell her that I let you out of my cab and that your epoch ended with a crushed mess of blood and pulp and bones? I don't fucking know you, Melody, and you very well may not want to ever know me. So tell me why I should care. Tell me why I *do* care. Is this some sort of cruel fucking trick? Are you out there somewhere, laughing and taunting me? Do you even exist? Will you please, please, let Geddy live?

Chapter 47: NICK

A WEEK HAS PASSED. Tim is conscious now but the stroke has done a number on him. He can move his eyes and twitch his limbs, but all basic body functions are still monitored and controlled via machine and medicine. He isn't a vegetable but he won't be up and at them any time soon. More waiting, the doctors say. If he doesn't have any more strokes in the near future he may return to his old self. We just have to wait it out.

Meredith asked me to take over the crew for now. When she asked I wasn't entirely sure if she meant the contracting crew or the other crew—which I guess is all but gone now anyway. I take on the construction work. I get up at obscenely early morning hours and lead the workers in any number of simple but tough tasks. The hours suck and the heat is near torture but at the end of the day the only thing I bring home with me is weariness. I like that.

Rebecca and I sit in bed. We smoke in bed. We talk for hours about what it was like, what happened, and what it's like now. She tells long stories. Her smoky voice gives her stories a fairy tale feel. Her words float in the air as I run my fingers over her perfect skin. I sit with her and covet her presence. I've never felt this way about a girl before. Not even close. I talk into the dark. I have the urge to unload the days and events that have passed since I left the tents. I want to tell her about this strange and unexpected odyssey, how I found myself again by letting whatever moral and ethical barometer I had fall to a level just above sociopath. But I can't tell this sort of truth to a sweet little girl I'm crazy in love with. I can't tell her that mere days ago I beat people within an inch of their lives, that I spent sweat–soaked evenings in the middle of the desert with stone–cold killers and big piles of money and guns and trouble everywhere. How could I tell someone so perfect that I'm really fucking flawed, that the heart of me is flexible in disturbing ways?

Rebecca and I fuck all the time. I sometimes look up at the ceiling mid act. I eye the vent where that big rotten bag of money is stashed and I wonder what in the hell to do with it. The sex with Rebecca is as good as it gets, but even the best sex in the world doesn't create the blood–boiling lust that money does. I had that initial revulsion with the money and its history, but I have since come to the conclusion that money is money, and that if I'm really going to go straight it will be a hell of a lot easier with a little cash in my pocket. Besides, every fucking dollar bill has some sordid history to it, doesn't it? Isn't that what makes it so precious?

CHAPTER 48: NICK

Three weeks later.

I'M TAKING ON BIGGER PROJECTS with Tim's contracting business. He used the contracting as a cover for his "real" work, but that's all gone now. There is no reason why the legit business can't make a few more honest bucks. I get in good with a few banks around town and get constant offers for foreclosure cleanups and rehabs—one booming industry in the current financial free fall. It sucks to be the one that has to wipe away any memories from a house that was recently someone's home—not just a house, but a home—but I have seven hard workers that count on this gig to keep them afloat, so fuck it. We work hard. We endure. We turn homes back into houses. I come home every day to a nice new condo full of toys and a gun safe packed with cash. Rebecca sleeps over a few nights a week. We sleep in a big bed. We sleep well.

Tim's getting better by the day. He can now move his arms and point his hands. The muscles on his face are partially paralyzed for now and he can't speak, but at least he's here. The person has returned. This person, I realize, is someone I really don't know at all. The Tim

I knew at work on the job site or in the streets or the desert—I gather from talking to Meredith that that was more of a role he was playing than anything.

"But Tim adores you, Nick," Meredith tells me. "We had two daughters and Tim never said it but he wouldn't have minded having a son, so he gets his heartstrings tugged on a bit when he meets a young man like you. Jordo never did that for him because, well, Jordo is Jordo."

The name makes my skin crawl. No word about Jordo. No body, no info whatsoever about where he is or what happened. Nothing. Same goes with Grey. The fed's identified all the other bodies, and it turns out that my buddy Grey is the other mystery. No clue as to what happened to him either. I hope they are both dead. I really do. If they're still alive, they'll come around sooner or later. I keep the .357 on me at all times.

Granges calls me once or twice a week. I'm still not clear on the nature of his relationship with Tim, or "Geddy," as he calls him. I figured Granges for a dirty cop at first, but the more I talk to him it's clear that isn't the case. Quite the opposite actually. This guy lives and breathes for his work, for busting the bad guys and justice or whatever the fuck you want to call it. His love for his work makes his relationship with Tim that much more bizarre—how the fuck does a cop not just associate with but *love*; love a guy like Tim, someone who has spent years on the other side of the law? I don't ask. I don't need an answer to that mystery. I have taken on the task of giving Granges the updates on Tim's health, and after that's done we shoot the shit. Our conversations come naturally. I tell him about my past, how I got a pretty good grasp on this sobriety thing right now and I'm committed to playing it straight from now on, no booze, no drugs, and no illegal shit. "I just want to be fucking normal for once in my life," I tell him, "I just want to fucking feel normal." Maybe I talk too much. When you spend enough time in AA meetings and talking to AA people you tend to forget that normal people don't unload on others the way that recovering drunks do. But Granges is more than willing to listen. I guess Jordo was right; I really do have daddy issues. Granges has an odd way of looking at things. His responses sometime baffle me. I tell him about how I never want to be close to that edge again, or do the things I've done, those acts that now I look back at with dread, baffled that I was able to do them. I tell him how I can't believe I did this or that and how I'll never do that again. I'd expect someone like Granges, a superstar cowboy of a cop, to give me a stern remark like, "That's good, son, you be sure to be true to your word and never make those same mistakes, I'd hate to see you go down that route," but he never says stuff like that. When I talk about my past, my guilt, and my desire to change, he responds with cryptic comments like: "Don't try and predict the future when you still don't understand that past," and other similar baffling shit. I want to shout at him, "I need a little fucking stern reinforcement here, can you please tell me, lecture me even, that the things I did were not okay under any circumstances; put the fear of God in me that if I ever do them again I am fucked nine ways till Tuesday!" Is that so much to ask from a fucking cop?

I don't understand this Granges guy, but I sure as fuck like him. He is truly a magnificent human being, and the fact that he and Tim have this strange relationship or connection or whatever you want to call it—it makes life that much more confusing and exhilarating. And this Ohio guy that sometimes comes up, the way he talks about him—I hope to one day to get at least part of the story about these three guys and what it is that binds them, beyond the simple, "We spent some time in a war together and then lost touch. Years later, we found each other again." That's how the story starts and ends, for now.

CHAPTER 49: NICK

One week later.

TIM IS OUT OF THE HOSPITAL. He's walking with a cane and slurs his words a bit, but he's back. Another stroke is possible and always will be, but as he says, "the possibility of a fucking fatal car crash or meteor landing on my head, or a freak bathtub accident or total apocalyptic nuclear war is always there as well, and always has been, so I'm not going to walk around afraid of something I have no control over."

Tim has chosen to retire, retire from everything. He actually laughs when I offer to buy the contracting business from him. I tell him that retirement will be a hell of a lot easier with that money, but he laughs it off.

I'm bringing him to the storage yard to gather some tools he wants to keep and we have this conversation again. I plead with him to let me buy the company; that it's worth more than I can pay. He again insists that I take it as a gift and that I keep using that money in my safe as a head start on my new life. He confesses that he hasn't even thought about money for years and the truth is that his work made him a millionaire over ten years ago.

"I have enough money to do whatever I want really—" he says. He stops mid–sentence to correct himself when the slurring gets bad. "Funny thing is, I don't want much. Yeah, I could buy that monster house on Camelback Mountain or in Paradise Valley, I could buy a Ferrari or three, I could live the rest of my life in the lap of fucking luxury. But I've never been about the money. It's never been about that. Me and Meredith, all we want is to move up north a ways, maybe Prescott, get a nice little piece of land and live in peace for once, away from this fucking city. That's about it. So you take the business, you keep that money; you carve out a nice little simple life with that young lady you're so sweet on. I'm sure you two are going to be married one day. I am sure of that. It's in the cards, Nicky, trust me."

I chuckle. "Oh yeah? You read my fortune? You catch a glimpse of the future?"

"Something like that," he says. "I just have a hunch."

It's dark by the time we get to the lot. Tim is getting tired. He gets tired easily since the stroke. He gets out of the car and I take a moment to reflect on our conversation. I want to ask him why, if he never did work for the money, then what was the point? What did he get out of it? Was it just for the thrill? Why the hell would you do the things he did if it wasn't for the money?

Now is not the time for that heavy of a conversation. He's too tired for that. We'll just get those tools and I'll bring him home to Meredith. After all, as Gary always says, I don't have to know everything. Nor should I.

I unlock the gate and open it. We pull in and get out.

"You miss this lovely piece of paradise," I say, holding my hand out to the yard, presenting the battered shed, the rusted garage, the scattered car parts, the weeds and the blight, to the dreary industrial land that surrounds us.

"No. This will be my last time here, thank God."

"Well I'll keep it the way it is in case you ever get sentimental and want to come back for a visit."

We laugh, and I'm about to make another joke when he quiets suddenly. I watch his face turn back to that cold, rigid look of the Tim I used to know, that role he used to play. He stares directly ahead. I follow his gaze to the shed. Two figures emerge from the dark and step toward us.

"Hello, Uncle. Hello, Nick."

Jordo.

Jordo has a Glock aimed at Tim; Grey has one of those SMGs leveled on me.

"We've been here for two fucking days, waiting in this fucking lot, nearly sweating to death in that fucking shed—waiting for you, Nick. We knew you'd be back here soon enough. We visited Dante a few days ago. He wasn't a very gracious host. He didn't seem very happy to see us. Can you believe that? He wasn't much in the mood for conversation, but after Grey got to working on him he sang. He sang beautifully. He told us all about your wonderful new life, Nick. Nick the contractor, with his new business. I'm so happy for you, Nick. You've really dug out a nice little future huh, Nick, putting in long hours with your hands, making a good honest wage, strong productive member of society, huh, Nicky? So we knew we could hide out here and you'd come by eventually. But Uncle Tim, we didn't think we'd get to see you, too. Dante told us about the stroke and all, we figured we'd have to come by and pay a visit some time, check up on you and your recovery. Saves us a trip I guess. It's good to see you, Uncle."

"What do you want, Jordo?" Tim asks.

"I have to tell you, Uncle, it bums me out to see you like this. Uncle Tim, badass Uncle Tim, shot caller, mean motherfucker, now crippled and slurring his words. Total bummer."

"What do you want, Jordo," I ask.

"Nick. I've been excited to see you; I mean truly treasuring this moment for two months. You see, I was pretty disappointed in you that night you sucker-punched me like a little bitch and bailed on us with our money. I was pretty disappointed in you. I felt like I had raised a cute but dumb little puppy only to have it bite me when I looked away. I really thought you'd come around, but Grey was right. I was stupid to think you'd come along for the ride. Shit, I was stupid to let you live. I should have just buried you next to Tick. I guess the coke made me a little reckless. There, I admit it; I might have overdone it with the partying. By the way, you ever come off a week–long booze and coke bender in the middle of the fucking desert? Not pretty, man. I almost died from that alone. I crawled, Nick—I fucking crawled my way back to the wash. The stupid fucking feds didn't find us and they didn't find the ATVs. We rode out straight to old man Jake's spot. I got a helluva memory; thank God, probably saved us. I knew the way."

I take a step toward him. "Jordo, if you want the money we can go get it."

Grey walks up and puts the barrel of his gun between my eyes.

"Shut the fuck up, Nick. We'll get to that," says Jordo. He turns back to Tim. "I'm sorry, Uncle, but we had to off your old friend Jake. I always liked him, but it had to be done. We offed him nice and quick, he didn't suffer, and we hid out in his spot. We were going to go down to Mexico, but we ended up just staying at his place. Talk about fucking boring. Almost two fucking months of sitting in his dump of a house, doing jack shit, just waiting it out. We figured there was no way you'd tell the fed's about Jake's place. I guess we were right, huh? No way you'd have them crawling all over an old con's home. Who knows what they'd find on that piece of land, huh? So we waited for the heat to die down, which it did. I guess the fed's got other things to worry about."

"I wouldn't be so sure. You guys shot a border patrol agent. They don't forget that," I say.

"It doesn't matter. I don't care. I don't give a fuck. Really. And seriously, Nick, shut your fucking mouth. If you talk again I'm going to have Grey go in the shed and grab a pair of those pruning shears and remove your fucking tongue. That's your biggest problem, Nick, you put way too much trust in that dumb fucking brain of yours. You aren't that bright, Nick, hate to break it to you. I mean, I liked you, you're a good guy to have around, but you're always going to be more of an extra than a feature performer, know what I mean? But you did disappoint me, bro. I don't think you know how upset I was when you took off like that. I wanted to go after you, but Sean was smart enough to point out that we were minutes away from a rather large deal, and we'd have plenty of time to find you when that was over. Big dumb motherfucker like you, you'd be easy to find. So we did the deal and then out of nowhere came that fucking helicopter and the feds. We made a good go of it, but they had us pinned down. Trevor got dropped, then Saul. Grey got away right when the shooting started, then me and Sean took off. Unfortunately Sean got exhausted and couldn't go on and I wasn't going to leave him like that, just waiting to get picked up, and they could make him talk, I knew it, so I had to put him down. By morning I was stumbling, then crawling. I gave up. I really did. I was ready to go. And would you believe it, here comes Grey on the ATV, trying to find his way out and he found me instead. Very lucky."

"Why are you telling us this, Jordo?" Tim says. "It doesn't fucking matter. Just tell us what you want."

"Uncle, I spent the last two months sitting in that shithole house of Jake's thinking that Nick dropped the dime on us. I spent every fucking minute thinking about all the things I was going to do to Nick to punish him for what he did. I had it all planned out. You wouldn't believe the things I was going to do. Pretty fucked up, I will admit. Then I get up here and go have a talk with Dante and he tells me that you, *you*, Uncle Tim, you called in the cavalry on us. I couldn't believe it at first, an old–school guy like you, talking to the feds, snitching? No way. But Dante got into some heavy shit about you and this cop, Gredges or whatever the fuck it is. I think Dante was kind of losing it at this point from all the pain; Grey really did a number on him. It wasn't pretty. Dante starts telling us this story about you and this cop and magical powers and shit, it was pretty far out stuff, and to be honest, I even started to feel sad for Dante, I guess we fucked him up so bad that his mind started going haywire, so I put him out nice and quick. I always liked Dante. Well no, I didn't actually. Fuck him. Anyway, that's not the point. The point is you saw it fitting to set up your own fucking flesh and blood, your family? Why? Because I did a few jobs behind your back? Because I didn't follow your every order? Because I have a fucking mind of my own, unlike this zombie fuck?"

He points his gun at me.

"You were looking to take me out, Jordo. What did you expect me to do about it?"

"I don't know, be a fucking man? Battle it out like a fucking man? Maybe I was going to come up here and take over, but the man I thought you were, he would have fought tooth and nail, not run to his cop buddy and squeal like a fucking faggot. You lost your edge, Uncle, and I was right to want to take over. It was the right move, and everything got fucked. I actually blame you, Nick. You came around and started following around my uncle like a lost puppy and he gets all soft and comes unglued. You both are fucking insects, you know that?"

Tim steps forward to Jordo, so Jordo's Glock is just inches from his chest. "What do you want, Jordo? You want to kill us, just get it over with. No need for any more talk. Just get it over with."

"Well it goes without saying that both of you are fucking dead. But just killing you—that's not very satisfying. I would like you both to know and appreciate the extent to which I am upset with you. I can talk all night, but talking doesn't do shit. We're going to go on a little trip tonight, go visit some people so I can show you how upset I am. Show you."

"What do you mean?"

"I'll leave your daughter's alone. I always liked my cousins. But Meredith, she never liked me, did she? That was obvious. Maybe when you're watching Meredith gasp for her last fucking breath you can see—"

Jordo doesn't have time to finish his sentence. Even crippled and weak, Tim gets on him pretty quick. Jordo isn't much in the strength department. Tim gets his arms around Jordo's waist and drags him to the ground. They hit the dirt and Tim starts to get the upper hand as he struggles to free the pistol from Jordo's hand. Grey moves the barrel away from me and points it down at Tim, but they're moving too much to get a shot off. Grey fucks up and stops paying attention to me. I have that .357 in my waistband. I get it out and with no hesitation I level it at Grey and pull the trigger twice. One shot misses, the other gets him square in the chest. He flies backward, dropping his gun. He lands right next to Jordo and Tim, and for a moment they stop wrestling and they stare at Grey, who starts to sputter and spit up blood. I move toward them to help Tim. Jordo takes advantage of the halt in action and gets the Glock to Tim's stomach and pulls the trigger three times. I freeze. The sound of the three shots echoes in the streets. Tim lets out an *"oooomph"* and goes completely limp, his body smothering Jordo. Jordo struggles to get the weight off him and frees the hand with the Glock. I take a step away and another three shots go off. I hit the ground with this burning, biting pain in my shoulder and in my calf. Two more shots go off, both miss me. I roll over and aim my gun toward Jordo. He has pushed Tim's body off. I'm about to squeeze another round off when I notice that Tim is still breathing. I can't take the shot at Jordo, not with Tim so close. Jordo peels off a couple more shots, but I make it to the side of the shed without getting hit. I take the .357 and blast two shots around the corner, aiming up well above them; it buys me a couple seconds to grab the SMG from Grey's body in front of the shed. I hear footsteps and peer around the wall to see Jordo run around to the other side of my Jeep. He puts his hand up over the hood to squeeze off a shot and I let out a long pull from the SMG, burying at least half the clip into the hood of the car. He stumbles back. I duck down the driver's side of the car and Jordo pops up and squeezes the trigger frantically until his mag is empty. A round shatters the window of my

Jeep. Glass flies everywhere. I catch a piece in the eye and am blinded for a moment. I hear footsteps again and I pop up, half blind, and with the good eye I watch Jordo sprint out from behind the car and through the open gate. I raise the SMG and spray the rest of the rounds after him. I miss. He runs off. I start to go after him. I stop when I hear wheezing in the sudden silence. Tim is still breathing. I fall down next to him. His eyes are open. His breaths are shallow. He stares up above.

"I—was right about not worrying about the strokes, huh," he says. He laughs and then wheezes.

"You're going to make it. I'll call an ambulance. But Jordo got away, I gotta go get him."

I stand up and he puts a hand on my ankle.

"No. Stay here. Don't worry about Jordo. He'll get his. He'll get his. Stay here. I don't—"

He coughs and then grabs his stomach. His white tee shirt is slick and red with blood; there are at least two or three gunshot holes. I take off my shirt and put it on his stomach. I dial 9–1–1. There are already sirens in the distance. That many gun shots—somebody heard and called the police. I tell the 9–1–1 operator to get an ambulance here ASAP, there's been a shooting.

"Fuck, I dodged all those fucking bullets in the jungle and now my own goddamned family kills me," he laughs again, mists of blood shoot from his mouth with each word. He chokes and gasps for air.

"Bullshit, the ambulance will be here any second," I say.

He makes a strange slurring noise and then convulses violently. He goes still.

I shake him. No response. I shake until I feel dizzy—fuck, I've been shot twice—I shake and I shake and his body is limp and ragged but then his eyes open again and he looks at me with an incredible lucidity. He speaks without any slurring or wheezing.

"I'm terribly sorry to do this Nick, but it has to be done. I have to pass it on, I know that now. I'm so sorry to have to do this to you."

He grabs my wrist and squeezes it with surprising strength; I don't think I could free myself from it if I wanted to. It's that strong. An incredible feeling of heat comes over me, starting from my hand and then spreading to every inch of my body; it amplifies the pain in my shoulder and calf a thousand times over, and I gasp with the pain, then the heat disappears into an incredible chill, like being plunged into an ice bath, the pain is gone for a moment, everything is gone for a moment, and the heat returns again, only for a split second, and then it all ends with an incredible blinding–quick jolt of electricity that surges throughout my body.

I collapse and gasp for air. I look up and expect to see stars but see the polluted fog mist instead. *You have been shot Nick,* I tell myself. *You might die. You might bleed to death on this ugly lot of land.* No thanks. I gather the strength and rise up on my knees. Tim puts his hand on my knee. He smiles at me. "I'm sorry. It had to be done. You'll learn to live with it. It had to be done Nick, you'll get it eventually. You just be sure to keep that girl close, she's the one for you, she'll always be there, I prom—"

He dies mid–word. It isn't like the movies where death comes quick and dignified. He gasps and trembles and oozes and coughs, then finally goes limp. I don't bother to shake him or beg him to come back.

"Help," a ragged voice calls out.

I turn toward Grey. I guess he's still alive. Blood spews from his mouth. He coughs and gurgles his words. "Help me. Please help me. Plu hep me…"

I stand up and tower over him. Our eyes meet. He begs me. I raise my foot over his head and stomp it down right on his face. I do it over and over. I do it over and over until he is stone cold fucking dead.

Chapter 50: HACK

NOT GONNA FIND THIS MELODY. Not ever. I don't find people. They come to me. Sorry, old lady, I put some muscle behind your case, it's the best I could do. Sometimes the streets chew you up but they don't always spit you out. I drove all over this fucking city, through every shitty street, past the crack houses, the junkie flops; I smiled at the low-rent whores, winked at the Mexican gangbangers with face tattoos, had a staring contest with the dead, money–hungry eyes of the brothers, I honked my horn at the skittish white trash meth peddlers; I crept and crawled and hemmed and hawed. I shucked and jived; I flipped rocks and wasted time. But at least I tried. I'm sorry it was all a waste. I tried to get down and look at it all from the ground up, my face pressed against the shards of broken bottles, fast food wrappers, cigarette butts, sand and dust bunnies, condom wrappers…fuck it, I cared as long as I could.

Enough slumming it. I dropped off a fare at a tow lot and now I'm heading out of this rotten red–light industrial wasteland, back to the bright lights of college and commerce. Tonight I am going to ferry college kids from bar to bar and I am not going to read a single fucking person. I want, for one night, to feel like everyone else and have that sweet and simple one–track mind of money, money, money.

A pedestrian flags me down after I pass an iconic strip club. I didn't plan on stopping but I do. Old habits die hard. This guy doesn't as much get in my car as he explodes into it. Someone is in a hurry.

"Drive!"

I take one look at the panic in his eyes and let him know my rule: "Tweakers and crackheads pay up front."

"Christ," he says. "Do I look like a fucking crack or meth head to you?" He's right about that. He doesn't. He might be sweat soaked and disheveled, but he's wearing designer clothes. He digs into his pocket and pulls out a Franklin, tosses it at me. "Drive.'

"Where to?"

"Fuck. I don't know, just go, fuck, just take me to AJ."

"Apache Junction? You sure? That's an expensive ride."

"Just fucking go!"

I do as he commands. I take the exit onto the 10 and head east.

"Where in AJ are we going?"

"It doesn't matter."

"Okay, anywhere in AJ it is."

I avoid looking in the rearview mirror as long as I can, but this smell in the cab is really starting to get me. It brings back a lot of memories.

"Hey buddy, you sort of smell like gun powder, you know that?"

He coughs. "I'm surprised you can smell anything over the fucking reek of this cab. Do you live in this fucker or something?"

"It feels like it," I say.

I light a cig, offer him one. He accepts it without a word.

"It's polite to say thank you after someone gives you something," I tell him.

"Thanks for the lesson, Mrs. Manners. I gave you a hundred bucks already; forgive me if I don't offer to blow you for one of your shitty cigarettes. But hey, if you have anything to drink, I will definitely thank you for that."

"Sorry, man, I gave up the bottle years ago. We can stop if you'd like."

"Fuck it, just get me to AJ."

I glance at him through the mirror and nod. In that split second, it all comes together. It always does. I see. I see everything.

The 10 turns into the 60. Traffic is light. I flip on the radio and try to ignore the manic explosion of thoughts that race in my head. I shut the radio off. Fuck it. It has to be done.

"You like girls?"

"What?"

"Girls? You were at the titty bar right?" I ask, even though I know he wasn't.

"Sure. I like girls. Why?"

"You like black broads?"

He laughs. "Sure. I like them all. Why? You got jungle fever, old timer?"

"Something like that."

He laughs again. "As great as talking about women sounds, I think I would prefer to spend the rest of this ride in silence. I've got a pretty wicked hangover coming on, so please, just get off on Tomahawk and make a left on Baseline."

"You got it, Jordo," I tell him.

I get off on Tomahawk, head south toward Baseline.

"What's the address?"

"I don't know. Just take a left on Baseline and I'll remember it from there."

I don't. I blow right past Baseline, heading south on Tomahawk, past the edges of AJ and on toward open lands.

"Hey, moron, you just passed Baseline. I said take a left on Baseline."

I don't respond. I put my foot down on the pedal and rev it up from forty–five to fifty–five.

He slaps the back of my seat.

"You having an aneurysm? You missed the turn. Turn around, fuckwad."

I gun it up to seventy in response. He utters a few obscenities and the slaps me on the back of the head. I gun it up past ninety.

"Don't want to touch the driver," I say. "We're doing a hundred. These old cop cars have some juice left, but at this speed I move the wheel just a little too much and we're going for a roll, Jordo."

"Wait, how the fuck do you know my name? Slow down! Slow down, you cocksucker!"

He emphasizes each word with a slap on the back of my seat.

I get it up to a hundred and ten. This road doesn't lead to many places. There are no other cars. I pull into the middle of the road and watch the speedometer max out.

"Look, I don't know if you're having a stroke or this is your idea of fun, fucking with me like this, but you don't pull over and let me out right now, I'm going to rip your fucking throat out. Got it? So take a deep breath and pull over. Now."

I light a cig and shrug my shoulders.

"Let me out," Jordo tells me. "I got money on me, you can have it all. Just let me out."

"You got it," I reply.

I pump the breaks and slow the car down to seventy. I spot a trail spur ahead leading off the paved road. At the last possible second I swerve onto the off road. The car screeches and fishtails, slides halfway around, I spin the wheel just in time to keep from flipping. Jordo rolls around in the back. I get control of the cab and point it in the right direction. I gun it again. The wheels scream against the rough dirt road. We catch air a couple of times. It gets dark fast; we head into the nothingness of desert, no ambient light, the lights of civilization blur in the distance. I can only see about ten feet ahead of us. I don't know what's next. I'm letting go; we might hit a rock or a rut any moment and crash a violent crash. Faith keeps me going. Jordo lets out an ear piercing, desperate, shrill scream, the scream of a man fully aware that he has no control over anything anymore. That's what I'm looking for. I hit the brakes hard.

Jordo slams into the back of my seat. I can always count on that. No one ever wears a seat belt in a cab. The cab comes to a complete stop. I slip my brass knuckles onto my hand as I get out. I open the back door. Jordo is sprawled out, half on the floor. I pull him out by his ankles. He hits the ground.

"What the fuck is this?"

He tries to get up off the ground but I give him a good push with my boot and he rolls over. He sprawls back and makes another effort to get up, grabs my leg and tries to wrestle me down. I crack him hard in the ribs with the brass knuckles. He releases his hold on me and gasps, grabbing his ribs. He coughs and swallows air.

"What the fuck, you robbing me? Fine, just take the fucking money." He pulls out a rubber banded wad of bills and pushes it toward me. I take the cash and pull one bill out at a time, rip each up and let the pieces sprinkle on top of him. "What the fuck is this?" he asks.

He scoots backward and then shouts "Help!" three times, each louder and longer than the previous.

"No one is going to hear you," I tell him.

"Just tell me what you want, you crazy fuck." He shakes his head and spits. "What do you want? You don't want money? What the fuck is this? What the fuck do you want?"

"I want you to tell me a story," I tell him.

"What?" He props himself up on his forearm. "What do you mean?"

"I want you to tell me a story."

"I—I don't understand. What the fuck is this? Are you some sort of fucking psycho or something? You don't know who you're fucking with. You try to pull any more shit with me—"

I pull my pistol out from the small of my back and aim it down at him.

"Oh fuck," he says.

"Tell me a story."

"Okay, okay, but, okay what do you want, I don't get it. I don't speak fucking crazy, okay? Explain what you want from me, and I'll do my best."

"Tell me about Melody."

"I—I don't know what that is! I, I, I don't understand—"I swing to the side of him and kick him in the arm then dig the toe of my boots against the bone. "Not what! Who! Tell me about Melody! Tell me the fucking story about Melody!"

He grabs his arm and writhes, shaking his head. "I don't know, I don't know," he repeats.

I put my boot down on his chest, lean down, and put the barrel of the gun on his forehead.

"I want you to tell me about that night you partied with Melody, that pretty black stripper. You and your friends had that escort service deliver her, remember?" I put some pressure on the barrel so it digs into his skin. He pulls his head back until it's on the ground. He has nowhere to go. I push the steel into his skull, increasing the pressure every few seconds, repeating "Melody...Melody...Melody..."

Finally he holds his hands up. Dust settles around us from our commotion. There are lights in the distance but they might as well be a million miles away. Everything is a little colder out here.

Jordo speaks. "Okay, okay. I remember. It was a couple months ago. We were in a motel. We got fucked up and we were supposed to go to meet up with these girls but we decided to pre–party some more and we called the escort service and she came and danced and we offered a little extra and she fucked us. Why? Why do you want to know this? What is this? What the fuck is this?"

I pull the barrel off his forehead. He puts a hand up to his forehead and rubs at the mark the barrel left, then scoots back a few feet. I give him a moment. He turns his head and looks all around. There isn't much to see.

"Thinking about making a run for it?"

"Just let me go, man. Just let me go."

"Why?"

"Why what? Why what, you crazy fuck!?"

"Why should I let you go?"

"What else do you want? Just tell me. What else? I have friends, I can get whatever you want, trust me. Just let me go. I did what you asked. I told you about Melanie."

"Her name is Melody," I scream. I kick him again, this time in his hip. He flops around, makes another desperate grab for me. I kick dirt into his eyes and he falls back.

"Her name is Melody," I say.

"Fine. Melody. Who gives a shit?" He wipes the dirt off his face and chuckles. "Who gives a shit," he repeats. He falls back and sprawls out, looking up above. "Who gives a shit," he says again, laughing as if a punch line for a joke finally set in.

"I do. Her mother does. People do."

He looks up at me, his eyes bleary and red from the desert grit.

"I don't understand," he says. Then he screams: "just tell me what you fucking want."

"Tell me about Melody. Tell me about that night."

"I did! I did!"

I put my boot back down on his chest and sink my weight down on him. He tries to push it off but the kid is fucking weak.

"No, you didn't. You didn't tell me the story. You didn't tell me the true story. I want you to tell me about that night with Melody."

He howls. "Just fucking kill me. Fuck you. You want to give me a beating, you sick fuck? You get off on this shit? Go ahead. Give it your best. Kill me, you pussy. Fuck you!"

"I'm not going to kill you. That's the good news. The bad news is that I *will* break bones. I *will* push the barrel of this gun into your eye socket until your eyeball is mush and dead. I *will* do everything and anything up to the point of killing you, to the point that you might actually crave death just to not have to feel so much pain. So again, I'm going to give you one last chance before it gets a lot worse for you. Tell me about Melody, Jordo."

"Fucking Christ, how do you know my name!? How do you know?!!"

I shrug.

He wraps his hands around my boot and makes another pathetic attempt to push me off. I laugh. He gives up, grunts, and then drops his hand to his sides.

"Fine," he says. "We got fucked up and she came over. She danced for us. We got a little too hands–on and she tried to leave. We apologized and gave her some more money. She danced some more, gave us lap dances and all that shit. We gave her booze and coke and she danced and danced. We got bored. We tried to give her money to blow us; me, Sean, and Grey. She refused and tried to leave again. I got a little carried away. I hit her. She clawed my face. I got a little worked up about that and I started smacking her around a bit. Then, well—"

He trails off, stops speaking.

"What happened next, Jordo? What happened next?"

"How do you know my fucking name? I never told you my fucking name! Please, tell me what this is. I need to know what this is! Please. Please. Please! This doesn't make any fucking sense." He screams for help again. The sound doesn't even echo.

I lean down and start to press the barrel of my pistol into his eye. He tries to twist away so I put my knee down on his throat, holding the back of his head with my free hand.

"Stop! Stop!" He tries to shout, his voice weak and hoarse from the pressure on his throat.

"Finish the story," I tell him.

I move the barrel out of his eye socket.

"Okay," He says. "Okay!" He screams. "We fucked her! We fucked that bitch every which way! We pinned her down and we fucked her every which way. We fucked her up the ass until she bled, and then we gave her some downers and when she passed out we took her out and dumped her off in a parking lot somewhere! Yes! That's what we did! We ran a fucking train on her and then dumped her off in some fucking parking lot. So fucking what!?"

"Are you sorry?"

He laughs at me. "No. I'm not. We got a little rough with some dope–head whore. It comes with the territory. Big fucking deal. You think anyone gives a fuck about some fucking street trash? Big fucking deal." His head falls back on the desert road and he starts laughing. He cackles. He howls. "So fucking what!"

I step away from him, bringing my gun down to my side. "That's all I wanted to know. You can go now."

He pushes himself up to a sitting position and looks up at me. "Are you serious?"

I nod. "I'm getting back in the cab and driving away. You can follow this old road back to the paved road, head north, and you're back in civilization. Maybe you get lucky and thumb a ride. It'll be a bit of a walk, maybe a little dark, but you're free to go."

He studies me for a moment. "What are you?"

"Just a cab driver."

I turn around to walk back to the cab.

"No!" He shouts. "You have to tell me what this was about! Who are you? What is this! You have to tell me!"

"No, I don't, Jordo. I don't have to do anything," I say. I get to the cab and open the door. "Well, there is one more thing," I say.

"What?"

I walk back to him and point the gun at this head.

He shrieks. "I thought you said, you said you weren't going to kill me!"

"I'm not."

With his eyes on the gun I bring up my boot and slam it down on his right hand. The little bones in his hand snap like twigs. He screams and rolls over. I take the opportunity to stomp on his other hand. I stomp until both of his hands are a shattered mess.

"That's for Geddy." I say. "That's for your Uncle Tim. Good luck on the walk home."

I leave him there, screaming and writhing all over that desert road. I start the cab and blast the AC. Holy fuck, am I sweating. Drenched. I sit in the cab and watch Jordo through the rearview. Jordo spasms in pain, holding his crippled hands in front of him. I turn the AC off and roll down the window. I want to hear his suffering before I go. I want to hear just a bit more. His screams go hoarse and he starts to moan from the pain. After a couple of minutes he rolls into the fetal position.

I want to stay. I want to stay and wait, wait for him to get up, wait for him to start the walk. I want to follow him as he walks into the dark. I want to watch it happen. I want to hear his screams when the end comes, comes so slowly; he will feel and know intimately every bit of pain for what will seem like an eternity, even though it will all be done in less than a minute. He will experience the pain all the way down to a cellular level, each tiny rip and tear as his body is torn apart from the inside out, like a million fish hooks planted deep within and pulled apart in one furious, masterful frenzy. I want to wait and watch the show, but it's not my role to see that. My duty leads them to that dark walk, but what happens after that is theirs alone to experience.

Jordo struggles to his feet as I pull off. I pull away slowly, watching him through the rearview mirror. I watch him until there is no more light, not for him, not anywhere.

W

Epilogue: GRANGES

"YOU HAVE TO LISTEN TO ME, NICK. No, don't say anything; you'll want to ask questions. It's better if you don't. There are a lot of questions I can't answer. There are a lot of things I don't know or understand about this whole thing. I guess we aren't supposed to understand it. I don't know. Let me focus on what I do know.

"I know that this story started during that rotten fucking war–imagine spending a year of your life alternating between epic boredom and loneliness versus pure terror and despair, I guess it's no wonder that in the heart of such a place, smack in the middle of roaring napalm fires and Charlie running across the wires straight at the heavy machine–gun bunker, firing his Kalashnikov from his hip, he had no chance of survival, but he was okay with running straight at the roaring M–60s and grunts with M16s on rock–and–roll, no problem taking the kamikaze route, all because Uncle Ho said it was the right thing for him to do. So imagine an entire nation full of booby traps and bombs and gooks and Americans screaming or praying with their last bits of life breath, imagine children howling from napalm burns, of sons, brothers, fathers and loners collapsing into rice paddies filled with human shit, of simple, primitive people watching planes bomb ancient forests, hearing the distorted chaos of rock 'n' roll from a GI's radio, good ole boys from the heartland wasted on morphine in the middle of the jungle, nodding off against moss–covered rocks while the dinks were just a few klicks away.

"Yeah, sorry, I try not to think back about it all; once I do it's tough to get off that train, you know? We came home and expected a hero's welcome, like our fathers got after World War II or even Korea, but there were no parades for us, no confetti, no cheers, nothing. We dodged bullets and crawled through human shit, we watched our friends die, we killed people, and most of us, like me, didn't ask to do this, we were told to, and we did so because we grew up in a time when everyone loved the US of fucking A and all it stood for, so when they asked me to go halfway around the world to off some commies in some jungle, I said no problem and I puffed up my eighteen–year–old chest and pretended to be a man. You know what I came back to? I came back to lily–white pussies with soft flabby stomachs and long hair, sheltered and book smart but world dumb fucking hippies–they wore peace sign buttons but had no problem screaming every foul world under the sun in my face, rabid and angry, spit flying, and when that happened, Nick, I'm going to be honest, I thought about the gooks we killed and the gooks that survived. I was pretty damn sure not one dink went home after the war to anything but a loving welcome. I thought about that, then I thought about how I would gladly go back to Vietnam if I could bring a few of these faggoty hippy protesters with me, if we could introduce them to Vietnam via a forceful shove off a bird onto a hot LZ, with AK rounds whizzing through blue flare smoke, to watch them shit and piss themselves with their first glimpse of what humanity looks like when you peel just a layer or two back and look at it in its purest form. You can't learn that in a fucking classroom.

"Anyway, I have a point I'm trying to make, well, it's a story really, and like I said I don't have answers or explanations but I have thought about it plenty, so I guess you can say I have theories or assumptions, but I don't *know*, Nick. You can only think so much before reaching a conclusion, but there are no conclusions here...just more questions. I thought, and I still do, I still think about all the great artists, the poets, the writers, the musicians, the leaders of men, the inventors, the prophets, et cetera, I think about how so much of their genius came from a dark place, how they struggled with the dark spots in life, whether it was abuse or neglect, addiction or apathy, war, love lost, sickness of the mind or body, poverty, inherent nihilism...whatever, take your pick. Shit breeds beauty sometimes.

"You see, Nicky, it was me, Geddy, er, Tim, we called Tim 'Geddy,' his middle name, because there was another Tim in our platoon and about three more in our company. Everyone had nicknames in 'Nam. So it was me, Geddy, and this kid, Ohio. Ohio was a real mean motherfucker, we all looked up to him, he was the guy that would take a shit detail no one else wanted, the guy who would hump some of your gear if you were dragging ass, and not say a word or expect anything in return. Ohio was the guy who would crawl up to the wounded and try and drag em' back when the gooks were trying to bait the medic up to the front so they could take him out. I don't think we ever heard a complaint out of him, no matter how clear it was that we spent a lot of our time as bait, bait to draw the dinks out of the jungle so the big guns and birds could blow them to bits. Ohio came to the war tough as shit. No idea what his life was like before, what the first eighteen years of his life were all about...but I don't think they were good. Not at all.

Me and Geddy, we thought boot camp toughened us up before shipping us out, but after a day or two in country it was pretty clear we were soft and scared and I know that I cried for my mother at night, quietly, but I did it just the same. We got tough fast. We were thrown to the wolves right away, or actually, we *were* the wolves. Just a week or two in we got word that a crew of VC hotshots were headed straight toward us. We set up an ambush choke point. They walked right into it. It wasn't pretty. Those that didn't get blown to shit by the claymores were more or less defenseless as we mowed them down, I was scared as shit, barely able to handle my rifle in my sweaty, shaky hands, but I quickly found myself joining the howls of 'get some!' 'get some Charlie!' 'die motherfuckers die!' And we survived, excelled really, during our first firefight; that toughened us up, but as the weeks went on the true thick skin, even if it was somewhat of an act we put on, that came with watching fellow grunts get shot to shit, the sudden permanent awe of death, the gurgling blood mixed with their last words, and Ohio told us that he had it figured out, that if you just throw yourself into the thing, expect the worst but bring your best, never hesitate, that if you did this, if you disconnected yourself from the emotion that comes between the thought and the action, then we could lose the luxury of fear and worry, and his theory was pretty damned spot on. Of course there were scary nights and days, horrifying really, and there was sadness, epic sadness that made us doubt memories of what life was like before the war— there was no way things were actually that simple and good somewhere in the world, at the very moment, no, no, no, we were human after all, we were scared and angry and sad and terribly bored, but that all got pushed so deep inside, we became incredible actors, it was tough at times, but we did it. We did it because Ohio told us to. He taught us that the best ticket to our survival was indifference.

"And at one point, I'm sure, we actually stepped foot on the precise center of everything that made war so uniquely human and horrific, the consciousness of how inevitable it was for human beings to maim and kill one another for whatever reason, to use grand and sweeping knowledge of science and industry for the sole purpose of finding bigger, better, and more exciting ways to kill and destroy, to alter and pervert history with great bullshit stories and artistic representations of brutality, to keep the politicians and storytellers well fed and adored.

"War crimes? Yes, it's as stupid as it sounds. I don't admit it, but to this day when I hear the jackoffs on TV talking about the 'war crimes' in Iraq or Afghanistan, anywhere, I always root for those under suspicion or indictment, not to say that I'm in favor of someone offing civilians or torturing people or using 'banned' weapons or whatever the fuck it is, but you don't blame a drop of rain for being a part of a hurricane, do you? The people who decide what is or isn't a war crime are typically soft pathetic fucks that have never squeezed a trigger or smashed their faces into mud and prayed those whizzing bullets stayed a foot over their heads; you get it, everyone gets it. But no one admits it, that the whole concept of 'war crimes' is the biggest fucking joke in the history of mankind. The 'rules' or arbitrary decisions and guidelines, the words on paper, the well thought out and reasoned expectations, the do's and don'ts, the fucking ten commandments, all this bullshit goes out the window when that first shot rings out. No shit, huh?

"I'll tell you, Nick, I am a war criminal. So was Geddy, and so is Ohio. I don't lose sleep over it. I never have and I never will. You know about me, decorated law enforcement officer, respected, hell, I've even had offers from both the parties to run for political office under their banner. I've had people filling my head with shit that with my looks and charm and decorated record as a peace officer, the sky is the limit, city council, mayor, governor—I can go as far as I want. Of course I said no, the same reason I've never taken the offer to move too far up the chain in the police force. I'm perfectly happy where I am, and though I was certain my skeletons would never come out of my closet, no way, unlike most shithead politicians, I know they're there, and that's reason enough to not waste my time convincing people I'm something I'm not. I admit, I did chuckle to myself when these politico jackoffs kissed my ass, blabbered on and on about my excellent and clean background, never knowing that I had done things that would make them shiver. Shiver. But like I said, I sleep just fine at night.

"It happened about six months into my tour. We were on a patrol near the border with Laos, helping the ARVN keep an eye on a known VC supply route. Shit, some of those ARVN fucks were VC themselves, which explained the frequent attacks we found ourselves in the middle of. It was particularly bad one day, and we walked into a mortar barrage and had to double back quick, then sneaky Charlie swept in from the other side and we got it pretty bad: two dead, three wounded. That was probably the closest we came to dying in the war, me, Geddy, and Ohio, and at one point, as we took mortar fire from one direction and small arms fire from another, it sure as shit did not look good. We ran low on ammo from shooting into the trees, just hoping to hit something. We hunkered down on some low ground. The dinks had a pretty good bead on us. They had us trapped. If we moved up we moved right into the reach of the mortars. If we moved back or out in any other direction, the other dinks had a bull's-eye on us and they might as well have been on the moon; we had no fucking clue where they were. We were fucked and knew it, but our big guns finally got the right coordinates and took out the mortars and laid enough fire in the general area of shooters that they packed up and left. We lost two men.

"I wish I could say we did what we did next out of the blind hate that comes with losing your own to the enemy, but war doesn't have that honorable bloodlust and revenge they show in the movies. You curse your enemy and you curse God, but the concept of revenge is difficult in a massive war involving millions of people…it's too tough to differentiate revenge from duty.

"Grief didn't inspire us. Our dead didn't haunt us. The helplessness we felt in that ambush is what really got under our skin, the weakness we felt while pinned down by the dink's mortars and small arms fire—that hurt the most. The dinks had us beat in certain areas. They were more committed to the cause, for one, and they didn't have a set timetable for their involvement in the war. There were no tours for them. They fought until they died or the war was over, and their simpleton minds offered no resistance against the propaganda wielded by their rulers. Maybe ours didn't either…but when they did engage in that suicidal behavior, like the dinks that cut the razor wire on the perimeters and ran into our camps, firing from the hip and screaming, running straight into certain death, I suppose they truly believed they were going to survive their bold and stupid attack, that we were cowards and would surrender, just as their leaders had said.

"The dinks were sneaky. They knew the land and were experts in ambush, booby traps, espionage. But we had the one thing that trumped it all, and that was the big mean fucking war machine we brought with us, the howitzers, the bombs, the planes—the machinery to kill a fuckload of people fast. We dropped seven million tons of bombs in that war. The war would have been over in a week if it had been a straight–up firefight. So when we got pinned down and helpless like that, outgunned and without the familiar and expected aid of the birds and the big guns, it was pretty fucking scary. We got away from that ambush, the fear died out and was replaced with—I guess I'd call it embarrassment or emasculation. We could take fear. We could take grief. We could embrace the endless anger. But they took our balls, and that was one thing we couldn't handle.

"The day after that ambush we nutted up and went out to do some shit kicking. We knew we were probably not going to find a damn thing. The war didn't work like that, and that was the worst part about it—just when we wanted to deal out some ass whupping, on our terms, the dinks disappeared and we were left chasing shadows. Sometimes we'd stumble on something, maybe out of dumb fucking luck, maybe it was just our day. This was one of those days. The engineers cleared the supply route road of mines and traps and we set out for a small village that we thought to be a stop–off point for the VC that attacked us. Humping on that road felt real hairy. It had been bombed to shit by both our guys and theirs, was one of those strips of land that had been fought over and handed back–and–forth constantly since the beginning of the war. Another ambush was likely. The engineers usually did a good job of clearing the road, but even the best engineer occasionally missed a mine or trap here and there. But we were angry and we didn't give a fuck. In war, anger is a double–edged sword. On one side, that anger gives you a little extra stamina to keep going, to fuck shit up. Anger is motivation. On the flipside, the more anger clouds you the more you're likely to not pay attention to the small things, like the fact that your head is four inches higher above the sandbag than it should be, or you forget to check the ground in front of you as you walk, and you miss that mine or that pit or that tripwire, or maybe you just get so dumb fucking angry that you don't give a fuck and you put yourself straight in the shit because it's the only place you can be…fuck the consequences.

"This was an easy walk, though. No ambush, no resistance, no traps, and no mines.

"This village was like any other: thatch roofs, odd wood and earth for walls, a well, pens for livestock, and some crops…meager but peaceful, pathetic or humble, depending on your mood. We'd seen enough of these villages to know that looks can be deceiving, Charlie was skilled at building tunnels and hiding storage areas in these villages, and, cunning fucks that they were, they had an admirable talent in booby trapping them as well. We stomped right into that village. The locals didn't flinch. They watched us with bored eyes as we ransacked their homes. The village was noticeably short on men of service age, and that was the first clue that our hunch was right, that this village was in play to Charlie and that its young men and women were off in the jungle with our blood on their hands. We searched around for an hour until we hit pay dirt. Geddy found a dugout on the edge of the village, a hole that held a heavy mortar tube and its components, two shells, and a few other heavier weapons that the dinks had likely dropped off to make their escape into the jungle quick. We rounded up all the villagers and sat them down at the advice of our rifles. Our translator was less than efficient at their native tongue, not that they would say shit one way or another, but we tried. Frustrated, we had everyone but the three combat–age villagers march off with orders to not return until the sun came down. We promised to not burn the village or kill the pigs and goats, and with that they marched off without protest.

"You see, we had no way of knowing whether these three men were VC or VC supporters. Charlie wasn't like us grunts; he didn't wear tags. He could be out in the jungle one night sniping at us, and the next day he's back in his village playing the peasant role. He was a fucking ghost most of the time. The way we saw it, the people in this village were guilty of supporting the VC at the least, and someone had to pay for their little ambush the day before. This wasn't My Lai; we didn't go off the charts and waste everyone in the village. But we did, without discussion or hesitation, execute those three villagers. We marched them down the road about a half a klick and then opened up on them while they had their backs to us. Of course, this was a major violation of the rules of war; we weren't supposed to go around executing suspected enemy or POW's. I mean, it happened in that war, who knows how much, things get real in the shit, but that didn't mean you couldn't get your ass nailed to the wall by the brass for doing it, so we took the bodies into the jungle and we buried them deep and then wiped off our hands and went on our way. That day made us all war criminals; maybe only in our minds, but this was a crime according to some words on paper somewhere. It wasn't a big deal. Even if we'd been busted for it I doubt anything would have come from it. No one did more than house arrest for the My Lai massacre for Christsake. Those of us that had some remnants of a conscience—and not all of us did at that point—knew what we had done was wrong. Sure, we had killed, killed the enemy, maybe killed civilians and innocent people, but that was always 'collateral damage' or 'friendly fire.' What we did that day was a straight up execution.

"We didn't feel bad about it. I know for me, Ohio, and Geddy, it just became part of the whole experience, there wasn't a whole lot of time to sit around and reflect on our sins when we were in a firefight every other fucking day. And, I'll be honest, after that day every time we saw one of our own get killed or maimed made what we did seem more and more like it was just part of the world we were in, routine, and you can't blame us for doing what we did no more than you can blame a dog for being a dog.

"I guess there isn't any reason to tell you all of this shit; it's more about what we felt than what we did or saw. You see, you just have to understand war, or *that* war at least, has a way of getting in you and just rearranging you, maybe in subtle ways, maybe for some they'll never be okay and the rest of their life is doomed, and—

"Fuck it; I'll talk myself hoarse trying to explain this.

"We came home. Ohio, Geddy, and me, we were sure we'd all be best friends for life but we lost touch once we all came home. I guess we just wanted to get back to our lives, and the only thing we had in common was the very thing we were trying to forget.

"So after the war I'm a beat cop in my home state of Wisconsin. I'm living a relatively boring, normal life and out of the blue I get this insane, unshakeable urge to flee, to quit my job and pack my stuff up and move across the country to Phoenix, for no reason other than Phoenix was the first place that came to mind. I had no way of knowing this at the time, but in that same month Ohio and Geddy had that same weird itch and they ended up packing up their shit and moving to Phoenix, too. Like me, the urge came to them, and like me, they went with it.

"So what do you think are the odds that three old war buddies, who haven't spoken in years, one day get an urge to pack up and move to the same strange city, a city that none of us had ties to? That's a rhetorical question.

"So I moved to Phoenix and I got on the force here. There was a little more action here than in Madison, Wisconsin, and fuck did I love it. I worked as much as they would let me; it was all I really wanted to do. I didn't have any interest in finding a wife, or having a family, or hobbies, or any of that shit. All I wanted was to be on the streets in the middle of the action, I didn't give a shit if I was on traffic duty—I felt at home. I fucking loved it. Then things started getting weird. It started about two months after I moved here; you see, at first I thought I was just getting that sixth sense type shit that some cops get, where you start to understand these streets and the people, you get to understand the mind of the criminal, their desires, their habits, their motivations, their strengths and their flaws, you absorb and appreciate their nature and use that to do your job, but it didn't stop for me there. I crossed a line at some point. I'd pick up a guy on a domestic or a shoplifting charge and then when I got close to them I started seeing things, sensing things, I'd close my eyes with a perp in the back of the cruiser, my partner driving, and I'd actually start to see the memories of the perp in the back, I'm watching his past like I'm watching a movie. At first I was sure I was losing my mind, that all the shit with the war, all the shit I had shoved down and buried and cemented over and ignored for a decade had finally sprung a leak and now it was wreaking havoc on my mind. Yeah, I was scared; I thought I was going to end up full tilt insane and strapped to a gurney in a padded room. I didn't tell anyone, of course, I kept my shit together and played the role of a good, normal cop, but these visions got clearer and clearer, and as time went on I had to accept the fact that these were not delusions or hallucinations or daydreams or any of that shit—I was in fact seeing actual events from the lives of actual people. Somehow, someway, I had developed the ability to look into a person and get a first–person view of their crimes straight from the source, a mini–movie crafted from their memories and screened solely for me. No shit.

"We took a call one day for a burglary in progress; an insomniac happened to look out his window in the middle of the night and saw a guy breaking into a corner business. We caught the crook coming out of the store. He didn't even have a chance to run. So we're driving the guy to the station for processing and this movie starts playing in my head, I watch this guy in the backseat breaking into a restaurant somewhere, I watch him open the back door to the kitchen with a crow bar. I see the dim room he walks into. He looks around. I see what he sees. He walks into the dining area, studies the area, then goes down a hallway to a door marked OFFICE. I see his hands push on the door. It's unlocked and opens. I see through his eyes as he walks around the room and looks for a safe, a cash drawer, anything. I'm with him when he bumps against the small sofa and realizes that someone is asleep on it. This sleepy head pops up and mumbles something and I watch the perp freak out and he starts hitting the guy with the crowbar, over and over, I hear the awful sound of the metal bar hitting the guy's skull. I watch until he stops swinging the crowbar, the guy is dead, and he bolts out of the room, down the hallway, through the kitchen and out the back door. He runs out of the back lot and down the street and then the movie fades to black.

"We process the guy for the B and E, and I get off shift an hour or two later and find myself pouring through recent robberies involving an intruder attacking someone in a restaurant. I stay up all night until I find something from two years before. I leave the file and a note on a detective's desk and I head home, half thrilled, half terrified, all exhausted.

"The detectives followed the lead and they leaned on this guy. He eventually confesses to breaking into that restaurant and killing that guy on the couch, the poor sap was sleeping in his office after a fight with his wife.

"That was the first time I used that little movie in my head to bust someone for something they were sure they got away with. I've been doing it ever since. The skill—its power—it comes and goes sometimes, like for six months it will be crystal clear and booming, then it fades for a while and isn't as strong. But it always comes back.

"Later on I learned that all the times my little talent went away or faded always coincided with Ohio being out of town. Ohio didn't have the smoothest transition back to the world after the war. Hell, he didn't want to go home, but he took a bullet in his leg and they wouldn't let him serve another tour, so he came back to the states and had nothing to do but hit the bottle. He struggled with that for years; he cleaned up for good like seven or eight years ago I think, before that he was drunk on the streets and drifting from city to city and state to state, sometimes putting the bottle aside for a short while to work whatever shitty job he could get. He came to Phoenix the same month I did. He tried to leave, went as far away as Oregon or Washington, but he always came back. It wasn't up to him.

"Ohio spent years running. He ran from himself; he ran from those crazy visions he saw in his head. He was sure at first, just as I had been, that he was losing his mind, that his unquenchable drinking habit had soaked his brain wet. He ran from his shadows in and out of Phoenix and all up the west coast, and after a while he realized that drunk or sober, the visions were here to stay...and they were real. He wasn't crazy, no, and no matter how hard he tried he couldn't drink the truth away. You see, Ohio has probably the strongest sight of all of us. He glances at a person and in an instant he sees their most private and haunted moments, and unlike me he sees it all, he sees the names, the numbers, the emotions, and the intimate details—he sees it all. He'd be stumbling drunk on some shit street in the city and look up to a person walking past him, and in a blink of an eye he'd see the skeleton's in that person's closet. Sometimes it was nothing, a white lie or a minor shoplifting habit, but sometimes, sometimes often, he saw the real shit: the murder, rape, major fraud, neglect, and abuse in every imaginable and despicable way. You see, *my* sight, it only works on the true evildoers; I can only see into those who have done something seriously wrong. But Ohio, poor Ohio, he sees into everyone, even if the worst thing they've ever done was cheat on their wife or steal a book from a library or not stop after they hit a parked car, he sees everything. Now imagine trying to live a normal life with normal relationships when everyone is that open to you, all their faults, their history, their weakness—it's just not possible. Poor Ohio is cursed that way, and he gave up the drink and keeps his other demons at bay, but Ohio will never be able to share his life with anyone. That's his punishment, I suppose.

"Geddy came to Phoenix the same month we did. He's never left. Geddy dug into this city and went to work right away. You see, Geddy came back from the war with a taste for violence, and the way he saw it was that as long as he had a jones for it he might as well put it to good use. He went into a life of crime but his prey was always fellow crooks. He kept what he earned. He didn't feel a need for his financial gains, but he kept it out of compulsion, as a means of keeping track of his work. Before he came to Phoenix he spent his time knocking off dope houses and shit–kicking pimps and stick–up crews; he had a proficiency in crime unlike any other, a unique discipline, and an incredible drive to fuck over those who fuck over. And if he had to, if someone tried to snap back at him or make him pay for what he did, he handled business, yes sir, he handled business. But the streets of Boston got dull one day and like Ohio and me, he felt that strange urge to pack up and move to the desert. So he did.

"He came here and he set up shop, got the run of the city, and went to work, always staying just under the radar of the cops and the big timers. I tell you Nicky, Geddy was a real fucking pro. Of course, he met that good woman and she understood what he was before he even did, Lord knows how, he met a hippy chick with a God jones and she prayed for him to return home safe when he was out handling business. He had those kids but they didn't slow him down. He was a loving and kind husband and father, but when he hit those streets he flipped the switch, and if he crossed your path and you were doing work, he made sure that you paid the toll in cash or in blood.

"Geddy had the gift too. His was a little different than ours, but he had a gift nonetheless. He was a seer too, but he didn't get as clear as a picture as I do and he never got the details that Ohio does. Geddy had an almost sixth sense about what to do, where to go, who to go after. He had a sixth sense about trouble, how to dance in the world of crime but never pay for it. Some greater force guided him toward his marks, the criminals that he worked over. Everything was laid out right in front of him. All he had to do was follow.

"His punishment, of course, is that he never wanted to rob, to kill, or to maim, even if he did only target scumbags, he never wanted to do what he did. He did it because he knew it was the right thing to do, the thing he was supposed to do, and maybe he did like it just a bit, and when he came across a true evil fuck, he saw that evil glowing around them, that tainted aura; he read people and he knew what had to be done. Imagine never having to second guess yourself, but hating it all the same. That was Geddy. Geddy came to the war a goofy, fun loving guy, the class clown, the prankster, and I suppose that a part of him stayed true to his former self, even up to the day he died. I don't know if it was the war or his gift, but Geddy was forced to turn his back on his true self and he became that man that you knew on those late nights, that incredible powerhouse of violence and discipline. But you saw it, Nicky, didn't you? You saw the real Geddy poke out toward the end? You saw the real Geddy when he let out that smile, when he finally let his guard down and the cloak came off and Geddy was just Geddy, not the man that *it* forced him to be? That was his punishment. Poor Geddy... he had to wear that heavy mask for all those years.

"Huh? What's my punishment? Yes, you're right; Geddy and Ohio paid a price for their gifts. And I do too. Mine is hard to explain. I guess the word would be, uh, existential? You see, I don't—well; there's a reason why I work so hard. If I don't keep my mind occupied all the time, this powerful feeling of nothingness takes over me. You hear about people that live to work or that work is their lives, you know, but that's not in the literal sense; but it is for me—my punishment, this punishment is that the moment I shut off my mind from work I start to drift, I can't focus on things, my body feels like its floating—not a comfortable float, but a listing, uncontrolled and anxious. I get off work and I drive home thinking about work and the moment I stop thinking about work I just drift, aimless really, there is no connection to anything, I eat and sleep and bathe like anyone else, but when I'm not at work or thinking about work I'm really not here, at least not enough to sustain a relationship or master a hobby or spend time thinking of anything other than crime and justice…and it's worse sometimes than others, but there is a reason why I only work, eat, and sleep—I sleep thick, dreamless sleep. It's really all I can do. And the scariest thing is that I'll have to retire one day, sixty–five is the mandatory age of retirement for police officers, and that's not far off. I don't know what I'll do when the day comes, and I pray that maybe I'll be able to live life again, be a normal fucking human being, but I doubt it. I really do. Let's just say, I'll be honest with you Nick, I'll probably put a gun to my head if…well, you know.

"You don't get it? Don't worry, neither do I. The three of us ended up in this city around the same time, not by chance, no fucking way, I guess we were a triangulation of sort, a tripod for some great signal, for our gifts work the best when we're all close, close but *not* close; we all fit together somehow, me a man of law, working and using my gift to bring scumbags down, and Geddy, he was on the other side, I guess, but he did the same thing I did, only he had to lie down in the muck and crawl around with the snakes to bring them down. And Ohio, he drifts around this city and happens upon those whose time has come, the time to pay for their deeds. Together, the three of us; and our paths did cross, sometimes it was blatant, sometimes I suppose it was so subtle we didn't even see it, but we were all intertwined somehow, part of something…something. I don't know what it is. I don't even try to understand it anymore. I hit a wall there.

"A year after I moved here to Phoenix I awoke in the middle of the night to this address in my head. I tried to go back to sleep but it got louder and louder, this thought, this address. I'd learned to trust my gut by then so I got dressed and got in my car and I drove to the address. I'd never been there before but I drove there like I had, it was instinct;

I drove to this empty lot in some random Phoenix neighborhood, I got there and I got out of the car and there wasn't a full moon but it seemed so bright out, I walked to a patch of grass and stood and waited and a figure appeared in the distance, walking straight toward me, and I instinctively unlatched my revolver and put my hand on it, and this figure closes in and I got that fight–or–flight shiver, but when I saw who it was I burst into tears, I don't know if they were tears of sadness or joy or both, but it was Geddy, fucking Geddy, he walked onto that lot like a ghost, and we hugged one another and didn't say a word — fuck, what could we say — and then moments later this straggly figure appears and at first we didn't recognize him, he just looked like your typical down–on–your–luck drifter, but it was Ohio, yes it was; he was dirty and beaten down, a discarded and worn version of that bad motherfucker we knew in the war, but fuck it was him, it was Ohio, and we hugged and we cried in that empty lot in the middle of the night, we didn't have to talk about it, we just knew, right, we just knew that we all had that same calling to come here, that we'd all been drawn to this city, the same city, that we all had this thing, this thing, this gift or vision, or whatever the fuck it is... we just knew. We didn't know the first thing about it, where it came from, why we had it or what it was, whywhywhywhy, but at that point this became clear, that the three of us were linked together beyond any comprehension of science or logic, and whether we liked it or not, we were put here in this city to use it, to fulfill some need or desire or eventuality. Fuck, Nick, we didn't know shit honestly. This whole thing was thrust upon us and there was no point in trying to figure something out when it was all out of our hands anyway.

"No, we didn't see each other much after that. You see, we all had experienced random bouts of sickness — nausea, migraines — at random times before that night, and after about ten minutes of us standing there in that lot, in awe of one another, of that great fucking truth we were now privy to, we all started getting the headache and the sick. After that, if we ended up in one another's company for too long, the sickness came; shit, if we even happened to end up in the same mile or two of each other, the sickness came. In the years that followed we'd talk on the phone at times, we shared our stories and our experiences, but even over the phone made us sick sometimes, not as bad as it did if we were close to one another, but sick nonetheless, sort of like the sickness that comes with overindulgence of particularly rich food. So we couldn't talk much, and it was always painful for us to know that we were in the same city, doing the same thing, suffering in our own way, but never truly being able to be in one another's lives the way we wanted to. Ohio in particular, he drifted off and on, like I said, but even when he was in town he made himself almost impossible to get ahold of. We wanted nothing more than to be friends, to be part of each other's life, to do all the simple and wonderful shit that friends do. We couldn't. We might as well have been on opposite sides of the world. So that's the way it was until that night, that night I saw Geddy, the night I met you. That's when it all came apart. I suppose we weren't supposed to see each other, I think that's why Geddy died, no, I'm sure of it, because I saw Ohio a couple days before that night and we both got sick, sicker than ever before. Fuck. I never would have gone to that lot if I'd known… anyway. I guess it was meant to be. It always is. You'll see that."

"What Nick? I don't know the answer to that question," Granges answers. "Like I said, we all thought about it, over and over, until it drove us half mad, and the best we came up with is, it goes back to that village in Vietnam, that story I told you about our crime, when we killed those three Vietnamese. You see, me, Ohio, and Geddy, we were the only people to touch those men after we killed them. We buried them. We each grabbed a corpse by its wrists and dragged them into that hole in the ground, and at the time we all had the same strange thing happen to us, when our hands touched their skin, their dead skin, we all felt that strange, unearthly sensation of hot and cold, of electrical jolts. I'm pretty sure that was how it all started. I don't know if it was a gift or a punishment or neither, maybe it was just fate and preordained, maybe it was pure randomness; who knows if those dead Vietnamese had the vision too, and in their death it spread to us because we were the ones who touched them. It doesn't matter. The why's and how's don't matter. It's so far beyond that. I—

"Nick, I thought you had a right to know, know what's coming, know what that sensation was when you touched Geddy as he died. Have you felt it yet? It starts as a tickle, a hint; you'll see things, you'll feel things, and these foreign images, thoughts, ideas, feelings—you'll start to trust them, inherently trust them. It develops over time. I suppose we came to grips with it in our own way. I'm telling you all this so you can avoid that period of terror we all felt, to spare you the fear that you're losing your mind. I can't give you much, but I can give you that. I can take that off your shoulders. But there is no turning back. There is no turning it off. It's here to stay. I'm sorry. You'll come to believe. I promise you will. And there is a satisfaction in knowing that you're part of something, something so fucking mind blowing, so fucking important, I mean, shit, can you imagine what this city would be like if Geddy and Ohio and I weren't here all those years, doing our thing? In the grand scheme of things, whatever work we've done may have only put a scratch or a dent in the big picture of crime or evil or whatever it is, but shit, you spend as much time on the streets as I have and you see the insanity and the despair—the awfulness out there... I shudder to think about a world without us, Nick, without people like *us*, Nick. There are more of us, there has to be, in every city perhaps, or maybe wherever we're needed, wherever the fringe needs to be tethered and controlled.

"Okay, enough talk. The more we talk about it, the more we think, it...it just doesn't help. Don't think. Don't. Try and just feel, just do. Try to put yourself on autopilot, Nick.

"Easier said than done? Yes, without a doubt. But trust me, Nick, the day will come, soon, you'll look at someone and you'll see, you'll see it, and you'll have never felt as sure about something in your life. You will instinctively, truly know it for the first time in your life. You might not like the places it takes you, the things it makes you do, or the way it makes you feel…but fuck, Nicky, who else gets to spend their life half demon and half angel…to wake up and know that you are one of the most powerful motherfuckers in the world, and while the rest of mankind scurries around and merely exists, you, you are gonna be out there living, living with your hand wrapped around the very heart of the world at its rawest and most human form.

"Good luck, Nick. Go ahead and run headfirst into that darkness. It's the only thing you can do now."

About the Author

WORLD OF VACANCY is Charles Schmidt's debut novel. He lives in Arizona and works in the behavioral health field. He likes X–Box and Faulkner.

You can visit his website at www.charlesschmidtbooks.com

or on Facebook at http://facebook.com/worldofvacancy

www.ingramcontent.com/pod-product-compliance
Lightning Source LLC
Chambersburg PA
CBHW050013180626
46810CB00002B/395